I0589380

About the author

Donna Maree Hanson is a traditionally and independently published author of fantasy, science fiction and horror. She also writes paranormal romance under the pseudonym of Dani Kristoff. Her dark fantasy series (which some reviewers have called 'grim dark'), *Dragon Wine*, was published by Momentum Books (Pan Macmillan digital imprint) in 2014. *Shatterwing*: Part One and *Skywatcher*: Part Two are now re-published independently in digital and print on demand. *Deathwings*, Dragon Wine Part Three and *Bloodstorm*, Dragon Part Four were published in 2017.

In April 2015, Donna was awarded the A. Bertram Chandler Award for 'Outstanding Achievement in Australian Science Fiction' for her work in running science fiction conventions, publishing and broader SF community contribution. Donna also writes science fiction romance, with *Rayessa and the Space Pirates* and *Rae and Essa's Space Adventures* out with Escape Publishing. *Opi Battles the Space Pirates* was published independently in 2017. In 2016, Donna commenced her PhD candidature researching Feminism in Popular Romance at the University of Canberra. Also, available is her epic fantasy series the Silverlands, *Argenterra*, *Oathbound* and *Ungiven Land*. Donna lives in Canberra with her partner and fellow writer Matthew Farrer.

You can contact Donna at her blog http://donnamareehanson.com

Or on Twitter @DonnaMHanson and Facebook

www.facebook.com/donnamareehanson

And if you like to keep in touch and hear about special offers, then consider signing up for my newsletter, Wing Dust.

Also by Donna Maree Hanson

The Silverlands (Epic Fantasy)

Argenterra, The Silverlands Book One

Oathbound, The Silverlands Book Two

Ungiven Land, The Silverlands Book Three

Dragon Wine Series (Dark Fantasy)

Shatterwing, Dragon Wine Part One

Skywatcher, Dragon Wine Part Two

Deathwings, Dragon Wine Part Three

Bloodstorm, Dragon Wine Part Four

Love and Space Pirates (Science Fiction Romance)

Rayessa and the Space Pirates

Rae and Essa's Space Adventures

Opi Battles the Space Pirates

Skywatcher

Dragon Wine Part Two

By
Donna Maree Hanson

Copyright Information

First published by Momentum Books, Pan Macmillan Australia 2014
Published by Donna Maree Hanson 2017

Copyright © Donna Maree Hanson 2014 and 2017

The moral right of the author has been asserted

All rights reserved. This publication (or any part of it) may not be reproduced or transmitted, copied, stored, distributed or otherwise made available by any person or entity (including Google, Amazon or similar organizations) in any form (electronic, digital, optical, mechanical) or by any means (photocopying, recording, scanning or otherwise) without prior written permission from the author.

National Library of Australia Cataloguing-in-Publication entry

ISBN 978-0-6480415-5-9 (ebook)
ISBN 978-0-6480415-7-3 (Print on Demand)
Cover design by www.crocodesigns.com
Edited by Brianne Collins
To report a typographical error, please email donnamareehanson@gmail.com

Dedication

To hope

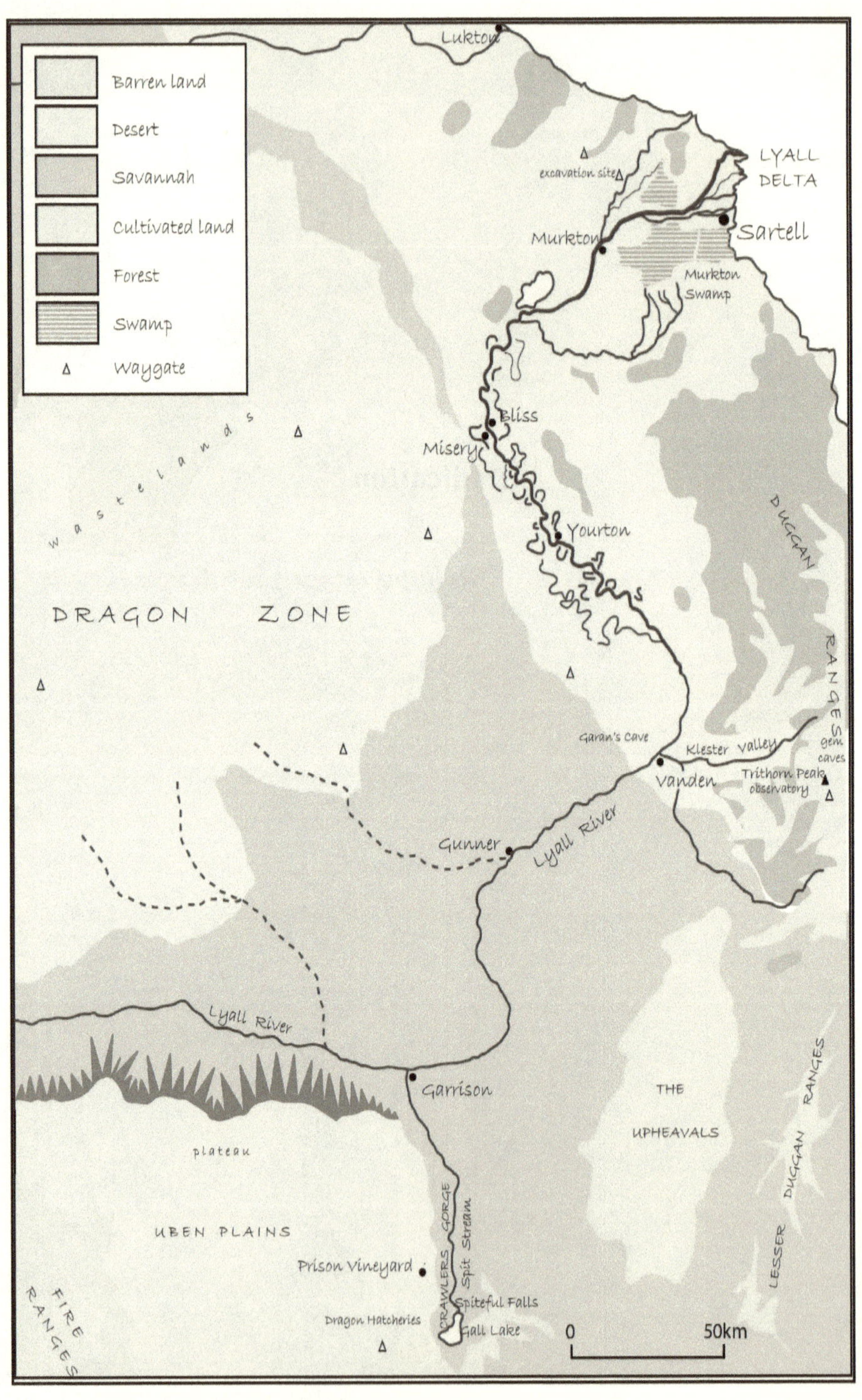

Barren land
Desert
Savannah
Cultivated land
Forest
Swamp
Waygate

Luktor
LYALL DELTA
excavation site
Murkton
Sartell
Murkton Swamp
Bliss
Misery
DUGGAN RANGES
Yourton
WASTELANDS
DRAGON ZONE
Garan's Cave
Klester Valley
gem caves
Vanden
Trithorn Peak observatory
Gunner
Lyall River
Lyall River
Garrison
THE UPHEAVALS
plateau
CRAWLERS GORGE
Spit Stream
LESSER DUGGAN RANGES
UBEN PLAINS
Prison Vineyard
Spiteful Falls
Dragon Hatcheries
Fall Lake
FIRE RANGES
0   50km

Prologue

The light of Belle moon burnished the surface of the planet to mauve, gently caressing hills, a valley, a filthy river. Above, the air seethed with heat as the meteor cut through the atmosphere. The city below trembled as death fell from the sky. A shaft of power burst from a scope only to miss its target. A Skywatcher failed and wept.

Part 1

Even a sober man must drink his fill of dragon wine

Chapter One

WELCOME TO BARRAHIEM

Fingers of cold air stroked Salinda to consciousness. There was no pain. The cadre within her glowed with satisfaction, its essence like sipping sweet nectar. Eyes closed, she inhaled the pristine air: no odor of dust or sulphur or vine leaves or even the stink of sweat. Free air, she thought as she held her breath and then let it slide out of her slowly.

Recollections of torture, of pain, of overwhelming humiliation flashed like lightning across her mind. She shuddered and knew those memories would forever haunt her. But in this place of quiet and safety she was able to master them and put them aside. Her task now was to deal with them and move on.

Like a welcome friend, the cadre pulsed silently, feeling like a part of her—less obtrusive and more malleable than it had been before. For a second, she doubted what she was feeling; the peace and serenity within her were strange. Was she dead? In that moment of panic, she snapped open her eyes and stared.

Overhead lay cream-colored vaulted ceilings, with veins of brown threading through the pale stone. Decorated in swirls and hollows, the ceilings merged with the walls and ran into murals carved out of the rock. The murals depicted people in flowing robes performing rituals Salinda could never hope to fathom. Each of the five walls had arched doorways, as if this room was a nexus. The ambient light was not bright, though sufficient enough for her to see her immediate surroundings. High up and in the distance shadows draped the corners of the room and the unseen corridors beyond.

Salinda was awed by what she was seeing. No tales, no histories, few as they were, told of such a place as this or mentioned the people described in the scenes surrounding her. The cadre throbbed excitedly the more Salinda looked around her. It ate up the sight of the murals, the ceilings and corridors as if it had hungered a thousand years for such a feast. She wondered how it could recognize the significance of this place. Was the cadre that old? Salinda's brow creased in puzzlement. Surely it could not be, and yet...

That strange being Nils did exist. He wasn't a figment of her imagination. Where was he now? Had he abandoned her in this otherworldly place? Anxiety made her heart beat painfully until reason calmed her down. He would not have saved her only to abandon her.

The urge to find him was all the impetus she needed to sit up. It was then that she noticed her healed body. She didn't know what had happened to the ragged remains of her clothing, but being naked seemed entirely natural. Running her hands down her arms, she marveled at smooth skin unmarked by a decade of hard labor. The brand on her upper arm was gone. Somehow years of exposure to sunlight had been erased. Her skin looked new and young and was two shades lighter.

Next she touched her lips wonderingly and glanced down at her breasts. The red was gone; no more whore taint. Tears pricked her eyes and a sob lodged in her throat. It was astonishing. At that moment she was moved to weep for all that had been erased. What manner of being was this Nils of Barr that he could perform such miracles of healing? She noticed something beside her. It was a folded, pale blue cloth. She glanced around, half-turning on the tray, seeking Nils among the shadows, but he was not there. The wall behind her had blinking lights down the center. A machine? On either side were wide arched doorways that led to further mysterious rooms that seemed to be dark chasms. Unfurling the cloth, she examined the garment, which was a simple full-length tunic, stitched down the sides. An ornate belt tooled in silver and beads sat on the tray with her. Underneath the folded tunic was a cream-colored outer cloak and what looked like underwear.

Clutching the clothes in her hands, she glanced up. The people depicted in the murals were dressed thus. She shrugged and pulled the tunic over her head, tugged on the underwear, fitted the belt and picked up the cloak, which she draped over her shoulders.

At first she was light-headed as she took her first step onto the cool marble floor. She clung to the healing tray and waited for the sensation to pass. On the floor were some slippers. Slowly, she knelt to pick them up and examine them. They were handcrafted and stitched with an iridescent thread in a pattern that echoed the theme of the walls. After she slid them on her feet, she realized Nils must have made them for her because they fit her exactly.

The memory of when she'd first spied him across the square in Gunner came to mind. His skin was so white, his eyes so eerie and silver, as if they glowed in the dark places of Margra. The cadre warmed to that thought. It was as if the essences of those within it whispered to themselves: *Dwellers of the dark places...keepers of knowledge...the Hiem.*

And? She queried the cadre. But there was nothing. Either that was the limit of its knowledge or she wasn't asking the right questions. Neither thought worried her because she would find out—eventually.

She made her way through the right-hand doorway into an even larger room, more like a meeting hall. The air was cooler there and had a faint smell of earth and rock. She stood still and gazed upward. A glimmering plant hung down from the ceiling, obscuring the intricate panorama of images. Between the buttresses were scenes depicting beasts and planets and abstract designs, which Salinda could not fully interpret. To her mind it was a confusion of ideas and the only thing of beauty within was the craftsmanship. The ceiling glowed, too, like starlight, and so too did the fabric of the walls.

Nils stepped from the shadows and stood still. His clothing was identical to hers, and he looked even more alien than she remembered standing as he was before the old and majestic murals.

Her first instinct was to rush forward and wring his hands in gratitude, but she held back, unsure of how he would respond to such an effusive greeting. Instead, she contained her emotion and spoke solemnly. "Thank you for your help, Nils of Barr." Then, lifting her eyes to his, she added, "I would never have thought such healing possible. You have restored me."

Knowing her words to be inadequate, she searched her mind for some other expression of respect. As she walked slowly and deliberately forward, he didn't back away, but nor did he speak. When she was within two steps of him, she lay flat on the floor and kissed the hem of his tunic. The cadre purred, satisfied that she had acted well. Climbing to her feet, she waited for him to react.

Nils took a step back, his robe swirling about his feet. Cocking his head to one side, he said in his strangely accented voice, "The machine healed you, although it took an interminably long time."

Salinda noticed now that his voice had a light, pleasing timbre that went well with his accent. Bowing fractionally to her while opening both hands, palms facing up, he added, "I have been keeping myself busy in the archives."

"The archives…? Nils, what is this place? Why is it so quiet?"

"My kin are gone. They are all gone, every single one except me. You are standing in Barrahiem, the capital city of the Hiem people. We are—I should say were—the record keepers. You are the first Sundweller, if I may call you that, to enter here."

Salinda's mind was a whirl of activity. The cadre glowed warmly in response to Nils's words. She herself had not heard of the Hiem or of any record keepers, but the cadre obviously had. "You are alone here then? How?"

Stepping back, he pointed to the archway behind him. "Come, I will take you somewhere more comfortable. These halls are hallowed and haunted by memory. I can scarce bear to be here for I can remember how it was. The loss is all too new. Follow me."

"I don't understand. You're alone here but the loss is recent? What happened to the people who lived here?"

His silver eyes settled on her face. "They died after the world was sundered. They did not escape your ancestors' fate."

What did that mean? It seemed contradictory. She went to ask another question but Nils lifted his hand for silence. He glanced around him and said, "Later. Now I would like to leave this place."

Salinda nodded, quite ready to use her newly healed body, and took a step toward him. Nils turned in a swirl of robes and strode through the dark doorway to the right.

Out on a wide balcony, she saw that the city spanned out in circular terraces, widening as the buildings crept up the concave walls of the cavern in which it was situated. Awestruck, Salinda noted that the cavern was a vast space, entirely underground. Overhead the roof of the huge cave, supported by thick columns of rock, sheltered the buildings, walkways and open spaces. The houses were formed from the same pale stone that she'd seen in the large hall. From what she could see, Barrahiem rivaled the city of Sartell in size. The thick central pillar, again decorated in the alien designs she'd seen elsewhere, served as a focal point to the city's grandeur. Muted light revealed dark round windows in the many houses. All was still, eerie and quiet. Salinda found the absence of sound quite disturbing. Her gaze slid to Nils. "So empty... How can you bear the aloneness?"

Nils halted and faced her, his strange eyes widening and the silver in the irises glowing fractionally. "What makes you think I bear it?" Those silver eyes held hers. "You and I are all that is alive in Barrahiem. An interesting sensation, is it not?"

"Yes." Salinda shivered and followed behind Nils as he continued on. His cream-colored cloak billowed out behind him, occasionally revealing the blue tunic beneath. They walked deeper into the city, through halls and walkways occasionally lit at floor level by soft glowing lamps placed along the skirting. Low archways, many of them in rows, circled large halls with vaulted ceilings, each with its own unique designs. The stairwells were like tubes so perfectly round that Salinda couldn't guess how they'd been made. She'd once seen a lava tube that was similar, but it had not been made from this marble-like substance. Trailing her hand along one of the walls she detected the change in texture from smooth to rough where the brown veins variegated the surface.

At last they arrived at what appeared to be a small terminating node. They stood in the center of a room ringed with six small archways. The ceiling was less ornate there, though the designs were intricate and beautifully wrought. "Welcome to the hall of Barr. It is small, but it serves."

"Barr? Is that your family name or the name of your city?"

He glanced around. "Both, in a way. This city is called Barrahiem. My people collectively are the Hiem. I come from the line of Barr, which is an old one dating back to the first settlement here."

"So your family built this city?"

"Founded, rather than built. It took thousands of years to delve into Margra and shape the city thus. Although I should say that there were already buildings and artefacts beneath the surface, relics from the previous inhabitants. There are many branches of Barr...were, I should say." He turned away and pointed to one of the archways. "My dwelling is that one. You may choose one of those three as they have been cleaned and are in relatively good order. If you need anything else for your comfort I will see what I can manage. However, you must realize there is no industry here. Some food, yes, which is easily gathered or retrieved from the storehouse, and there is water aplenty..."

Just then something happened within Salinda's body, something that both alarmed and thrilled her. With sudden haste, she said, "Thank you so much, but could you excuse me for a short moment? There is something I must see to." She dashed away to an archway of one of the homes Nils had pointed out, bent down to ease through the doorway and went inside.

The dwelling was small, only three rooms. Luckily the ceiling itself was high, in stark contrast to the entranceway. A bed was in one room with a handmade cover over the top of it. She had the feeling that Nils had made it, along with the shoes. Another room, much smaller and more like an alcove, was a place to wash, and the other was a common room with a low table and a sofa with cushions. She turned in a circle, looking at the creamy substance of the walls and the few bits of furniture. It was so still, so empty of warmth that she had a sudden longing for the vineyard. How long had it been since she'd had a proper roof over her head? Ten years at least. She couldn't help feeling closed in.

Her mind clicked over and she began to search. She needed something to absorb the blood flow. The urge to weep nearly overwhelmed her. Although inconvenient, her monthly blooding meant that she hadn't conceived—that she did not carry a child of rape. She would not bear a child to remind her of Ange. On the third shelf in the bathroom she found some cloths sufficient for her needs. When she'd dealt with her immediate problem, she took in more of her surroundings.

In the main area, she saw a beveled-edged mirror set in a carved stone frame. Her image mesmerized her. Other than glimpsing her reflection on the surface of water, it had been years since she'd seen herself. Her skin was olive, but creamy-colored and smooth as if she hadn't been roasted year after year in the hot sun. Her brown eyes glinted with health, her hair was lustrous and long.

Her body? With a quick glance at the door to ensure her privacy she lifted up the edge of the tunic and pulled it over her head. She turned side-on so she could see her back, and what she saw made her weep anew. They were gone. The scars that her husband had etched into her skin with such malice had disappeared. Her skin was whole and new and young, regrown. All of her body was healed. Salinda was uncertain what such a transformation meant. The memories were still there; the thought of them clenched her brow with a frown. But what really startled her as she wiped the tears away and put her clothes back on was that she appeared elegant. Not pretty, nor classically beautiful. The clothing and the color of her skin and the angle of her eyes all combined to make her pleasing to look upon.

Her reaction to her appearance surprised her. Danton had told her she was beautiful, that somehow she had kept her youth in the vineyard. Although pleased by his compliment, she had not really believed him. Her thoughts turned to Danton as she wondered if he was well and whether Brill had found the rebel leader. Life in the prison vineyard seemed so long ago.

A soft rustling sound at the door roused her. Nils stood there, his facial expression neutral and wide, pale brow distinctive. He bowed in his strange way, hands outstretched and palms up.

"Is the house to your liking?" he asked.

"Yes, I thank you." She stepped back, allowing him to enter. "Will you come in?"

Nils seemed to hesitate in spite of her invitation. Then he bent over nearly double to enter through the low doorway. Once inside he played with the folds of his tunic, a mannerism she thought indicated unease.

"Why are the doors so small when your people are so tall?" she asked.

"One must be humble to enter another's abode. The smallness of the doorway forces one to remember."

"I see." She turned to seat herself on the sofa and arranged the cushions behind her back. She wasn't sure what kind of hospitality he expected. Luckily, he stepped into the breach. "With your permission I will prepare Pardu, a kind of tea."

"Thank you. That would be most welcome."

Nils went to a niche in the wall and his slim-fingered hands coaxed a flame from a single-burner stove and set a kettle on it. "I have only recently cultivated the Pardu and set it to cure. This will be my first taste for a long time." The water boiled quickly and he added it along with powder to a square container. Once it was sealed he shook vigorously, then poured the liquid into a pot. He arranged it and two square cups on a tray that he brought over to the table. He sat across from her, closed his eyes and appeared to meditate. Salinda contemplated the pot, too, while she waited for Nils to say something.

"The Pardu is ready. As this is your house it is your duty to pour," he said quietly.

With a quick glance at him, she poured the white, frothy liquid into the cups. Nils picked his up and sipped, first from one edge and then another until all four points of the compass, north, south, east and west had been covered.

"Should I drink in the same manner as you?" she asked.

"If you wish. For me it is a blessing to sip the Pardu thus. Margra provides us shelter, food and water and a place to hold our souls. Sipping the Pardu in all the directions of Margra symbolizes its all-encompassing nature."

Salinda had to look away, lest he accuse her of staring. What kind of creature was he? She decided to follow his example. The cadre was quiet on the matter, as if soothed merely by being here. The Pardu tasted odd; not like a leaf brew at all. The liquid was slightly muddy in taste and the pale white froth had the consistency of pond slime. Yet she drank and noticed that her spirits lifted immediately.

"How do you like Barrahiem?" he asked, leaning forward, unable to hide his eagerness.

Salinda couldn't help smiling. "I never knew such a city existed."

Nils's lips pursed together and he sighed. "Your face speaks of your wonder. I mentioned that I am the last of my kind. Not long ago I woke from a long, long sleep to this emptiness. You cannot imagine how I felt to find myself alive when all the others are dead. And me so unworthy."

Salinda took what he said at face value. If he had a machine that could heal her injuries then he could possess a machine that allowed him to sleep through his people's demise. But how must he feel? What emotions must roil within him? He knew the world before, a vibrant world if the murals held true, and now he saw this empty city.

"Unworthy? How can you say such a thing? You saved me—helped me, though you barely knew me. That makes you worthy to my mind. That makes you great…"

Nils looked down at the table top and turned his cup around and around absently. "I cannot say such an act makes me worthy. I did save you from death, that is true, but you offered me something in return… do you remember?" He glanced up at her, his eyes flashing silver.

"Yes. I remember your words now. You have no faith in humankind. I must admit to having a similar feeling when I was at the mercy of the people of Gunner. But I believe there is hope."

"Hope?" Nils ceased playing with his cup and stared at her earnestly.

His direct gaze gave her pause. She swallowed a hasty mouthful of Pardu. "Yes, hope for many things: survival, redemption and…"

Nils leaned forward again, his eyes searching her face. "You wish for these things? Strive for these things?"

"Yes." Salinda didn't want to go into detail about her hopes and dreams. In spite of everything he'd done for her, Nils was an unknown, his motivations difficult to comprehend. She had to tread carefully and she sensed that the cadre supported her choice to do so. "You wanted to know about dragons."

"Yes!" he answered with overt enthusiasm. "I have so many questions."

Salinda frowned. "Dragon lore will take a long time to tell. I know a small part."

"Yet, you converse with the dragons."

"I wouldn't call it conversing, exactly. We communicate, and usually it's only with Plu. I raised him from a hatchling. His egg was displaced from the nest during a rock slide. I cared for him with the help of my friend and mentor, Mez, before we moved him back to the dragon hatchery. We couldn't keep him at the vineyard."

"Vineyard?"

"Nils—may I call you Nils?"

"Yes, you may."

"I worked in a prison farm, a vineyard, growing grapes for dragon wine. The prison was an isolated place, difficult to reach and virtually impossible to escape from. There was a dragon hatchery nearby, along with a large herd of adult dragons. Their presence was the reason prisoners couldn't escape...dragons eat people."

"I see." He looked thoughtful at this. "You said you raised Plu, but how did you know their language? You brought other dragons to save us."

Salinda scratched behind her ear as she gathered her thoughts. "Mez taught me all the dragon language he knew. He explained that the words form pictures and simple ideas for the dragons. Plu doesn't talk to me, for example. As for calling others, that was the first time I'd tried it. I felt their minds—that hasn't happened before..." She trailed off, wondering. What had changed in her to allow her to sense other dragons? Was it the cadre growing stronger or was it something else, something the Inspector had done? Could that foul liquor have altered her abilities? Had he truly distilled the essence of dragons?

For a person without eyebrows, Nils demonstrated a fair impression of surprise in his facial features. "You sensed some power from them?"

Salinda frowned. Power? He could sense that? She considered it best not to reveal too much about the cadre. "I detected their minds, their powerful presence. Do you truly not know where they came from? Dragons have been with us since Ruel split, or so it is said."

"I have slept these many years—countless years. When I closed my eyes, Ruel was whole in the sky. There were no dragons then. When I woke my world is how you see it now."

Salinda stilled, her eyes widening. He had hinted that he had slept for a long time but until that moment she hadn't fully grasped it. "You are...you are truly ancient. That must have been more than a thousand years, surely."

Salinda trembled with excitement, with awe. This being was from the time when the world was whole. It was hard to imagine, to even contemplate. The city around her and Nils's form were so alien, so different. She knew she had to try to accept and to comprehend. In her heart, pity stirred. How lonely he must be. But the things he must have seen! Civilization at its height—architecture, technology, culture, art. She only had vague tales of these from Mez and an occasional image that filtered through to her mind from the cadre, as if something she'd seen or experienced had jiggled it loose.

He inclined his head. "Even longer. I said before that I am of the Hiem. Knowledge of our existence had sunk mostly into myth even in my youth, even though some of us walked the lands above in that time. We are—were—the keepers of knowledge. All around us are the works of my kin, the ancient knowledge of times past, dating back to when this planet was settled."

"Settled?" Salinda shuddered. "By the Wing! You thought me a witch, but such words as these would see you burned. It is the common belief that Magol brought us forth to Margra from the source and only through him will we return."

"Yes, I know my words appear heretical these days. Luckily there are none here in this city who would perform such an act as to burn me. I trust that you will not seek to destroy me."

"Of course not."

"But this Magol you speak of fascinates me and so too does the mention of a source. How one of the First Ones rose to the status of godhood I do not know."

"First Ones?"

"I wonder if...No, I must speak of what I know. This planet was settled by a number of Sundwellers and Hiem. They built a colony. They used to be referred to as the First Ones, the progenitors. Why they came here is a mystery, one of the reasons I think that my people became focused on recording everything in the archives. But Margra has a long history. Our ancestors were not even the first to come to this place. Why, those who bound Ruel in bands of power pre-dated even our ancestors. We call them Moon Binders, but not much is known about them. Their physical appearance, for example, is an unknown, but they left many relics and a small portion of technology behind."

"Nils, that is intriguing. I can see how what you say meshes with some of the tales my mentor told me. To tell the truth, people did think he was eccentric." The cadre throbbed with warmth and understanding, prompting Salinda to accept what Nils was telling her.

"But tell me, Salinda, what do you know of your heritage? Who were your parents' parents?"

"My parents were from Sartell, though I think my father was from Stoli stock; he was fair where my mother was dark. She had some Lim in her but also something else, Arvoli maybe. I'm not sure exactly." She shrugged. "Everyone is a bit of everything these days.

With the continent of Arvoli being submerged and Strega destroyed in Moonfall, there were many refugees. Now it is hard to distinguish people's heritage. Beyond that, all I know of my ancestors is that they lived and they died. Life is hard, too hard to worry about personal history." Surprise, disbelief and awe were warring in her head. She was actually talking to a being who had lived before the moon split. One who knew not of Magol's teachings, or if he did, discounted them. Mez would have burst with pleasure at meeting such a being.

Nils looked at her again, his pale eyes flitting from her hands to her head. "You are part Hiem."

Salinda blinked once. "What did you say?" The way he looked at her and what he had said made her go cold. Her hands shook so much that her cup rattled on the table top. Such a statement was unexpected. She'd gone from meeting a being from the past, from a race she hadn't even known existed, to being told that she was related to him somehow. It skewed her sense of self, her sense of what she knew of the world, more personally than any of the other revelations so far.

"The healing tray produced a report saying you had Hiem blood. I think we share ancestry. There is a chance, too, that the machine mingled Hiem blood with your blood as it healed you, but I'm not convinced of that."

As she withdrew her fingers from around the cup and placed them in her lap, Salinda said, "I am a...a blood relative of yours?" She breathed deeply a few times to calm down. "But I don't understand. I don't feel any different—I can't believe the machine changed me—so it might be true that we are distantly related."

"My people were good at hiding themselves. We did not mix easily with your kind. If someone interbred with Sundwellers then circumstances must have been dire. And if it was the machine...what can I say?"

"Nothing. It healed me, saved me..." She stared into her cup, collecting her thoughts. When so many people had mixed blood, what did it matter that she had some other kind of blood within her? People had had to survive, and intermingling was often the only way they could, sharing resources, knowledge and blood. Yet she desired to say something more to Nils. He'd lost so much that a small thread of kinship, no matter how tenuous, was no doubt important to him. "I would be proud to be part Heim, Nils. From what I have seen, your people were a great race. I will gladly tell you what I know of dragons, as I promised."

He inclined his head, an eager brightness is his silvery eyes.

Salinda folded her hands in her lap and began. "Legends tell us that dragons rose from the wound of Margra at Moonfall. No one is sure if they were within Ruel or deep within Margra itself. Many fear them because they eat the flesh of man. You probably saw the harpoons on the walls at Gunner. Dragons apparently only attack if a human—my kind, those you call Sundwellers—goes on or near their territories or if they are really hungry. The prison where I was held was naturally isolated because of its geographical position, the geothermal activity around it and the presence of the dragon hatcheries." She saw his puzzled look and added, "To my mind the dragons live near volcanic vents for the warmth and the minerals. It is where they breed."

"That does add weight to the theory that the came from within Margra...but my people have lived beneath Margra for thousands of years and never encountered them."

Salinda reached for the last of her Pardu, which had now cooled and thickened. "The dragons are more than just flesh and blood—they have properties, strength, power...I'm not sure what you would call it, but it is true."

"Properties? I felt something in their presence, but I am not sure it was anything more than a sense of awe. When one is fascinated by something as I am fascinated by dragons, the mind can easily create a corresponding phenomenon. What makes you so certain of these properties?"

Salinda met his slightly mocking gaze. "I know this from the dragon wine."

Nils sat back and one side of his mouth curved up in an almost smile. "Why would a wine named after dragons be anything more than crushed fermented fruit? You mistake the euphoric effect of alcohol for something greater."

Unwaveringly, Salinda held his gaze. "I do not." She swallowed, trying to moisten her now dry throat. How was she to convince him of something she knew to be true when she could provide no objective proof? "I have felt the wine work on me. I've seen it heal, bring life where life had been waning. The dragons have something that we need to survive—"

"Forgive my skepticism. I have come from a time when there were no dragons. I find them astonishing, true, but I'm not ready to accept any far-fetched tales about them."

Salinda flushed, partly from anger and partly from the hot drink. "Dragon wine is sourced from grapes grown in dragon dung. Even the vines themselves have properties. I have seen the wine's power with my own eyes—felt it, felt it heal me."

"I would have to experience this phenomenon myself to even begin to entertain this idea."

"What I say is true. We need dragon wine to survive. It is the only thing that keeps us alive."

"Dung and wine? This is not what I want to hear. I want to hear about dragons—how they fly, how long they live for, how they birth their young."

"I can tell you those things, and I will, most happily. But you must hear me first. I need your help. The Inspector—the man who harmed me—had a lot of wine. I have to ensure it reaches the people who need its life-giving properties."

"Help you? You want to help those lowlifes, those who are a mockery of the Sundwellers of old?"

"Yes, I do."

Nils stood up, gathering his robe about him. "If all of your kind were to pass away, then so be it. Margra would be a better place, a place for dragons."

Tears filled Salinda's eyes as she stood to face Nils. While his words were devoid of empathy, they were laced with truth too. "I believe we will rise again. I hope to prove to you that we are worth saving. Please do not...do not give up hope," she said in a low voice.

"I have no hope. Even if your humans could mend their ways, time is against them. When the rest of Ruel falls—because fall it must—then this place will be fit only for dragons. The Sundwellers are doomed no matter what they do, but dying sooner will spare them witnessing the death of their planet. So I will hear what you have to say about dragons, then I will take you out of Barrahiem and back to the world above. I will write down all that you tell me and put it in the archives."

The cadre turned to ice in her mind and she staggered, reaching out to the wall for support. The rest of Ruel fall? It could not be. That would be the end of everything. She fought her grief and formed it into fury. She stood straight, dropping her hand from the wall and taking a step toward Nils.

"Archives? What good is an archive if it is not used? Who will read your records? Who will care about what happened today or yesterday or a thousand years ago? No one, because they will all be dead. Your work is pointless!"

He squared his shoulders and lifted his chin a notch higher. "There is no higher calling than the work of my people. Who I am to judge the ultimate purpose of our great store of knowledge? You speak in anger."

"Oh, yes," she replied vehemently. "I am angry—disappointed too. For I thought you worked for the greater good, but that is not so. You work for your own selfish, grief-twisted ends—ends that serve no one but yourself." She meant to provoke him. As she spoke it dawned on her that the suffering she had endured and the experiences that had nearly ended her life need not have been in vain. She had found Nils and the wonder that was Barrahiem, and she knew she had an unparalleled opportunity to garner Nils's help before all was lost. She wasn't about to settle for his indifference and indolence.

Nils stood absolutely still for a long moment. She thought he would rage and yell at her, but he didn't. When he finally spoke it was to say, "You speak truth. My heart is filled with grief and many other darker feelings. You cannot know what I feel."

Her heartbeat relaxed back into a steady rhythm as calm returned. The cadre glowed at that moment, and words came into her mind as if it had sent them. She repeated them: "Ward yourself well, do all with care, for the knowledge makers are near."

Nils brightened. "The world above did not forget us. That is some recompense. Many feared us, even then. As it is now, I dare not be seen."

She went to reach out to touch him, to reassure him, but dropped her hand. "It is true. Your looks would instill fear into the hearts of my fellows; they would kill you before even asking your name. Sense has fled. Fear rules the hearts of men. How it pains me to know it."

"But not you. Fear does not rule you."

She had to look away, couldn't bear to focus her anger on him when she owed him so much and knew him so little. How could she admit that fear had ruled her? She had nearly died with a heart and mind laced with ripe, red fear.

"No." Salinda fell quiet. "I have known fear intimately, but it does not rule me anymore. I have you to thank for that." She dared not tell Nils of the cadre and its ability to recognize one of the Hiem. She wondered whether she would have been afraid of Nils without the cadre's help. Glancing up at him, she saw he hadn't taken offense at what she'd said about his work being futile. Yet she wasn't about to give up the fight. She had to have Nils's assistance: she had to help him find some hope.

"It was fortunate I was in a position to help." His face softened and he smiled. "I am not sorry for it."

Salinda grinned in return. "Will you show me more of the city while we talk? It truly is a marvel."

Nils bowed and gestured to the doorway. "Follow me, and see the wonders of the Hiem."

Chapter Two

A REBEL'S TRAIL

Danton and his selected rebels had ghosted along the river on foot on the Gunner side until they'd realized that it curved in a large arc and that a shorter overland route would be both faster and safer. Danton suspected that the Infra-pact rebels would exercise caution now they were on the main waterway, perhaps leaving more traps or men to deal with curious onlookers or any party that looked vaguely interested in the wine. It had meant a week-long trek through the foothills. Brill suspected it may have been shorter, distance wise, but it was far more arduous. One advantage had been that they did get the occasional glimpse of the river without being seen by their quarry. Unfortunately, there had been no sign of anything unusual until late the previous evening. It was then that they had decided to investigate.

Under cover of the early morning mountain haze, Brill, Danton and ten of his rebel band descended from the foothills of the Duggan Ranges to gain a better view of the small town below. The remaining eleven men, led by Danton's deputy, Merl, were deployed to scout the area, lay low, scrounge supplies for their onward journey and keep their eyes and senses sharp. A rendezvous point had been chosen. Brill was content that if things went wrong with his group, the wine trail would be pursued by Merl's.

"Is that it then?" Brill asked as he lay on his stomach in a hollow next to Danton, surveying the town through a viewer. Two other rebels, Joss and Harden, rolled into their cloaks to take a much-needed rest.

The small town of Vanden was situated at the foot of a mountain valley that fanned out to meet the Lyal river plain. Smoke billowed from a few of the burned-out houses within the walls, and they'd seen rebels and guards engage in a few skirmishes throughout the morning. Through the viewer Brill saw that a few of the farms outside the walls had been destroyed as well, and there appeared to be bodies piled by the main gate. He could confirm, too, something Danton had suspected—that Infra-pact rebels with the distinctive red band on their shirt-sleeves patrolled the walls.

Lying on his back facing the sky, Danton stretched, lifting his arms over his head. "Yeah, looks like it. We'll have to wait for Stinger to get back to verify it. But I reckon the Inspector has split the cache into three parts. The smaller one he's left in Gunner. A larger portion is stored in the town down there and the other, the main part, he has sent downriver. I don't know exactly where yet, but I will find out. The good news is that he's split up his men. Has to protect the wine and himself." He rolled onto his side and scratched under his chin, where his beard irritated him. "Anything else of interest?"

"Not much at the moment...wait." Brill lifted the viewer to his eyes and peered through it again. "There's something... Men are heading for some empty barges. Looks like they are crossing the river."

Danton took the proffered viewer and directed it at the line of men departing the town. Brill watched as his friend stilled and lowered the instrument.

"What is it?"

Danton rolled back over onto his back and swallowed uncomfortably. His complexion was pasty. "Him. It's him. Sorry, I shouldn't be reacting this way. It's just that I haven't seen him since..."

Brill took the viewer and searched the line of men for the Inspector. He felt a jolt of surprise and a spark of fear when he found him. "He tortured you, too, didn't he?" he said quietly to Danton.

"Had me for three days," he said as he made a fist and thumped the ground beside him. "Drugged me. Used me. Made me his personal pet. By the source, I don't want to remember it. I won't remember it."

Brill reached over and squeezed Danton's shoulder.

Danton's bravado dropped away and there in its place was a man who had been hurt, who had suffered, and the pain was still raw. "You can probably guess what the Inspector made me do. He paraded me around in front of his men and the other prisoners...fondled me...in front of Salinda."

"The Inspector is good at humiliation," Brill said dryly.

Danton nodded, acknowledging their shared experience.

"I thought I was over it until I saw him there, striding along confidently. It makes me feel as though it were yesterday. You know, if it hadn't been for Mez's intervention I would've ended up his permanent pet or dead. He thought me...pretty." He chuckled, though there was disgust in the sound. "That was in my younger days." Danton rubbed his hand over his face, fingering his eye patch thoughtfully. "Afterward I couldn't face Salinda, couldn't bear to see the pain in her eyes. But before Mez got me out of the vineyard I finally fronted up to her and asked her to come with me—she wouldn't, or couldn't."

"You know she cares about you, thinks about you still."

"Does she? For a long time I wondered about that. I thought that what she'd seen me become might have changed her opinion of me, eroded what love she might have felt. The source knows I hated myself."

Danton turned back onto his stomach to observe the deployment of men from the town. The rebel leader ground his teeth as he watched the men continue to issue from the gates.

"Something important must be afoot if the Inspector is leaving the town and the wine. I wonder what it is?" Brill ventured.

Taking the viewer once again, Danton studied the Inspector and his men. "Keeps one step ahead of us all the time. Despite splitting his force, there are a lot of men down there. We've too few to attack the cache in Vanden. Our best chance to recover the bulk of the wine is to follow the main part downriver."

Brill held Danton's gaze. "You may be right, but can we outsmart him? I have the kernel of an idea...but I need to think about it some more. Need more information too. Reckon I should head into the town and look around. What do you think?"

Danton's expression turned grave. "Not a good idea. Wait till Stinger gets back. He's good at what he does. We'll know more then." The rebel leader took another thoughtful look at the town and a smile played around his lips. "Can't risk you. Not unless I have something to gain from it."

Brill laughed. Danton was good and true, like Salinda. "I'll wait as you suggest." Brill took the viewer from Danton and trained it on the Inspector's line of men. There was something familiar about a particular rebel, but he couldn't get a clear look at him. Brill re-sighted and kept looking as the men walked in to closer range. He adjusted, refocused and then nearly dropped the glasses.

Alerted by his hastily drawn-in breath, Danton asked, "What is it?"

Brill shook his head, not quite able to speak.

Danton propped himself up on one elbow. "Looks like you saw a ghost."

Still mute with shock, Brill took another look at the rebel—a tall, thin man, straight dark hair and a hooked nose. There was no mistake. Sweat broke out on the back of his neck, and blood drained from his face. He glanced at Danton, who was watching him with his good eye. "Found your betrayer most like," Danton advised sagely.

Brill swallowed, his mouth suddenly dry. "I...don't understand. How could he be here? I thought he was dead. We were together when I was taken."

Danton frowned and shook his head. "It's the way of it," he said, his gaze sympathetic. Brill stared at him until Danton nodded once.

"No." Brill was shaking his head, so full of denial he felt ready to land a punch on Danton's knowing face. He slapped a fist into his palm instead. "I've known Henley all my life. He has been a family retainer since before I was born, worked for my father when he ruled Duval and was a most ardent follower of his Highland Confederacy. He looked after me when I was young. I trusted him with my life—the same way I trust you."

Danton reached over and squeezed his friend's shoulder in solidarity. "Look, Brill, I know it hurts, but every man has his price. He betrayed you...and he lived. But think—we now have an in. We can use this."

Brill sat back and let the viewer drop from his hand. His thoughts and emotions were in turmoil. Danton was sanguine, and it was easy enough for him because his best friend hadn't sold him out. Remembering the Inspector's torture, and how Brill would have said anything in the end, he realized there was a limit to what a person could endure. Yet Henley appeared untouched, with no visible scars. "What do you mean by an in? Henley? I don't know if I..."

Danton sat up, keeping his head low. "You may not, but I do. We'll follow the Inspector and your friend. Could be that we can gain both our objectives through the same means. I must admit I'd like to see how you handle the betrayer, Henley, you said his name was...I'll bet you won't find his excuses sufficient. When you do face him, be careful. He has betrayed you once and won't hesitate to do it again."

Brill nodded and swallowed spit. "And then what?"

"We will find out why the Inspector is trotting off onto the plains when he's just won himself a town."

The sound of footsteps caused them to halt their conversation. As Stinger approached, Joss and Harden roused themselves and made room for the damp rebel spy. Stinger, a small, wiry man, dripped river water as he slid into the hollow to report back. Joss's keen dark eyes glittered with interest as he sat up to listen. Harden brushed ginger curls off his forehead, his hair a stark contrast to his brown skin and pale green eyes.

"So, what's the news?" Danton asked.

Stinger flopped himself down on the dusty ground, the dirt turning to mud on his wet clothes. "As we thought, the town's Vanden. Near enough a farmin' place and no' very 'portant neither. A convoy of twelve barges packed off downstream at dawn, with 'bout fifty men. Five full barges at the rear o' the town, bein' unloaded."

"The wine?" Brill asked.

Stinger nodded. "Sober bunch, I'll say. All that wine and no drinkin'."

"Did you notice anything else?" Danton asked.

"Town's seen a bit o' action of late. Lots o' old fires, some new ones. Plenty of bodies piled on the riverbank, raisin' a stink."

Brill shivered once and wondered how Stinger could have stood the smell and the threat of disease. He took another look at the river and the tendrils of brown ooze that spread out behind the town.

"Right, I want Earl and Riken to remain here and keep an eye on Vanden. Stinger, you take the other five men with you and follow the wine discreetly. Pass on my orders to Earl and Riken. They are down the hill there a ways with the others. Report to Merl at the rendezvous point and then keep going. Borrow more men from him if you need to. Joss and Harden, you come with me."

With a nod, the two young rebels went to ready their gear, chatting quietly as they did so.

Brill shook his head, perplexed by Danton's deployment of the men. "So only four of us are following them? We can't hope to overpower them."

Danton smiled lopsidedly. "Yes, but with the help of your friend we can infiltrate them, or at the very least get close to them."

Brill was doubtful that any intelligence could be gained from speaking to Henley. Even so he picked up his gear and secured his short sword. He cast a grin at Joss and Harden even though his mind was troubled. No point in upsetting them with his fears.

Following the path of the Inspector's rebels was not hard. They left a wide trail, oblivious of or indifferent to attack. There was no rearguard, no one scouting behind. Brill's heart raced. There were at least two hundred men in this band alone, perhaps more still in Vanden. The odds against their success were daunting.

Danton took no risks, though, and made sure that they stayed well hidden. He and Brill traveled together, with Harden and Joss staggered behind, ready to assist if need be, but effectively splitting them into two groups. When the Infra-pact attacked some bandits in a ravine, Danton wouldn't investigate further, even though they burned with curiosity. Instead they took cover for the night some distance away to avoid being discovered by scouts.

Time etched a slow path across Brill's mind as the sounds of battle and death diminished and fell away. It had been quiet for an hour or so when he found himself still tossing and turning, too alert and too impatient to relax or sleep. Although there were sounds of men moving during the night, it seemed the force from Vanden had not withdrawn from the ravine.

After dawn, Danton went off to find a clear line of sight to make a signal to Joss and Harden. After he'd crept back through the undergrowth he began, "It's time, Brill. Things have settled down in the ravine and there is a reasonable amount of cover to hide your approach. Draw your man away from his companions if you can sight him. I'll try to keep you in view." Danton tapped his viewer and lifted the left side of his mouth in a quirky smile. In spite of his attempt at cheerfulness his remaining eye held an expression of concern.

Brill nodded once and turned away. He was both excited and scared that things could go terribly wrong. He found that the mere thought of falling into the Inspector's hands made sweat trickle and itch between his shoulder blades. With one backward glance at Danton, he stepped into the scrub and headed toward the ravine.

Crawling through the undergrowth, he bobbed up to check his bearings and then changed direction so that he should emerge near the edge of the ravine. He had to be careful and quiet. Soon it became apparent that the place was alive with rebels. He navigated ahead, nudging his way toward a rocky outcrop—a ledge, something that would give him a wide view of what was happening below.

The ledge was unstable so Brill lay flat on his stomach and prayed that the slight rock fall would not attract any undue attention. Pushing a branch of prickle out of his face, he caught his first glimpse of the scene below. The Infra-pact rebels had executed quite a number of men; even now some were being skewered or bashed. Brill bit his lip. It was a savage business, the kind you undertook when you didn't want witnesses or an enemy at your back. Even as slaves or indentured labor these men had some value. Killing them was a waste.

Then his eyes fell on the Inspector, who sat with his back to the rock face. Of course, the Inspector valued no one. The cruel bastard sat cleaning his nails in that fastidious way he had. Brill couldn't help the clench of his gut when he saw him, so unmarked, so untouched by any hardship. How had that man done it? Escaped a burning vineyard, crossed a field of dragons? He frowned when he realized that the only explanation was the dark-skinned woman with the kind smile and soft voice. What had that animal done to Salinda?

A commotion up one end of the ravine snagged Brill's attention. A tall man and a slender girl were being pushed and dragged forward. Brill shifted his gaze to the Inspector, who after receiving a message ceased cleaning his nails and headed toward the pair with a lithe and sure stride.

The captives didn't look like rebels. The tall, broad man was wearing some kind of uniform and the girl a strange admixture of clothing. Her bearing, though, was that of a lady. She was no slave. However, something about the girl made Brill start. She was beautiful for one thing, but there was a faint glow in her eyes. He hadn't seen anything like that since Salinda had called the dragon, Plu. Was it possible that there were others like Salinda?

Brill swallowed the dry lump in his throat. This changed everything. The Inspector had had Salinda and done unspeakable things to her. Now this girl, who held on to the young man so tightly and who appeared to be no more than a child, was in his hands. If this girl was like Salinda, then the Inspector would have access to power— an unknown quantity of power. Brill fought his outrage, breathing slowly to calm himself and to get his brain to work.

Taking his eyes off the scene, he scanned the area for Henley. A man was walking out of the ravine, quite alone, heading down a pathway. He knew that walk. Scuttling back on all fours, careful to keep his weight even across the ledge, he found himself on solid ground. He sighted ahead of him and decided to follow the edge of the ravine, which appeared to narrow until only a crack separated it from the other side. Brill was hoping that his luck was high and that Henley would remain on course and cross his path.

Brill moved cautiously, taking cover more than once to avoid rebels. He had hardly gained any ground before he became aware of five rebels about a hundred yards downwind. They chatted among themselves, eyeing the woods around them, their distinctive red arm bands visible through the breaks in the leaves. After drawing back into the cover of a bush and finding a vantage point from which to watch the men, Brill kept still and listened.

"Any word yet on when we can stop searching? I'm sure we've accounted for them all."

"Nah, no word yet. But I heard they found what they were looking for on the other side of the ridge. Now that he's got that we'll be heading back for sure."

"Well, I'm hungry...and it's been a bloody long march. I just want to put my feet up and enjoy what Vanden has to offer."

There was a chuckle. "Not much to enjoy in Vanden."

The others agreed.

Brill heard someone else coming along the track to his right. He peered through the branches as a shadow passed. Brill let his breath out slowly when Henley walked into his line of sight.

"What's the word? Are we heading out?" one of the rebels asked Henley.

Henley greeted the men with a nod. His gaze roamed over the

undergrowth as he stopped to talk. "Yes, prepare to head back. Any stragglers returning to that rebel camp will get a surprise—an explosive one. Any more of our men further down the track?"

"Well, Kit and Munch went past us earlier, but that's all. We'll head back. Had enough of chasing nothin'."

"Right. I'll go down a bit further and see if I can flush the others out."

Henley picked a leaf off a bush and chewed it while he looked around. The man's cloak was covered in red dust, as were his face and hair. Dust also covered the other men who began to walk away, heading back to the ravine. Brill couldn't believe his luck or how hard his heart was beating. Henley set off slowly down the track, stopping occasionally to look around.

Brill worked his way out onto the path and hurried after Henley, keeping his ears pricked for the presence of other rebels. He rounded a bend in the track and there Henley was, standing staring at nothing and pissing into the undergrowth. He heard Brill's step and jerked his head round in his direction.

"Well met, old friend," Brill said as emotionlessly as he could, keeping his expression bland.

Henley's face was a study of shock. He fumbled with his trousers to rehouse his goods and wiped his hands on his thighs, leaving a spray of droplets. "Prince Brilliant?" Then he recovered somewhat. "You're alive? But I... When you were taken, I was worried...I feared—"

"But you were taken also, weren't you, Henley? I distinctly remember that."

"Oh, but I got away. Thought you were right behind me."

"I see. Glad to hear it." Brill so wanted to believe him, but he knew—how he knew. He'd replayed that moment again and again. Brill shrugged and smiled pleasantly. "Well, that's all water under the bridge now. We're working for the same cause...the same boss."

"We are?" Henley's gaze roamed, looking for a way out. Brill could tell he didn't believe a word of it. "Don't recall seeing you..."

Brill decided to bluff it out, though he understood the risk he was taking. All Henley had to do was shout for backup. "You weren't looking too hard...I mean with the wine and all, and then chasing that girl and her friend. Such a large force and there's been hardly any time to socialize."

Henley smiled uneasily. "Yeah. It has been rather tense, hasn't it?" Sweat beaded on the man's upper lip and another trickle slid down behind his ear, leaving a clear trail in the reddish grime. Henley hadn't relaxed at all. Brill sensed he wasn't falling for his story—his former friend was worried about something. Perhaps worried that Brill would kill him...had come to kill him. And kill him Brill should.

"I wonder what the fuss over that girl and the lad is about. I mean, isn't Vanden prize enough?" Brill sauntered forward. Henley stiffened at his approach but didn't move. His eyes darted everywhere, though, returning regularly to Brill.

Sweat was beading on the traitor's brow now and he swallowed. "Yeah, I was wondering too...Lenk has his balls in a knot about it, what with the bandits attacking him and then Gercomo waltzing in and taking over. Girl's got some kind of power. Never saw the boss so excited."

"Well, he doesn't usually get excited about much, does he? Particularly about women."

Henley's brows drew together as if he were trying to reconcile Brill's presence with the information he was divulging.

"I reckon not." The sound of men approaching in the distance challenged Brill's acting ability. He stayed put, close to Henley, almost close enough to kill him, and remained calm. He'd have to brave it out. He smiled once, a flash of his former princely charm, and folded his arms.

Henley suddenly looked as if he were preparing to move. "Here!" he yelled. "Traitor!" The footsteps drew closer and sped up. Henley made a lunge. Brill was ready and he deflected the knife blow and elbowed Henley in the jaw, stunning him momentarily. Whoever was approaching began to sprint at the sounds of struggle. Brill kept to his purpose and kicked Henley in the head. He felt a moment's exhilaration. "Traitorous bastard," he spat. "Your mother was a red-lipped whore!"

Henley swung his leg up and kicked Brill in the gut. Brill went down as a whoosh of air was forced from his lungs. Henley rolled on top of him and hissed into his face, "You're a self-important prick. Wait till the boss hears about what I've caught. We've had a great time listening to his tales around the campfire...how you squealed like a stuck pig when he interrogated you, how you wanted his guard to keep pounding your rear like a lovesick whore."

Bastard! At that moment Brill hated himself even more than he hated the Inspector. But his anger gave him strength. He rolled and shoved, dislodging the older man. Both got to their feet, circling each other in a crouch position. Henley got another boot in, sending Brill backward, before Henley grunted once and slouched sideways to the ground, the handle of a hurling blade protruding from the side of his neck.

Brill dragged himself to his feet, his breath coming in heavy pants as he swayed. He turned to see Danton, who stood poised with another hurling blade at the ready. "You all right? Sorry I killed him for you. But you were taking too long and our other friend is moving out. Time to put your brains to work."

Brill spat on Henley, whose eyes stared up at an unforgiving sky. "Yeah, thanks. He knew the bastard...I don't know how I didn't see through him, back then. I was a fool..." Brill recollected that his father had trusted Henley too. Perhaps he'd betrayed Hubert and the Highland Confederacy as well.

"Time for recriminations later. Did you find out what's going on?"

Brill forced his mind to focus on the present situation. "That girl has some sort of power, the same kind Salinda has, I think. From what I could gather they had escaped from Vanden."

"They?" Danton's eyebrow rose.

Brill concentrated on his friend, aware that he felt shaky. "The lad and the girl captured by the Inspector. Did you see them in the ravine? The Inspector wants her...got excited when he heard about her. That's reason enough to rescue them. But if she's like Salinda, she'd be useful to us, too."

Danton considered this. "You have a plan?"

"Blend in, but keep our distance. If you've finished off the other men Henley was looking for then we can use their cloaks." Brill went over to Henley's body and pulled off his rebel cloak. "If the Inspector was heading out, he won't be in the ravine. With him gone, there is less danger of either of us being discovered and recognized."

Danton signaled into the forest. Joss and Harden emerged from the shrubs where they had been listening in, brushing dead leaves from their clothes and hair. Joss smiled, his uneven teeth giving him a feral look. "Be careful, but fetch those cloaks and bring them back," Danton instructed.

At a nod from the rebel leader, they went back down the track for the cloaks. "Let's hope he doesn't have more of our former allies in his ranks. It won't take long for them to return to Vanden, and once they do, any attempted rescue will be nearly impossible."

"That doesn't leave us much time, does it? If we ghost along the line while we have cover, we can get close to the lad and the girl. But we'll need to create a diversion at the right time. Got any explosives?"

Danton patted a small pouch attached to his waist. "Yes. And what happens if we run out of cover and don't get close to them in time?"

"In that case we blend in and pretend we belong or..."

Danton grinned. "We shoot arrows and toss explosives and hope for the best. Joss and Harden will be able to do that while we integrate with the line, extract the boy and the girl."

Brill frowned and shook his head. It was a hasty plan, after all, with a few too many holes for his liking. "Let's just aim to get to them before we lose cover."

Danton slapped him on the shoulder and led him away from Henley's corpse. "Knowing the Inspector, he won't wait once they are inside. If I was him I'd kill the young man...or use him as leverage to get what he wants from the girl."

Brill frowned and rubbed his chin. "I agree. I don't understand the nature of the power Salinda and this girl seem to have, but it is important. Salinda stayed in that vineyard all those years to keep her power hidden. All I know is that the Inspector shouldn't get his hands on it, or on them. I want to stop him corrupting innocence. I want to take a stand now."

Danton guided him forward, his hand still lightly on his shoulder. "I don't know much about power either, kid. But Salinda thought it was important and that is enough for me." His expression soured. "And keeping those innocents out of his hands is a powerful motive in itself—risky though it is. When I think of Salinda...with him..." Danton's voice filled with emotion and his good eye moistened.

Brill frowned. "I know. Try not to dwell on it. I'm sure she's all right."

It wasn't long before Joss and Harden returned with the rebel cloaks. Danton deployed them to the other side of the ravine to survey the line and instructed them to be ready when the signal went up. They unhooked bows from their packs and strung them, before disappearing into the undergrowth. With the Inspector ahead, Brill and Danton set about infiltrating the enemy's line.

About half an hour later they caught up with the tail end of the rebel force and slipped into the cover on one side of the line, glad the rebel cloaks provided camouflage. Surreptitiously, they worked their way up the line, searching for the two captives. Seeing them up close, Brill didn't have any illusions about this force. They were professional. His heart rate notched up a beat.

One of the sergeants stood alongside the file, facing backward. "Anyone seen Henley?" he yelled up the line.

No one answered. The sergeant bellowed orders for a detachment to go back and search for the missing man before he scuttled away. The pressure was on now. Once the rebels found Henley's body, any chance Brill and Danton had of subverting the defenses around the prisoners was going to dwindle fast.

A ruckus erupted ahead. With a casual glance at Danton, Brill caught the other man's signal. This was them: the captives. Hopefully the young man still had some fight in him.

Danton gestured for Brill to take up his position. Brill edged as close to the rebel line as he could, and then he saw them. The young man had a swollen eye and blood from his nose stained his shirt. The girl looked thin and worried. The glow in her eyes was faint. Brill switched his gaze to the young man again. If anything the captive looked like he had something about him. Brill was drawn to his face, to his expression of concentration and the hunch of his shoulders. He could hear something too, a low buzz. Brill could not believe it at first. The man was humming.

Suddenly a blinding flash erupted from the young man's hand, followed closely by yells and sounds of confusion. Brill kept his eye on the man, who grimaced in pain while he tossed sparkling fragments into the air around him and grabbed for the girl. The men surrounding them reeled back; a couple stumbled and tripped others. The man and the girl were out of the line and heading in Brill's direction. Brill stepped back and let them pass. With a quick salute, Danton began hacking with his short sword at two rebels who had lunged after the escapees. Brill nodded and fell in behind the man's retreating back. Grunts and expletives receded as Brill followed the pair into the woods. He needed to make sure they understood that he was there to help them.

The ping of arrows letting fly sounded clearly, adding to the shouts. Danton's men had done their job, staying back and waiting for their opportunity. Brill drew behind the man and the girl and shouted, "This way. Quickly."

The young man swung around, fists at the ready, pushing the girl behind him. His eyes looked wild.

"Easy. I'm here to help. My friend is holding off the others."

The absence of rebels streaming through the woods obviously added weight to Brill's assertions. The youth nodded, though he remained wide-eyed. Brill moved in front of him and led the way through the woods. Before they had gained ground, Danton erupted out of the shrubs and said bluntly, "Move!"

With the man and the girl between them, Brill and Danton ran. As they took off through the shrubs, Brill doubted they had a chance. Their trail was easy to follow. All they could do was run and hide, run and hide, and hope for a bloody miracle.

Chapter Three

THE BREAKING OF THE WORLD

Deep in the warren of rooms beneath the city, Salinda watched as Nils rummaged through shelves and drawers of records. Some of the documents appeared to be made of parchment or paper and others out of a kind of metallic film. Strange symbols adorned them, some handwritten, others too evenly formed to be so. Nils handled them as if they were as fragile as eggshells, seemingly oblivious to her presence. Fatigue dogged her but curiosity kept her alert.

Nils had dragged her over the archives, his family's section in particular, for days at a time. Her head ached at the thought of taking in any more information. He'd said it would take a lifetime to go over the whole of the Barr collection and she believed him. There was one relative who claimed the bulk of Nils's attention, and it was this relative who was responsible for Nils's current burst of frenetic energy. Nils paused in his search, apparently having found something of interest.

Salinda's stomach rumbled loudly in the relative quiet of the room. "Nils, shouldn't we return to the city now? We have been here for hours and I must confess to being tired and a little hungry." The strange man didn't respond. Perhaps he had forgotten she was there. Moving a little closer, she noticed that his hands were trembling and his facial expression was frozen. "Nils? What is it?"

Peering over his shoulder, she saw that he held one of the metallic films. The symbols were strange to her. Without responding to her, Nils began to read aloud, his voice was wet with grief.

> *I was in the city of Newen when Margra shook on and off for a day and a half. We knew then that a large piece of Ruel had hit. The government's early reconnaissance told of the vaporization of millions on the continent of Strega. They ceased to exist within a heartbeat, and I knew that Stregahiem and all its Hiem would have been destroyed along with them. Soon afterward a howling hot wind lifted roofs, flattened buildings and whipped up the sea. Those of us in the shelters survived. Trell of Barr's model had predicted waves and quakes spreading out from the impact point, and time seemed to stand still as we waited for those. That Margra didn't disintegrate is a miracle. The last solution devised by the Seven must have worked. I can only surmise that the observatory at Trithorn Peak must have used the solution to reduce the mass of Ruel before it fell, and thereby lessened the impact of Moonfall. Yet the damage is done. The world as it once was is lost. That day billions died.*
>
> *In the week that followed, I walked among the dead, the bodies washed ashore, in the crumpled buildings and in the streets. I could have returned to Barrahiem and taken shelter with my kin, but in my heart I knew that this was a fate to share, a fate that none could escape. I helped those I found still living, though they feared me. Some called me an angel and others saw me as death incarnate and perished when I touched them. Weeping now as I look out across the remains of the city, I see that the ocean rises still, boiling and churning all that stands in its path. Miles and miles of our continent of Arvoli has already succumbed. The sky darkens and roils with dust—a cold hand that is death to sunlight.*

Nils paused, still peering at the entry as if reading ahead. "He makes another entry, perhaps a week later, although he was obviously too distracted to date it," commented Nils before continuing to read.

> *I cough and know the end is near. I cannot eat for the food is polluted and the water is contaminated by rotting corpses, which I can no longer smell. The sky is dark, the air thick. The Way Gate is blocked. I fear that no one will be able to retrieve my record.*

Nils lifted his eyes to the ceiling and uttered words that sounded like a prayer. "This record was made by Ryad of Barr, my cousin. I knew him well."

Salinda listened to the account, so sparse and unemotional yet entirely moving. Arvoli. That was the name of the continent that had sunk beneath the sea. She knew some considered it a legend. Yet, thinking about what she had just heard, she knew it had been real and those who had not escaped in time had died.

Finally, Nils looked toward her, acknowledging her presence. His face was awash with tears. "You do not know, cannot know. For you this is from a time so far removed—a fable, long wrapped up in mystery. For me it is yesterday. I closed my eyes to sleep and the world was whole around me, and now..."

Uncertain of what to do or say, she stood close to him. With her fingertips, she lightly touched his hair, stroked the back of his head. At her soft touch, Nils trembled, and tears leaked down his cheeks as his shoulders heaved with the effort to suppress them. Salinda moved closer, not embracing him, but letting him rest against her. To willingly hold a man, a strange man, felt odd. Yet she did not shrink from the task. His need outweighed hers. When Nils had composed himself, he slid the film back onto the shelf. Unobtrusively, Salinda backed away, always with her eyes on him.

"Can you explain the symbols? I don't recognize the style of writing," she asked him finally, hoping that something so ordinary as an explanation would break the bleak mood that had fallen on him. She hoped too that her hunger would abate so that she would not embarrass herself with her weakness.

Nils looked her way, not at her but at her feet. "It is a code—a single means through which to record events. There were many Sundweller languages in the past. We learned them all, but everything is recorded in this way. Languages die, but our coded archival language does not."

Salinda allowed her smile to show in her eyes. "So that is why you can speak my language?"

Nils lifted his eyes to meet hers, his apparent shame at showing emotion ebbing as he explained, "Yes, though what you speak is a hybrid of languages from many of the continents. It's a common tongue spoken in the towns I visited. Though your system of writing is less recognizable. In fact, it is very different from what it once was." Again he looked away, as if suddenly shy.

Nils turned back to the records, his fingers brushing the shelves lightly. "The archive is more than a collection of dry events. Written here are thoughts, analyses, science, learning, mysteries..." His gaze met hers once again, his eyes sparkling with his enthusiasm. "Thousands of years' worth."

With that look the cadre warmed. She was on the right track. There was a purpose or a use for what Nils had stewardship over. She wondered at the account he'd read. What or who were the Seven Ryad had spoken of? What was the last solution? What did it matter in any case? It was so long ago. Yet, there was a rich source of information in the archives. Source willing, in time, either she or the cadre would recognize it.

He sighed and turned back to regard the shelves. "You have lost much—technology, wisdom...perhaps it is all for nothing now."

Shaking her head, she said quietly, "No, Nils. There is hope. Please believe that. Try to understand that there is hope."

As if sensing her willingness to listen, Nils continued to talk. "We served the path of knowledge, reveled in the seeking out and recording of what happened. I preferred to research the unknown, to discover new truths such as those to be found in the stars. This is why I am an outcast historian—one of the reasons, at least."

Salinda laughed lightly. "You seem to be doing well for someone who is 'outcast.' You know your way around these records like I know my way around a vineyard."

He stared at her then, as if he couldn't believe that she had understood him. Perhaps he was too alien to understand. But she understood the loneliness that came from dedication to a task—the decisions and choices that must be made. She had given up a life with Danton for duty. She refused to believe that choice had been wrong. Nils continued to search the shelves, sinking once again into a reverie.

Thoughts of the vineyard led inexorably to thoughts of dragon wine. Her tongue recalled the taste of it and she swallowed an imaginary mouthful. Could she live without it?

Later, without preamble, Nils quit the room and gestured for her to follow him. Back in the residential node and after some prolonged verbal encouragement, Nils took a meal with her, some dried fungus soup. He barely finished before heading back to the archives. When he had gone, Salinda sat and stared into space. Another deep yawn convinced her it was time to go to bed. As she slid beneath the covers she wondered how Nils could concentrate for so long without rest.

Had he always been this focused, this driven? Her eyes closed and she considered whether all his drive and energy could be turned to her own cause.

Eventually, Salinda slept and dreamed of death. Those words that Nils had read about Moonfall swam around in her mind, calling forth detailed images of her ancestors' demise. There was so much to smell and taste and feel in the dreams. They were more like visions from the past, a gift from the cadre perhaps. Her bedding was wet with tears when she started awake. Nils stood on the threshold to her bedroom, a crease marking his bony brow. Had she called out during her sleep? She rubbed her eyes, but he had gone when she glanced up again. She sighed and shook her head. Nils was a mystery to her. Sometimes she felt drawn to him, at other times repulsed by his manner and his alienness.

Hurriedly, she threw back the covers and put on her robe. Determined to catch him before he vanished once again into the archives, she raced out of her abode and went into his. Even though he didn't appear to be within, she could hear his voice. Scanning the room, she realized that his voice emitted from a small box inserted into a niche in the wall. After hearing her name, she edged closer to listen.

It has been almost a month now since Salinda emerged from the healing tray. I find her mind most serious and her manner demure. Often we walk around the city and she tells me what she knows of dragons. It makes the desolation easier to bear. Her observations are interesting, based on empirical evidence rather than book learning. At times, I sense she has a natural affinity for these beasts, a capacity to communicate that I could never possess and can barely comprehend. Every time I think of that dragon flight, of how I sat astride the beast, Plu, of how I touched him, and the farewell I gave him, I feel exhilarated.

From Salinda's tales I am able to piece together some of the history and habits of these creatures. When they first appeared, they fed upon the dead, sometimes eating the remains of whole towns and cities. By doing so they reduced the spread of disease and decay, but in their flesh eating they also earned the Sundwellers' ire. The beasts increased in number, taking to the newly formed volcanic vents and geothermal areas to breed.

In the vineyard where Salinda toiled, a symbiotic relationship sprang up. Feeding the dragons kept them away from the prisoners tending the vines, provided that precautions were taken. Salinda's belief that the dragon wine has some kind of supernatural quality is hard to reconcile. Yet, she seems convinced. There must be some basis for this conviction for in other ways she appears to be logical and sensible. Then again, she has been brought up in a culture rife with ignorance and superstition. The only evidence she can tender is that the wounds inflicted by her captor had healed over, but I couldn't corroborate it myself because she'd been lashed again by the people at Gunner and had more wounds.

The dragons have some intelligence. How much I cannot say, but enough to respond to commands. Salinda said she touched the other dragons' minds. I, too, felt something that night when I saw my first dragon, some ethereal touch of mind on mind. At first I thought it was my imagination, but in my discussions with Salinda I am not so dismissive as I was before.

A noise disturbed her. She spun around and found Nils observing her from the doorway. He strode over and touched the wall where she'd been listening.

"I beg your pardon. I didn't mean to intrude. I was looking for you. I thought you might like to talk."

ｅｅｅｅｅ

They stood on the edge of the dark-watered lake that separated Barrahiem from the lesser city of N'Barek. Salinda could hear water spilling in and saw an aperture jutting from the roof of the cavern. Her gaze ranged out and saw more of them. Salinda gaped at the cavern roof so immense it housed both cities and the lake. *Spectacular*, she thought. The section of roof over the lake was like the darkest of nights with a spray of stars. Luminous lichen covered the cavern ceiling and their light was reflected in the waters of the lake. It reminded her of a jewel-encrusted velvet cloth of her mother's she had coveted as a child. Nils's voice chimed behind her, rattling off facts and anecdotes about the lake and the city they had walked through. So many stairs; she despaired of ever walking back up again. Already her calves twitched and her ankles ached. It seemed to have taken hours to reach the lake, the very heart of Barrahiem.

Something Nils said broke into her reverie. "I'm sorry. I didn't quite catch what you said."

"I was saying that this inlet was used for mating ceremonies."

"Truly?"

Nils crossed his arms over his chest. From her reading of his gestures this one implied frustration, even anger—though true anger from Nils seemed unusual. In her opinion, he did not feel deeply enough. One had to care before one could express anger. She detected a slight shudder in his shoulders as he drew a breath. This made her even more alert. Turning back to the lake, she sought what it was that had disturbed him.

"The essence of Margra concentrates here within this inlet. It is called the waters of Raenen."

"I've not heard of Raenen."

He gazed at her, his eyes dark pools. "I suppose you would call her a goddess, someone associated with fecundity."

Salinda chewed her lip and contemplated the water lapping against the shore of the inlet.

"When a couple join to make their vows, they must swim together here. Only then are other Hiem made. Only then is a true bond formed."

"You...procreate in the water? Or is it only ceremonial, the bathing together?"

To her eyes Nils grew even paler than he usually was.

"You mock me."

Stepping forward she said, "I do not. I only seek to understand your ways. We do not bathe to procreate. Indeed, you saw for yourself how little regard there is for the sexual act among my people."

There was something there in the glint in his eyes, a hunger or a need. He turned away.

"Have you ever bathed in the waters of Raenen, Nils?"

He didn't speak but shook his head once, a definite negative.

Oh! she thought, and said, "I see...and it pains you. That much is clear."

"I do not know what happens when one of my kind enters Raenen. It is a secret kept from me, a ritual of adulthood that I eschewed and now one that I will never know."

Salinda was wounded by his words. The mating act was no mystery to her. When she'd been a virgin, she had seen so much of the act that there were no surprises when it was forced upon her. Danton had told her that it could be a wonderful thing, joining with another person who you loved. But she'd never had that experience—not with Danton. When she had wanted to, he couldn't—the Inspector's abuse had destroyed him. Since then she'd experienced only the brutal aspects that required no sharing and no joy, only the will to survive it. Could it be possible that Nils didn't even know the mechanics of sex? Could his kind have been so prudish? She found herself blinking rapidly at the thought. "Do you regret that you never entered here with anyone? Can you not go in and experience it for yourself?"

"Again you mock me."

Her eyebrow arched with surprise. "Stop staying that. I do not. Why would I mock the one who has saved me, who has given me a body even more precious than the one I was born with? You, who have taken the physical scars and erased them. You, the great and wondrous historian, keeper of the very soul of Margra. I could not mock you if I tried."

Nils's eyes glittered with some emotion Salinda couldn't name. His gaze drifted to the lake and a look of longing passed across his features. While he stared at the lake's surface Salinda backed away from him. She trembled for what she had decided to do. She cared too much to let this moment pass. Nils was alien, but that did not make him less graceful or less handsome to her eyes. He was bitter, yes, but the source of that bitterness was a soul that felt too much. There was a great risk involved with her plan, the risk of rejection the most dangerous of all. And yet the cadre warmed the center of her, stroking her will with tendrils of encouragement, filling her mind with an echo of the sweet taste of rich, ripe fruit.

After easing her cloak off her shoulders, she jerked the tunic over her head and flung her clothes to the ground. Nils wasn't looking at her. The cold water made her skin pucker with goose flesh and her heart rate quicken. A wave of fear surged up her spine. She had never learned to swim. Already her breath began to catch as panic spread. The cadre urged her into the lake with flame-like intensity, setting her abdomen burning. The heat spread as the icy water rose higher up her body.

To her surprise the lake floor fell away quite abruptly. One minute she had Nils in her line of sight, the next dark water closed over her head. Fear threatened to overwhelm her—fear that he wouldn't notice she had fallen in. The cold water enveloped her, sucked away at her breath. With one thrust of her body, she struggled up and gasped for air with a great whoosh and splash. And then she went down under the surface again, lower this time, where the water was darker and more soup-like. With her breath held, her pulse throbbed in her neck and her lungs burned as they yearned for air. The surface was so near, almost within reach.

A flash of white streaked through the water next to her and air bubbles shot up to the surface. A pressure wave rocked her, sending her upward until the air stroked her face. She snatched a breath before sliding back under. Alive with power, the water tingled against her skin. Straining to see in the dark, she looked in the direction of the white streak.

A naked Nils swam toward her, hair floating in a nimbus cloud around his head, his thin body arrowing through the water as if born to it. There were slits in his neck, rippling like the gills of a fish. She'd never noticed these before. His eyes glowed in the dark water. She found that she could not look away from him. He was stunningly beautiful. Again she rose to the surface, this time lifted by his hands brushing caressingly against her skin. He held her up, then lowered her slowly back into the lake. There was almost a smile on his face as he drew her lower. He swam with her in tow, gently lifting her to the surface for breath as he powered through the waters of the lake. Salinda's body was awash with strange sensations, as if she were part cold fire rather than warm flesh. The feelings were exhilarating, and she longed for Nils to hold her and tow her deeper and further out into the lake. She wanted to sink to the very heart of the lake's bottomless depths. The core of her was responding to something in the water, filling her up with need. In her mind, the cadre pulsed like a heartbeat.

As if he was reading her mind, Nils lifted her high out of the water and from there she could see that she was in the center of the lake. As he lowered her down again, sliding her body along his, she took a deep breath. Then he propelled them lower and lower, so that Salinda's head felt ready to burst from lack of air. All the while, the cadre was pulsing and murmuring "yes" and "yes" like a whisper of water in her ears. There in the deepest part of the lake, Nils came to her. He slid inside of her, the press of his skin on hers like the touch of silk, his seed hot inside her, and then she felt the blackness descending as her air gave out. Sliding into unconsciousness, she was fulfilled and renewed and surrounded by Nils's beauty.

ᏅᏅᏅᏅ

When her eyes opened Salinda was in her bed. The soft covers enfolded her and her cloak was twined round her body. As she roused herself, she wondered if it had been a dream. Her hair was dry. She sat up and went to get water to drink. It had not been a dream, she realized, for she felt the remembrance of Nils's touch on her body; the rawness in her most tender flesh told her it had been real.

The water jug was full so she drank one or two cupfuls before deciding to make some of the Hiem tea. While she waited for the water to boil, she closed her eyes, not quite believing what she had done. She'd flung herself at Nils, seduced him at his weakest moment. She'd meant it as a gift, but now other thoughts intruded. The Pardu helped her to relax and think. Nils was nowhere to be seen. She wondered what he thought of her actions. She knew why the cadre had encouraged her in the way it had; it did not want the Hiem to disappear. If Nils was the last of his kind, it was her duty to preserve what she could and learn about his history, his people and the vast archive. Forcing a mating had been the optimal solution. Yet she felt something for him; he was alone in the world with no one to kindle hope. She couldn't allow Nils to succumb to despair. He had so much to offer, to give to the world. And it would wound her. In her heart, she knew her actions would divide her from Danton forever. If Danton still lived and still wanted her, that was. She was confused. Nils was not easy to understand and she had to admit that her own motivations for mating with him were obscured by a sense of duty. Yet, she cared for him. The recollection of Nils in the lake filled up her senses. In the water he'd been beautiful, as though unmasked, as though all of his pain had been stripped away.

After another sleep and some food, she went in search of Nils, because she knew it was time to take a stand and accept responsibility for what she had done. Continual avoidance would become ridiculous. She followed the stairwell from which he usually emerged. Down and down she went, all the while listening for him. There were catacombs, rooms etched from the very substance of Margra, filled with books, records and artefacts. Some contained machines, seemingly inactive, but when she approached they hummed to life and panels covered in lights twinkled blue and green. Lower and lower she delved, wondering if she had missed him in some passageway. At the very base, she found a desk and a light. There she saw his writings and the voice box he used to record his experiences.

40

As she was alone, she turned the recorder on. She wept when she heard of his awakening, wept harder when he recounted his despair, wept at the depths of his misery and what he had seen of the world above, her world. How different his words were to his manner and expression. How deeply and deftly he hid his pain when he was with her. She had thought that he didn't care. Now it was revealed that if anything he felt too much.

Next to his writings was an old handwritten book. The language was unknown to her. She queried the cadre and it too did not know it. On the desk she found more writings, some translations. A footstep behind her warned of his approach. She placed the book down gently on the desk and turned to him. Outwardly he was no different. The gills in his neck were closed and sealed as if they hadn't existed; his eyes, though bright, were no longer luminescent; his skin, though pale, no longer glowed.

Lifting her face she met his gaze. "I was worried about you, Nils. I came in search of you."

She saw straight away that he was different. Emotions once buried now seemed to ripple beneath the surface of his skin. He was angry with her.

"Worried?" He laughed, his voice full of bitterness. "What do you worry about? That I will abandon you here after what you did?"

Salinda cringed inwardly. He knew there had been a deliberateness in her act, no doubt about that. "I didn't mean...no, that's a lie. I did, Nils. I wanted to—"

He interrupted her. "I could have let you die, let you drown in that lake."

She arched her eyebrow. "But you didn't."

He looked away and walked to the desk, shutting his writings away from her gaze. "You have much still to tell me of dragons."

A smile threatened to destroy her attempt to appear calm and unemotional. He lied. Playing along, she answered, "Yes, that is so. But you know enough to find out the rest for yourself."

His head jerked up from where he had been putting things away. In that instant, she saw something raw in him, something that he didn't want to admit even to himself. Need. He needed her. "You wanted to enter the lake—I gave you a means to complete the ritual. You should thank me."

His eyes glittered with something akin to anger. "Is that so? You think you know my mind and heart better than I do. Luckily you are not Hiem enough to mate successfully. I will not be responsible for condemning another of my kin to live in this world."

"Really? How positive you are that the mating act was void. By your own reckoning, one of your kind mated with mine. Was that mating void also?"

The truth of her words registered with him. His mouth hung open then closed again.

"Preposterous! You know nothing about it. You could not even swim or breathe in the lake. I doubt there is enough Hiem in you for my seed to take. Yet, by joining with me in the lake you have an obligation to me, as I do to you."

Her own face went slack with surprise. There was a chair. She sat in it.

"Obligation?" Her hands kneaded her robe, rubbed the folds together, let them drop and then gathered them together in her fingers once more.

"Yes, you are now my mate...and with that role come responsibilities."

He sounded so hostile, yet she was sure it disguised his hurt. "Really?" she asked, lifting her chin and swallowing once, though her mouth was dry. Even she had her pride. She would not avoid the consequences of her actions. The cadre's role flashed briefly in her thoughts, but she didn't engage with it. "I will not shirk my duty. I embrace it fully. I care for you, Nils of Barr, though you are too proud to see that."

His gaze hardened. "Care for me? Your actions were too directed to come from emotion. This is part of some plan, some manipulation."

Her anger grew in her gut, boiling and churning. "And what do you know about it, Nils? You care for no one, therefore you think no one can care for you. Have you never loved anyone? Is it possible for one as self-consumed as you to love?"

He stepped away from her, backing out of the doorway. It was clear to her then that her verbal dart had hit a sore point. His face was a study of misery. Looking at her appeared to be a torture. "It was for love that I was imprisoned, Salinda," he said in an almost whisper. "I slept for untold years, neither breathing nor dreaming. The love of a female is a dry, bitter cup."

He spoke with such emptiness that it brought tears to her eyes. "I'm so sorry, Nils. I didn't know." With her head bowed, she studied her hands because she could no longer bear the grief in his face.

"You did not ask me why I did not enter the lake in my youth as the rest of my peers did."

Still looking at her hands she answered gently, "I saw only that it pained you. I thought—"

"It did pain me, but not because I was denied. I was destined to enter it with Acendrian, my appointed mate, but I preferred—loved another. You see, it was not only in my choice of profession that I was thwarted. Luca filled my night dreams with desire, yet when it came to the point, she spurned me. She did not have the courage to stand with me against our families and the elders. I was left with nothing but the guilt of having shamed Acendrian."

"I'm sorry for your loss." Her gaze lifted to his, her eyes moist with unshed tears.

"What loss? They are dead, and the enormity of my deed along with them."

He turned to leave, his robe tightening around his hunched shoulders.

She stood to go after him. "Please, Nils. I don't understand. If the Hiem did not mate for love, how is what I've done any different? What difference do my motives make?"

Stopping suddenly, he swung around and took a few steps toward her, not touching her, yet filling her senses with his presence, his scent. He whispered into her ear, his breath stroking her neck. "You risked much with your swim in the lake. You may yet regret it." He stepped back, watching her expression. His eyes glowed silver with emotion. "My seed might have taken. I could not bear to have made another as alone as I am. Yet we are mated. Together we will dwell here and you will have until final Moonfall to tell me of dragons."

Chapter Four

THE INSPECTOR'S WRATH

Returning from the hinterland on the back of a burden beast, Gercomo was confident that Fursten, his number one, would finish off the last of the bandits and then bring his captives well and truly trussed to his door. He might even have time to soak some of the grime from his body and find some clean clothes before he had to deal with them.

He reached the gates of Vanden just as Belle moon threw the first shafts of light over the mountain peaks. In the pale violet glow the town had an oily cast, filling with dark, creeping shadows as the moon rose higher. Gercomo considered Vanden little more than a village, and a pitiful one at that. Evidence of recent ruin clogged the streets and lay piled against the crumbling walls.

Further down the main street, the stench of the dead filled his nostrils. *Weak bastards!* he thought. A cool anger washed over him when he thought of the weakest fool of the lot—Lenk. The man had no impulse control and never thought things through before acting. Well, the foolish would-be prince would understand his peril. Not only had Lenk let the girl escape but he had killed the old man—the master and the true wielder of this supposed power.

Gercomo's senses reeled at the thought of this strange phenomenon. He had seen it in the girl's eyes and it had touched his mind somehow. Lenk couldn't tell him what it was or much about it at all because he didn't know precisely, but Gercomo could tell it must be a force of some strength, and important in ways he didn't yet understand. He paused before the mansion house and took a sip of his carefully distilled dragon elixir. It glowed faintly in the moonlight and slid down his throat like the knife edge of sharp ice. Its coolness spread throughout his body and his heartbeat slowed and steadied.

The two guards at the door pushed them open as he approached, and he strode through. He despised Lenk, because the man was a fool and because his grip on power was like that of a feeble old woman and not a true man. Not like his own. Lenk might have been useful as an ally, a provider of a safe haven, but no more. Some friend of friends. *Pah!* The lot of them were useless. They all depended on him for plans of action, for his powerful connections. He wondered why he bothered with any of them.

Gercomo laughed aloud, to the surprise of the guards standing to attention along the hallway. *Friends!* He had no need of friends. He looked about the sometime reception hall, ignoring the house guards by the door and seeing only the mess, the broken furniture and the soldiers' leavings after the ransacking. It only made his anger boil, made him imagine how he could temper it on Lenk's sad flesh.

When Gercomo had quashed the bandit attack for him, all that fool Lenk had been able to do was talk of his missing girl with the glowing eyes. At that moment Gercomo had found it difficult to restrain himself from crushing the man's throat. Yet when he'd seen the girl, he wondered what Lenk had been thinking. It had appeared as though she could barely stand as she clung to her young companion—not the force to be reckoned with Lenk had described.

For the young man, he had no use—he was pretty and expendable. Perhaps this observatory would want him back. He glanced up the mountain to where the observatory supposedly nestled, existing quietly at the very edge of human awareness. If they had any backbone they would come and enquire about the escapees. Yet rumor had it that they were weak old fools, full of religion and bizarre beliefs about Shatterwing, so removed from real civilization as to be almost mythical.

Lenk had said the Skywatchers were dependent on the town for food and supplies, another surprise. That would have to change if Gercomo stayed. He would brook no power above him and no hideaway to harbor opposition to his rule. The observatory may have been dependent on Vanden, but that did not mean that they would perish when Vanden no longer supported them. It was logical that they would find other ways to meet their needs. If Lenk was right, this power was connected to the observatory as well. It made Gercomo think how well their myth had been crafted and circulated. They wanted to be hidden.

As he turned on his heel to make his way to his rooms, the ones he had appropriated from Lenk, he heard whispering and a sensed a tremor of unease in the men in the hallway. Glancing back to the front door, he saw the guards tense as Fursten, his number one rebel commander, burst through them. Judging by the look in the man's face the news wasn't good.

"What is it?"

Fursten bowed his head. "Forgive me, sir, the line was attacked not far from the ravine. Henley was missing and we delayed while we searched for him. Then there was an explosion of some kind and the captives escaped."

"Escaped?" Gercomo did well to hold his temper. The moment his back was turned these idiots let things run riot.

Fursten bowed his head and nodded faintly. His red arm band proudly displayed his Infra-pact rebel status.

"Are you telling me a bound man and a bedraggled young girl who could barely stay on her feet escaped all by themselves, in spite of being surrounded by the most hardened rebels?"

Fursten raised his head and looked him squarely in the eye. His cheek twitched once. "I'm not saying they did it on their own. I found Henley. He'd taken a hurling blade to the neck, which took him out quickly. His cloak was gone."

"Do you know who did it?"

"Can't say naught but it's a rebel's weapon. The bandits we captured didn't use them."

The Inspector frowned. "Henley, the betrayer of Prince Brilliant of Duval, my, how interesting. Do I have a puny prince on the loose and following my tracks? I will not be gentle next time we meet."

"Do you know who it is, sir?"

"Perhaps. Tell me, Fursten, what have you done to recover my property?"

"Everything, sir. They are leaving a very wide trail for us to follow. We'll have them back in no time, I'm sure."

"And if you don't get them back? Do you know where they are headed? Where could they find shelter in this dust-infested hole?"

A new voice spoke from behind him. "I'd say they would head up the mountain—to the observatory."

Gercomo turned slowly and saw Lenk, unwashed and unshaved, standing further down the hallway. He felt an itch on his thigh and unclasped his riding crop from his belt. He rubbed it against the cloth of his trousers. "Why would you say that, Lenk?"

"Because that's where the old man was heading. That's where the boy was from. He is a Skywatcher from the observatory. He'd come to take her back there, or so he told me."

Gercomo considered this information. Perhaps it was likely that the young couple would head there, but would Brill head there as well? He wondered if Salinda had sent the young rebel to join Danton's band. If so, maybe they were after the wine.

If Brill had joined Danton they might have come looking for Salinda; she had planned to escape after all. He pictured what they would have found at the vineyard. Some hint of her fate, and about that of the wine cache. The evidence would have been there. His Infra-pact rebels were not subtle and the reports he'd received indicated they had done nothing to hide their trail.

He eased his neck, hearing the joints creak. That added some spice to the situation—Danton and Brill. Those two couldn't have many men at their disposal, otherwise the intelligence reports from Sartell would have mentioned them. Infra-pact had decimated their ranks through treachery and outright attacks in their bid for supremacy. He smiled to himself, confident there was nothing to worry about with those two except settling old scores and completing their destruction.

"Fursten, send two of your best men toward this observatory Lenk talks about. I don't want them seen, but I do want a full report on these people's defenses and the best possible attack approaches. If they see the escapees they should send word back immediately."

Lenk stepped forward, so close now that the stench of his unwashed body flowed over Gercomo. He latched on to Gercomo's forearm, dirty fingernails grotesque against his white shirt. "Are you going to let them escape?"

Gercomo could bear it no more. He flung Lenk off him and then swept his riding crop across the man's throat. Lenk went down in a tumble, half-wailing and half-gasping for air. Gercomo stared at him with neither pity nor disdain. "If you had been a better man I'd have no need to chase after anybody. You are a fool, Lenk. And that makes me a fool for trusting you. I can tell you this: I do not like to be seen as a fool." He stepped over Lenk and headed down the hall.

Fursten followed. "And the escapees?"

Gercomo turned abruptly, letting his anger flow over the rebel. He noted how the man flinched. "Make sure you get them if you can, but don't waste your men unnecessarily. If they do head for this observatory I'll be waiting for them, ready to gouge them out."

Nodding once, Fursten turned and headed out the door, yelling orders to his men as he exited.

Lenk was still rolling on the floor, banging his head on the skirting, hands clasped to his throat. "Bring him," Gercomo said to two of the guards who were looking on in dismay. With a smile he noted how they rubbed gingerly at their own throats.

Gercomo strode up the stairs two at a time and entered Lenk's old sitting room, the prince's before that. The overpowering smell of soot still hung over everything, and the furnishings, the carpets and even the walls were stained black. He sighed. He had lived in rough quarters for many years. It seemed he would have to abide more of it for a short time. The only emotion he felt on seeing the mess was boredom. He would have to think of ways to amuse himself, until he was surrounded by the luxury he deserved.

Lenk was suspended between the two guards. "Excuse me, sir," one of them said. "Where do you want the prince?"

Gercomo considered his former ally, still writhing in agony as he fought for breath. A smile lifted the corner of his mouth. Perhaps he did not have to let tedium rule the day after all. "Take him to the late prince's bedroom and tie him down on the bed. And I mean tie him down. I will look in on him later."

The men moved quickly, eager to flee his presence and his displeasure. Gercomo resisted another satisfied smile. Lenk would be a good example to the others. He made himself at home, pouring himself some wine while contemplating his later amusement. Of course, if by some chance his two escapees were captured, then maybe he would have something else to occupy him.

As he sipped a full glass of pure, well-aged dragon wine, he thought back to his escape from the vineyard and how much he had enjoyed destroying Salinda. How he had reveled in every one of her cries as he'd peeled away layer after layer of her dignity and hope. Watching that brute Ange repeatedly rape her had infused him with power. It was not the defilement so much that had thrilled him but the effect it had on her. It was like watching a candle flicker and burn as it strived to survive a blast of wind.

And knowing how much she hated being subservient to him had made her enthrallment through the elixir even sweeter. If he had had more of it, she would have been irreversibly his. Her intellect would have been replaced by slavish devotion and when her feeble body had finally succumbed to its addiction, it would have shriveled up and died.

The essence of the dragon so impurely imbued within the liquor eventually destroyed the body, rendering the organs nothing but lifeless slime. Or so his first three experiments had shown. All that was left of them had been fed to the dragons in a few quick gulps of useless tissue. Putting down his glass, he drew out his flask and sipped his own special brew, basking in its power. Only this elixir was free of those terrible side effects. It had taken long years to distil and then perfect pure dragon essence.

Seeing how Salinda had escaped the wonderful death he'd had planned for her, he would now have the opportunity of finishing the task of destroying her completely and utterly. A future time would throw her in his path again, of that he was sure. He'd detected something when she fled, something that he'd also sensed in Lenk's power maiden. How had he missed it before? He eyed the flask thoughtfully.

Within minutes, the lull the special brew induced hung over him like a shawl of ice around his shoulders. He liked this unemotional state. It took a lot to rouse him, to arouse him, when he was like this, and that in turn took him to new heights of pleasure. He could do so much more, see so much more. He hoped the prince was up to it.

When he entered the bedroom he saw that the guards had obeyed him precisely. He could see by the red hands and feet, full of blood, that Lenk was tied very tightly indeed. A red welt across the man's neck showed the path of the riding crop, and his breaths were sucked in painfully as if drawn reluctantly through a straw. Gercomo could tell that Lenk was aware of him by the slight hitch in the man's breathing.

With deliberate movements, he placed a chair in the corner and sat himself down in the shadow of a lamp. Then he took out his knife and pretended to cut Lenk's wrists. Lenk turned his head, straining his already swollen neck, his eyes large and afraid.

All at once Gercomo lunged, grasped the other man's shirt and slashed down the center and vertically down the sleeves. Lenk's breathing grew increasingly raspy and whimpers escaped him as Gercomo tugged off the remainder of the garment. Next he moved to the trousers and proceeded to do the same with those. When his captive lay there trussed and naked, Gercomo saw a glint of something in Lenk's eyes. Desire, anticipation, anger, fear. Gercomo drank them in as if they were a sweet wine. With a faint smile, Gercomo noted the man's pathetic erection.

The sight of it made the cool mood of the dragon essence come over him afresh. He jerked the rope tight around Lenk's left foot and Lenk stifled a curse. After waiting for five minutes or so, Gercomo loosened the rope and watched silently as Lenk bit down on the pain as the newly released blood once again pulsed freely.

Lenk shed tears as he watched Gercomo play with his bonds. Gercomo regarded him passionlessly. There was no pity in Gercomo and he could barely raise the interest necessary to keep Lenk alive long enough to provide amusement. At least Lenk hadn't started to beg yet or plead for mercy. Gercomo had to give him that. One word of that and he would have slit the man's throat. How to deal effectively with Lenk while providing a useful and informative lesson to those who might think to thwart him was proving to be a problem.

The thought of mutilation came to mind. He gazed upon Lenk and watched him harden further. As if Gercomo could be interested in such a pitiful creature; as if the sight of the man's cock could arouse him.

He enjoyed inflicting suffering on others, but it was more enjoyable still to manipulate others into doing it, to prolong the process so the fulfilment was as long and strong as the ultimate sexual climax.

Surely there was another way to satisfy his needs. Pity that he'd had to rid himself of Ange. His erstwhile guard had been a simple brute, but he had enjoyed himself and he had taken direction well.

Lenk was a man who enjoyed exploiting those weaker than him. Gercomo mused that this was the reason he lay there waiting for Gercomo to take his fill—he recognized Gercomo's superiority. An idea crystallized in Gercomo's mind. "You disgust me," he said, and left the room. If Lenk had preyed on the people in Vanden then his victims would be interesting to watch. He made enquiries and issued a few orders.

Within the hour he was back in the room and seated on a chair in the dark corner, looking on with satisfaction as Lenk saw the two slaves enter. The usurper prince began to struggle, though each tug on his bindings made him cry out in pain.

The slaves were interesting to watch, too. They no longer cowered and their eyes shone with animal lust. Watching from the shadows Gercomo realized that they no longer even registered that he was there, so absorbed were they in the sight of their former master, helpless and waiting for them to exact their bloody vengeance.

One slave was a man. He might have been young but he was slightly hunched on one side and his mouth was an embittered slit on his face. The woman was older, impossibly thin, and had fine wisps of hair on her head. Gercomo watched her. She almost slavered as she drew a rusty kitchen knife from her apron. With one glance at her companion she leaped between Lenk's legs. The male slave wrestled with her, urging her to wait, and poured suggestions into her ears. The woman's eyes widened as she listened, and then she nodded.

෨෨෨෨෨

Near dawn Gercomo repaired to the sitting room. He stood yawning and checked his clothes for splashes of blood. Lenk was still alive, though barely more than a bloodied heap of flesh. The slaves' imaginative torture had amused him for a while. It was more the bitter, twisted way they approached it that surprised him. He was neither satisfied nor moved by Lenk's punishment. It served its purpose, and that was all.

He lay down fully clothed on the settee to rest, but not to sleep. Sleep came harder these days. The more he imbibed the dragon essence the harder it became, yet he did not miss sleep. When he closed his eyes his mind was filled with visions of fire. His thoughts, though, did not burn or roil but hung like lead in his mind.

Just after dawn there was a knock at his door. Identifying himself, Fursten came in quietly. Gercomo sat up and reached for his riding crop, which he had left on the small table by the settee. He gazed at the leader of the Infra-pact, keeping his face bland.

"I'm sorry to report, sir, that the prisoners have not yet been recaptured. Though we did surround two rebels."

Gercomo's brow lifted. "And?"

Fursten swallowed and Gercomo enjoyed his fear. "Unfortunately, they killed themselves before they could be disarmed and questioned."

"I see, most unfortunate. Did you bring their bodies? I would like to inspect them. And the observatory?"

"We did bring the bodies. They are in the rear courtyard, sir. As for the observatory, the men we sent have not yet returned or sent word."

"Have you been able to find out about what they do up there, Fursten? Surely the people of Vanden must know something about it."

Fursten stepped closer and lowered his voice. "Yes, I did question some people, sir, in particular those who go up there to deliver goods and bring back the trade items. It seems they call themselves Skywatchers, and they shoot down asteroids before they hit the world. They study the heavens and live quite peaceably from what they say around here. They mine gems on the side and trade them for goods and a few children once a year."

Gercomo lifted an eyebrow in mock surprise. The trade information jelled with what Lenk had told him. The shooting down of asteroids was a bit harder to grasp. Try as he might he had no idea how such a thing could be done. He thought it odd that such an altruistic group of people existed in this world. Did their efforts mean that fewer asteroids fell? He stood up and gave a grunt of disgust. *Idiots!*

"They are merely a bunch of fools," he said to Fursten as he paced along the floor. He didn't want Fursten to see the doubt that had begun to grow in his mind. There had been the power hidden in that girl, and in the old man Thurdon who had been shepherding her around the countryside.

According to that miserable fool Lenk, who was no longer a man, there were rumors about Thurdon, who had always been ferreting after arcane items, books, technology...anything unusual. Then there'd been hints that his eyes had glowed, that he could do mysterious things.

There was more to this situation than he had thought before, Gercomo realized. He recalled the tales he had heard growing up, of strange lights in the sky and thunder when there were no clouds. Could it be that these Skywatchers had put those stories about to ensure that people left them alone? If they had pre-Shatterwing technology then they would have brought it to bear on Vanden as soon as the girl had been in danger, would they not? He did not really believe the tale Fursten had told him, but something was going on up on that mountain, and he would not leave them there, perched ready to prey on him.

As his mind returned to Lenk and the man's babblings, he smiled. He must make sure that Lenk didn't die of his injuries or it would spoil the fun. Lenk deserved so much more than death.

He turned back to Fursten. "When your men return with news of the observatory, draw up plans for an assault. And by the way, get the physic I put in one of the cells to tend to Lenk. I'm afraid some of his slaves held a grudge."

"Yes, sir, right away." Fursten left, his visage rather pasty at the mention of Lenk's fate.

Gercomo stood and stared out the window. He had power, contacts, the ability to reward and he had the wine. It was sufficient to keep these rebels bound to him, but it wasn't enough. Why did his need seem so great, so unquenchable? Even Lenk's torture had faded to nothing but a sour aftertaste. Salinda's had been more fulfilling, yet it had been years in the making. He stared at the mountain range in the distance, wondering about the girl with the glowing eyes. Would she entertain him? Could anything or anyone in this world have enough to fill up his need?

Chapter Five

FLEE!

Brill's breath ripped up his dry throat as he kept on running. The girl they had rescued was being dragged along, her grip so tight on her companion her fingers were white. Danton kept to the rear, casting regular glances over his shoulder and estimating how close their pursuers were. It wouldn't be long before they caught up, Brill feared. The sounds of pursuit followed them, growing ever louder. Without clear knowledge of where they were headed, Brill felt helpless. They put on a burst of speed, veering to the right through a copse of trees, and managed to put some distance between them and those behind. Their pursuers appeared to be heading off to the left, hopefully following the course Joss and Harden had laid for them.

When sounds of pursuit faded and Brill thought they'd gained a better distance, he called to the young man. "You there—where do we run?" he asked, panting between strides.

The young man eyed him suspiciously, but slowed his pace. After a pause, he said, "I need to get her back to the observatory."

"And where is that?"

The young man pointed to the mountain range dominating the far side of the river. "Up the mountain, through the Klester Valley...other side of Vanden. 'Tis the only way I know."

Brill tried to see exactly where the young man was pointing. There were lots of mountains, and they were heading away from Vanden, not toward it. "Which mountain?" A breath. "Vanden is out of the question. We can't go near there."

The young man stopped, letting go of the girl's hand. She bent over to catch her breath while scanning the terrain. "Trithorn Peak," he said breathlessly. "If only I could get my bearings. We need to rest. I need to think."

Brill nodded and swept his gaze around them. They could only afford a brief respite. "And what about you?" He caught the girl's attention. "Why are you so important?"

The girl wouldn't look him in the eye. They didn't trust him. He shrugged. After what they'd been through he didn't blame them.

"Not that the Inspector needs a reason to capture and torture anyone," Brill added.

Fear flashed into the man's eyes. Shutting his mouth tight, he stepped in front of the girl. The girl glared at Brill, the expression of horror on her face making Brill's innards clench in sympathy.

"You don't need to tell me anything. I understand."

The young man grabbed the girl's hand and then bolted. Brill followed, lengthening his strides to keep up. "Truly, I am a friend." The man nodded but kept up the pace. The girl was tiring, but didn't slow down. They ran for a few more minutes, until a whistled signal from Danton meant they were in no immediate danger. "You can slow now, for a moment, but keep moving," he called to the other two. They slowed to a stagger, the stress of the continued run making itself evident in the twitching of muscles. The young man introduced himself and the girl.

"I am called Garan, and this is Laidan."

Laidan held on to Garan, using his arm to steady herself. The sky was the color of smoke mixed with violet, muting the brown and red hues of the rough, rocky terrain they had stumbled onto. Provided they could survive the lack of general cover, the ground itself made their trail harder to follow. They kept walking, while Danton stayed behind them, periodically whistling the all clear. Brill wondered what had happened to Joss and Harden. Hopefully they were laying a separate trail to confuse pursuit.

It grew dark as they continued on, stopping occasionally to rest on the ground or next to a clump of bush. During the night, Garan and Brill took turns keeping watch while Danton scouted around. Laidan slept fitfully or paced numbly about. Brill found he was too alert to sleep soundly, even for short periods, and, he suspected it was the same for Garan. Danton whistled his regular status reports or occasionally put in an appearance. Even though the rebel leader had signaled an all clear, Brill urged them to keep moving after each rest break.

Near dawn, when the sun began to light up the tips of the mountain range, a great wedge of exhaustion lodged between Brill's shoulder blades. Whistling a message back to Danton, he slowed and turned full circle, taking in a clump of rocks. He peered at it a second time, realizing that it was a cave of some sort. Looking at Laidan's wan features and the fatigue etched around Garan's violet-colored eyes he said, pointing, "We'll rest there...out of sight." The cave was only a temporary option as it was an obvious hiding place. But what choice did they have? The girl was incapable of putting on any speed and the young man wasn't entirely certain of how to find way back to his observatory. Brill had grave concerns, too, for his rebel companions. Had they sacrificed their lives to allow Danton and Brill to rescue these two?

Garan stretched and nodded once in the direction of the cave. "I know this place. We sheltered here a few days ago. The river is not far from here. We should keep going."

Brill turned slowly, keeping his senses tuned to their surroundings, listening for followers. "The river current takes us away from where we need to go. We will have to think of another path if we are to backtrack. I'm thinking we'll have to go up to the foothills and over to get to this observatory."

The tall young man shook his head, jiggling the curls on his forehead. "I wasn't suggesting going downriver, but across."

"After the storm it is too dangerous to cross," Brill observed.

With a nod, Garan bent over to catch his breath and ease a stitch from his side. "There is one problem with taking refuge in here. We will be trapped if we are discovered. There is only one entrance."

"I know, but Laidan needs rest. So do we. We'll have to risk it." The girl had not complained, but looking at her, he could see she had no energy left. She sprawled on the ground, arms splayed to stare up at the sky. Her chest was rising and falling, her pale skin pink with exertion. She was done in.

While they talked Danton drew near and caught the tail end of the conversation. "Take advantage of the shelter while you can. I'll range around and send you warning if I see anything," he said. With a nod to Brill, the rebel leader headed away again.

Brill turned back to Garan. "We will have plenty of warning if they approach. Right now your lady needs to rest."

The girl sat up, her expression sour. "I'm not his lady," she said, even though she didn't resist when the young man helped her to stand up and move inside the cave.

Brill raised an eyebrow. The girl was very young, and despite the dirt and the dark circles around her eyes and her rather strange attire, she was appealing.

The look he received from the young man told a different story.

ඖඖඖඖඖ

Installed in the cave, Brill had a chance to reflect on everything that had happened, and he tried hard not to be overtly interested in Garan's ability to make explosions seemingly from thin air and sound. Also, he tried not to be disturbed by the fact that the Laidan's eyes glowed. He had indeed fallen in with odd company.

"Why are you helping us?" Garan asked.

"Why not?" Brill responded lightly, but then added, "We're interested in thwarting the plans of an evil man."

"Who?" Laidan asked. "Do you mean the man who calls himself Gercomo?" She shuddered visibly.

"Gercomo—he was known as the Inspector when I knew him. Couldn't let you two be taken by him. You, my lady, have something he wants—"

She drew in a breath. Garan sprang to his feet, poised for attack. "Move away from her."

"Rest easy." Brill smiled up at Garan, who relaxed slightly. "My concern is that she doesn't fall into Gercomo's hands. You see, I also know a woman who can make her eyes glow."

Laidan leaned toward Brill. "Another lady? Perhaps she can help me. Where is she?"

"Why do you need help? What happened?"

To his dismay, her face screwed up signaling her distress and she began to cry into her hands. After several attempts to get a sentence out, Garan interpreted her sob-filled phrases. "Master Thurdon, Laidan's guardian, was killed. He thrust some kind of power into Laidan, but she was unprepared. Since then her eyes have glowed, though the effect is dimming now. At first she could not even speak or move. She needs help to deal with Thurdon's gift."

"I want it to go away," Laidan said, before covering her face and dissolving once again into tears. Garan patted her on the shoulder and shrugged when he caught Brill's eye.

"Forgive her. It has been a trying time, full of threat to her person. I do not know how she has borne it as well as she has." Laidan began to calm, her breathing slowing and easing in step with the soothing strokes on her back that she was receiving from Garan.

"I see," Brill said, rubbing his chin with his hand. "Salinda called it a 'cadre,' some entity that is passed on through the generations from one person to another. I think she mentioned she had trained hard before she received it on her master's death."

Both Garan's and Laidan's jaws had dropped open as he spoke. Eventually Garan cleared his throat a few times before he said, "You know what this thing is?"

Their steady gaze was unnerving, and he rubbed the leg of his breeches absently. "Well...yes, in an intellectual kind of way. I've seen Salinda with her eyes glowing and saw her summon a dragon."

"A dragon?" Laidan went pale and would have collapsed if Garan hadn't been supporting her. He resumed rubbing her back and she smiled weakly at him in gratitude. When she was restored, she edged closer to Brill and said with a note of desperation in her voice, "Tell me where to find this woman."

"I wish I could. We lost her in Gunner and followed the Inspector—Gercomo—instead."

Laidan's hopeful expression clouded with disappointment. A trilling all clear sounded from Danton outside, so Brill advised Garan and Laidan to rest. With a nod, Garan, who was a rather large man, squeezed himself into a space and helped Laidan nestle next to him. He made sure his bulk protected her from Brill and the entrance. Both seemed to fall into an exhausted sleep straight away.

The light streamed in from various gaps in the overhead rock. Brill took his time looking around, confirming that there were no other exits, as Garan had reported. He noted the change in color of the rock and the strange portal-like structure at the back. While there was no obvious way out, the panel ringed in ornamentation certainly looked like a door to him.

He examined the ancient structure in detail. It was definitely pre-Shatterwing, and there was something familiar about it. As he studied it, he sifted through his memories, through the lessons of his tutors.

As far as he could tell, it was not just a relic of the time of Moonfall, but even older...an ancient thing.

A signal from Danton dissolved his contemplation of the doorway. The whistle was sharp and low, so he knew immediately that something was wrong. He strode over to Garan, but the big man was already propped up on his elbow, alert. Laidan was harder to wake. Danton appeared at the head of the cave. "Time to move, people. We have been discovered."

Brill hastily introduced the couple.

"From which direction do they approach?" Garan asked as he climbed to his feet.

Danton frowned, making his patched face appear even more disreputable. "I hate to say this, but from all sides. They took their time and made a wide noose around us, and now they draw it tighter and tighter. They are a smart operation. I'm sorry I missed the signs. I did wonder why it was so quiet. Not much I could do about it, except to work out how many there were."

Brill repressed a groan. "And how many are there?"

"Too many to counter—it seems the Inspector wants these two badly."

"What about our men?"

Danton shook his head. "They should have joined us by now. We took plenty of stops during the night to allow them to catch up with us. Perhaps they were too successful in creating a diversionary path."

A chill sped up Brill's spine. He glanced quickly at the two escapees and then at Danton. The rebel leader's face was lined with worry.

"We have to keep them out of the Inspector's hands," Brill said, surprised at the harshness in his voice. Garan and Laidan were young and innocent. Any fool could see that. He'd not let their pure spirits be warped by the Inspector. These were the sort of people he imagined he was fighting for, the sort of people who deserved a better future.

Danton nodded. "He's not having them if I can prevent it."

Garan was sweating and breathing heavily while Laidan's eyes were wide with growing terror. Garan grasped her shaking hand and squeezed it. Turning to Brill he said, "What are we going to do? We can't fight and we can't stay here."

Brill let his gaze dart around the cave until he was again drawn to the ancient portal. There was something about it...Heading for the rear of the cave he called over his shoulder, "Danton, take a look at this. I've found something."

Garan shook his head but stood aside to let Danton pass. "'Tis nothing helpful. Just some old relic from times past," he commented as the two rebels stood close together.

Danton clasped Garan's shoulder as he walked past and said, "Keep a lookout, but stay out of sight. Brill, whatever we do, we must hurry."

When Danton stood to examine the structure, Brill watched his friend as he blinked and whistled his surprise. "That does look old. Do you know what it is?"

Brill bit his lip in thought. If only he'd been a better scholar. Yet there was still a teasing memory of a verse and a legend. "It's a doorway of some kind, I'm sure. If only we could open it."

Danton ran his hands down the sides of the recessed panel, just visible behind a layer of caked sand and etched designs. The sand dislodged by his fingertips spilled to the floor. "Yes," he murmured, "if only we could open it." He withdrew his hand and shared a look with Brill. "Unfortunately we would have to destroy it once we were through. They know we're here and they'll find it as they search. Either way it could be our doom. We don't know what is on the other side. It could be death."

"A doom less immediate than the one at hand, though, don't you think?" Brill grinned broadly at Danton's frowning face. They'd been in worse scrapes. At least this one didn't involve a midden heap. Brill's smile faded as he regarded the door again. He hoped it didn't open onto a midden heap.

Danton smiled grimly. "Aye, if your brilliant brain can regurgitate some vestige of your private tutoring maybe we will be able to open it. Laidan, you should come closer to the rear of the cave. No point in having you so far away from us and too close to capture."

Laidan stretched her hands over her head and eased her lower back before she took a few wary steps in their direction. Brill thought she looked afraid of Danton, as she looked twice at his eye patch. When she neared and turned to face the portal something happened. After a slight gasp, all the expression left her face and her eyes opened wider as if she was surprised. The glow in her eyes brightened fractionally. Danton lifted a dark eyebrow at Brill. Concerned, Brill stepped closer to her and studied her face, mesmerized by how her whole body seemed transfixed.

"Do you recognize it?" Brill asked quietly from beside her.

For a moment she was unresponsive. Then, as if her voice were coming from far away she said, "I don't know. It is so confusing." Her calm state shattered and her expression twisted. Her body bucked and writhed as if she fought an unseen force. The light blazed out of her eyes and then faded.

Brill had to act quickly, had to use his instinct and his intellect. He placed his hand on her shoulder and squeezed lightly. Immediately she stopped struggling and the light in her eyes lessened. "Relax, my lady," he whispered. Then, hoping it sounded as if he knew what he was doing, he said confidently into her ear, "Let something of the cadre forward. Let it see the portal, and ask it if it knows how to enter."

Laidan glanced at Brill, blinding him momentarily with her gaze. Then her face contorted and she moaned as she stumbled over to stand in front of the portal. Her legs shook until she forced herself to stand straight. Part of Brill hated seeing what was happening to her. Salinda had been so calm about her cadre. This was so different; he worried for Laidan, and for her soul. There was something alive within and it seemed beyond her control. The very concept scared him, but he was unsure what else to do. As far as he could see, they had no choice but to ask Laidan to help them in this way.

Seeing that something was happening, Danton made preparations to seal the portal after they had made use of it, laying a line of small explosives he carried on him around the rocks and setting a fuse.

From his position by the cave entrance Garan called back urgently, detailing the shrinking noose of men surrounding them. "I don't think we have much time," he hissed.

Danton's whisper was like a shout. "If she can't open the portal, I'll blast it open and hope our pursuers are blocked from following by the debris. If they're a superstitious lot they won't want to climb into a hole in a wall in the middle of nowhere."

Brill eyed the support stones and the slab of rock overhead. Blasting might open the portal, but the rock fall that would probably ensue might kill them before they could go through it. He had hope that Laidan could find a way in, however. He had thought about what Salinda had told him. If what she had said was true, then it was perfectly reasonable that one of the former holders of the cadre would know about these portals. Of course, that was supposing that Laidan carried a cadre and not something else entirely. He decided that option wasn't worth entertaining at present.

Garan retreated from the entrance in a crouch. He was very agitated, flushed and breathing hard. But when he saw Laidan he paused, and his anxiety for his friend was etched across his face. It was obvious that Garan's heart belonged to this woman, no matter how strenuously she denied it. Brill cautioned himself to be careful. He found his attraction for her growing, and not only because she had a source of power that could help his cause.

"She reacted strangely when she saw the relic before. But the effect on her was much worse then. Do you think she can open it?" Garan asked solemnly.

"Don't know, but it's worth a try," Brill replied. He was straining to hear the rebels outside.

Laidan had been still, the occasional grimace the only indication that she was undergoing some inner turmoil. Then, as if in a trance, she twitched and lifted her hand, reaching out to touch four spots on the wall, one after the other. Brill strained to see what she was doing. With a groan, the door began to slide back.

"Quick, Danton! She's done it!" Elation flowed through Brill as he reached into the darkness beyond the door with his foot and stepped on a smooth floor. "There is something here. Do it."

His friend nodded and lit the fuse. Brill pulled Laidan through the doorway and Garan followed close behind. Danton darted through last, hissing, "Move, move."

It was pitch black inside the portal when the door slid shut behind them. Laidan's eyes provided some slight illumination. Brill could make out a corridor that was straight and had a flat, even floor. He walked along it, conscious that Danton's explosives were due to blow. With a shudder, he realized the ground dropped away ahead, and he fell backward into Laidan to save himself. Gingerly, he groped around, his fingers finding the lip of a ledge. Putting his foot on it, he discovered another one. A staircase.

"Laidan, look down here." Laidan's hands reached for his and he clasped one of them to his chest. He could see that the staircase continued on. "All right, there's a staircase here with even risers so we should be able to go quickly." Brill placed Laidan's hand on his shoulder and patted it, before beginning to descend. An explosion rocked the corridor behind them and filled it with dust. A loud rumble sounded as rocks and debris blocked the portal behind them.

When the noise subsided, Brill called out, "Is everyone all right?"

"Yes," Danton replied. "I think that did the job. They won't be able to follow through. Completely blocked."

"Indeed," Garan said, though he sounded uncertain. "I've used all my crystals so I can't make any light. I'm sorry."

Brill squinted into the dark. Who was this man who used crystals to make light? That would explain the little display that had enabled the pair's escape. He hadn't got to that topic of conversation yet. Shaking his head in wonderment, he decided there'd be time to think about those two later, when they were safe. He kept up the pace until the stairs became a platform beneath his feet. Then, standing still, he listened for any sounds of pursuit. It was too dark to run. Danton drew alongside, and Brill could feel the tension in him as they listened. Except for the trickle of smaller rocks and gravel settling into place, they didn't hear anyone else in the corridor with them.

After a few long minutes Danton sighed loudly. "That should serve to kill off pursuit—unless they have explosives. I'll take the rear, kid."

Brill nodded. "Then I'll take the lead."

Although dark in the corridor, his eyes gradually grew accustomed to the gloom, and Brill realized that there was some light emanating from the very substance of the walls around them.

Everything was black and gray, bled entirely of color, yet he could make out the six sets of stairs jutting out from the platform they were standing on. Beyond the stairwells there appeared to be nothing but blackness. There was a faintly musty smell, as if no one had traversed this space in eons. More eerie than that was the total lack of sound. Even their footsteps didn't echo.

Brill paused briefly to touch the ground beneath his feet. It had the texture of marble, yet it had an unusual warmth to it. For a moment he thought that he wasn't even underground, but then he dismissed the idea as foolishness. Nonetheless, it took all his efforts to stop himself from thinking about where they were and who had created this space.

This was more than pre-Shatterwing technology. This was something else entirely, and its existence stretched the limits of his carefully tutored mind. As he nudged in front of Garan to take the lead, he hoped that the principles of direction still applied as they did on the surface.

Chapter Six

TO OBSERVE IS TO KNOW

Nils came to Salinda's bed every night after their coupling in the lake. Her first impression was that he intended it as a punishment, a way of ensuring she understood what being his mate meant and that she'd have to be close to his alien body for the rest of her days. She did not find it a hard task to be with him. After so long alone, she welcomed his warmth in her bed. The city was so desolate that it reminded her of death at every glance. With Nils close to her, those dark thoughts were kept at bay. Yet he approached her with trepidation, as if he found touching her repellent, as if succumbing to some basic need was anathema to him. Often he wept silently after sex, as though he had left a piece of himself behind with her.

She pretended not to notice his misery and suffering. There was no denying that Nils's reaction to their intimate relationship tugged at her heartstrings, made her want to reach out to him. Yet she held back. He was vulnerable and needy and didn't really understand or accept that part of himself. Perhaps his need reverberated in her own emptiness. What she'd been through at the hands of Ange and the Inspector had changed her. That much she could discern for herself. Feelings of unworthiness, of shame, hampered her ability to speak frankly to him of how he touched her heart, of how much she cared.

Outright rejection would validate those negative feelings, which she was trying to shrug off. She told herself that the arrangement was a duty, and she understood duty best of all. Although Nils was challenging and difficult, that duty was not repellent to her. Part of her longed to explore his depths and to fill up his emptiness with hope—

her hope. Daily she saw him fight against the bitterness that welled up inside him, though he did not speak of it.

By day, Nils continued to teach her the Hiem archival code, and they studied the records together, though their purpose was different: he was searching for something within the records, and she needed to learn. The cadre contained a lot of knowledge and wisdom, if one but knew which thread to tug to unravel it. Often she would feel it warm when she read something, as though she had struck a familiar chord. Yet she couldn't discern Mez's personality or thoughts anymore, or feel his presence in her mind; it seemed he had merged with the others. When she thought about the cadre she realized what a poor receptacle for it she was. She had neither higher learning nor an acknowledged position in society. A true and willing heart was all she could lay claim to. And right now, she found Nils making an unwitting claim on it.

With reverence, he moved among the records. She watched him out of the corner of her eye and thought again that there was something moving about his air of aloofness and aloneness. A coughing fit seized him, hacking and continuous, shattering the temple-like calm of the small room.

"Nils?" she said. Alarmed by the intensity of the attack, she stood herself, ready to soothe him in any way she could. But he held up his hand to stop her until he'd finished coughing and leaned exhausted on his chair. He could not speak, but waved her away from him and pointing to the work she was doing.

At the table, she sat back down and practiced reading the Hiem code in front of her again, listing the words and expressions that she didn't understand so he could explain them to her after their evening meal. Surreptitiously she glanced at him, saw the sag in his shoulders and the movement of his chest betraying the effort it took him to breathe. Now that they spent most of their time together he couldn't hide it from her. He was ill.

Tenderly her hand hovered above her abdomen. There had been slight changes in her body. Nils's child grew within her, she was sure.

After an hour or so of quiet study, he stood. "Come," he said, "I want to pursue a partial record of my cousin, Ryad, who survived Moonfall. I have found a reference to it in my family's archive."

Without a word she followed him out of the room, around a bend in the path and down a few more stairwells. She entered the private archive quietly, moved by a sense of awe. Nils's whole family's lives were recorded there—their thoughts, their deeds and the actions and motivations of those they had observed since the time when records first began. To him it was like a shrine. She saw it in the way he touched the records, the way his shoulders hunched as if he was handling something alive and very dear to him. Suddenly it crossed her mind that dwelling on the past was not good for him. How could she change that? Moonfall was so new to him. It was practically irrelevant to her.

When he found the excerpt he was looking for, Nils sat down and read it aloud.

> *The survivors have moved up into the mountains. I follow along, though my heart is heavy with loss. I can see no way forward, for the worst is not over. At the shores of Lake Nester I found a Strega woman traveling on her own. She told me she had been left by her kin. She was small and dark and her smile in the face of her horror warmed me. I chose to aid her and hope, perhaps, that in her company I can win my way through to a Way Gate to send this message home.*

He stopped reading aloud and read on in silence. "I think I have found a link."

"A link to what, Nils?"

"Your Hiem blood."

"What?" Salinda felt her blood chill.

"It says here that after a while Ryad mated with this Strega woman. She bore him twins."

"Twins...but that doesn't mean I am related to him. She could have died. The twins could have died. So many of them did."

"I have a feeling."

"Really? I didn't know intuition played a part in making archival records."

Nils missed or overlooked her sarcasm. "It does...mostly in finding the records. And I wouldn't call it intuition. I would call it an application of intellect."

Just then they both felt a tremor in the earth around them. It was only a shiver—nothing moved—yet something had happened. A presence pricked her mind, a brief, sharp prod. Nils stood up and dropped the record he was studying. Salinda stood, too, stunned. "What is it?" she said breathlessly.

Nils held a hand to his brow, wincing as if he had a headache. "A Way Gate has been destroyed."

Salinda grasped his free hand. "A Way Gate? Do you mean that someone is using a Way Gate? But—" How did he know? Salinda couldn't detect that, but she did sense something else, a familiar presence of some sort. She shook her head in confusion.

Nils stepped away from her, his bony brow furrowed. "I hardly believe it is possible for a non-Hiem to use a Way Gate. Yet one has been opened and then destroyed. No Hiem would do such a thing, unless the need was dire. You perceived something—"

"Yes, I...something strange, just for a moment I..." Salinda turned her face away and sagged back into her chair.

"What did you sense? Tell me."

"I can't explain it to you." She lowered her head. She didn't want to lie to him, but it was the cadre that had recognized something. "Can you tell which Way Gate? Maybe we should investigate."

Nils pursed his lips together. She could see the indecision warring within him. It was clear he wanted to know what she had sensed. Likewise, she wanted to know how he could determine what had happened. Was he connected to the network of travel ways in some spiritual way?

"I am not sure it is necessary."

"But surely you are curious to know who has done this? Does it not pose a threat? Let us see what has happened." He was thinking it through. She could almost feel him weighing up his arguments. Will she try to escape from me? Can I trust her with more Hiem secrets? What is she hiding from me? Tentatively, she touched his arm and squeezed, making him turn toward her. In his gaze she could see all his fears before he lowered his eyelids and hid them from her.

"If humans have discovered a Way Gate, then won't that lead them here?"

He looked at her then, the silver in his eyes glowing with passion. "That cannot happen. I will not have them coming here, will not have their greedy minds see this treasure. I would die first."

"Then we must investigate and turn them from this path if this is where they are heading."

To her surprise he nodded once, decisively. "Yes, you are right."

Salinda smiled. "Don't worry, Nils. I will come with you and together we will succeed."

As they left the room, Nils was racked with another fit of coughing so severe he had to brace himself against the walls of the corridor.

"Nils, that cough is getting worse. I worry for you."

When the coughing eased, he replied, "It is nothing. Come with me and we will follow their trace."

Chapter Seven

THE WAY IS DARK

Once through the portal Laidan had to battle Thurdon's presence, which surged and expanded as if trying to break free of its restraints. Her mind filled with dazzling light, like fireworks exploding inside her head. With the light in her eyes once again rekindled, Brill was able to use their glow to illuminate a staircase in the dark corridor. It didn't matter that along with the light the pain had returned. Laidan was so scared of pursuit and of dying in the dark that it made a useful distraction.

Then Danton's explosives had blown in a shower of dust and noise, sending them reeling. She thought the corridor would crumble, that they'd all be crushed. Thurdon reacted as if he'd been stabbed through the chest, as though they had committed a sacrilege of some kind. In agony, she coughed dust while shoving soothing thoughts in Thurdon's direction. If only he would calm down so she could think.

Brill guided her slowly down the staircase as Laidan fought back sobs. It was time to be brave, no matter how hard it seemed. Once at the base of the stairs, Garan stood protectively by her side. She felt the warmth of his body and inhaled his scent. She found his presence comforting and in some way so did Thurdon. She sensed his anxiety lessen.

Brill and his friend, Danton, stood in front of them, peering into the darkness, discussing who would take the lead and who would come up the rear. Laidan glimpsed more stairs.

Garan spoke suddenly, rubbing his hand along her back. "Of the six staircases, I think we should take this one." He pointed toward one of the tunnels.

The one-eyed man grunted in acknowledgment and moved to examine the staircase that Garan had indicated. "But where does it lead?"

Brill went to inspect it, too, leaning over to peer down before turning back to face them.

Garran shrugged. "Away from here and toward the mountains. We have to move in case they find a way through the rubble."

"Are you sure?" Brill asked.

Garan rubbed his chin. "I've been paying attention and I'm pretty sure that's the best way to go."

Danton agreed.

They followed the staircase and it also terminated in a landing. From this landing stemmed three staircases, all heading down into the dark abyss below. Thurdon was quiet in Laidan's mind, seemingly awed by what she was seeing and experiencing.

As she stood in the dark she was suddenly pierced by a sensation, like an arrow to the brain, which appeared to originate from outside of her and end in what Brill had called the cadre. Thurdon reacted as if he had heard something and had suddenly turned his head. Turning her own head, she listened, too. It was like a vibration or an echo. She turned slowly on the spot, trying to locate the source, but it was vague, faint. She got a teasing glimpse of something, then Thurdon erupted again, jabbering emotions and words in her mind, filling her up until she was overwhelmed.

Garan's hand on her elbow steadied her, drew her back to what was going on around her. Each time she tried to get Thurdon's gift to settle, to give her information, it remained a confused, tight knot of pain and anguish. She had to clench her jaw against the urge to scream.

Garan touched her arm again and leaned in close to whisper, "What is it?"

She leaned in his direction so he could catch her words. "I don't know. I'm sorry." She shook her head though he couldn't see her.

Garan groped for her hand and when he found it, squeezed. "We should keep moving. This looks like some type of road. Perhaps it will lead to the observatory."

They kept moving. Brill and Danton kept looking around them, whispering observations now and then. The taller one loomed close to her. She blinked and Danton smiled. Then she realized that she could make out his face: white teeth in a dark beard and a dark patch over one eye. It was getting brighter. Glancing around her she could see that the light was coming from the walls, or what she expected should be walls. She couldn't tell if it was rock or mist that shrouded the walkway in a gray haze like the first glimmerings of dawn, but the ability to see was comforting after so much darkness. She sighed loudly and she noticed Garan looking at her with shadows where his bright violet eyes usually were.

At another intersection, the two rebels began to argue over which stairway to take. Garan paused and appeared to be taking his bearings, looking right, left and then overhead.

"What difference does it make?" Danton was saying. "We're bound to be lost whichever road we take. Who would have thought there were roads like this under the surface? I have a new respect for the world before."

Brill nodded. "Yes. I'm rather awed myself."

Garan edged past her so that he was square with the other two. "I don't think we will end up lost," he interjected. The two men stopped speaking and made room for him in their circle. With a nod from Danton, Garan continued. "If there was a doorway that leads into the place, then it is logical that there are others that lead out. I suggest we take this way, because it is the one that appears to be going in the direction we need."

Brill frowned, his gaze sweeping their surroundings.

"What makes you say that?" Danton asked.

Garan stood taller, his chest expanding. "I told you I've been paying attention. The river is in that direction and we need to get to the other side of it. My guess is this pathway runs under the river."

Danton faced Brill and nodded once. Brill brought his attention back to them and smiled. "Well, my lady. It appears there is more to your friend than meets the eye. Our choices have been mere guesswork. I say we follow along and if we do not end up where we need to be when we find a doorway, at least we'll be out of immediate danger."

"I'd be glad of that," Laidan replied. "It is a relief to be safe but I don't like it here."

Garan patted her on the back. "You'll be fine," he whispered. "I won't leave you."

He sounded sincere. Maybe he was sorry for abandoning her last year in the caves, just because she'd slapped his face. Looking around, she took in the eerie light glowing from the walls and shuddered. It wasn't natural. Thurdon's interest was piqued again and Laidan wrestled with him to keep him quiet. If this didn't end soon, she'd run mad.

In silence, they trod down the steep stairs of Garan's chosen stairwell until it met another corridor. Garan led the way, holding Laidan's hand and tugging her gently along with him. About half an hour later, the quality of the walls began to change and the noise of water cascading down rocks spilled over them. Ahead of them, the corridor appeared to end. Garan slowed and Brill edged forward to stand beside him.

"What is it?" Brill whispered to Garan.

Garan ran his hands over the walls. "We're in a natural formation of some kind—a cavern." He edged further in and peered ahead. "I can't see if the corridor continues on the other side."

Brill shared a glance with his friend. Laidan thought they did that a lot, communicating through looks and gestures alone. "Danton, can you give us some light?"

Danton came forward, gently easing Laidan out of his way and guiding her to stand behind him. "If you insist, but you know I don't like to waste them." He lit what appeared to be a fuse. Sizzling as it burst into life, it gave them their first glimpse of the cavern. The roof wasn't much higher than Garan's head and it was narrow. To one side was a waterfall and on the other side they could see that it tunneled through rock. Ahead was a bridge, forking into two dark doorways.

"There's a fissure there where the water leaks into the rocks below and flows along this tunnel. I'd say it mirrors the path of the river above, so that's the corridor we need to take," Garan said, pointing to the left-hand pathway.

Brill nodded and then the fuse burned down to Danton's fingers. He sucked them while surveying their surroundings. "I'll take the lead.

Garan, if you could assist Laidan across the bridge, Danton will bring up the rear."

Laidan stepped in front of Garan, preferring to be between the two young men rather than walking in Garan's shadow. Brill was very attentive to her, grasping her hand to assist her passage. As she crossed the bridge moisture sprinkled her face. By the time she was in the middle of the crossing, the droplets of water were more like drizzling rain, and she was able to lick the moisture from her lips.

Danton called a halt as he lit another fuse, which flickered light onto the dark water below. They all took the opportunity to look around them. In front of the corridor into which they were heading Laidan saw billowing mist, spray from the waterfall. Water also dripped from the ceiling. Overhead she could make out teardrops of white stone hanging down.

Brill urged them to keep walking. Laidan couldn't help an involuntary shiver as they passed underneath what Garan said was the river. Once in the corridor again, the second fuse having expired, they depended once more on the light emanating from the walls around them. It seemed to Laidan that they had been walking for hours and hours, perhaps even more than a day as they continued to follow Garan's lead along corridors, across landings and up stairwells, their feet making no sound as they moved. She wondered absently what the stairs were made of, as they appeared to be neither metal nor stone nor even wood.

Garan assured them at regular intervals that the path angled toward the mountains. After a while it became long and perfectly flat, yet the gray walls still hemmed them in. She began to have flashbacks to the time when Garan left her in the caves. As if he sensed what she was feeling, he put his arm over her shoulders and squeezed. "You're not alone. Don't worry."

"I'm not worrying." She shrugged him off.

Walking became harder as the muscles in her legs and lower back tightened. Luckily, Brill called for a rest break before she collapsed. Demurely, Laidan knelt down, though she felt like sagging straight to the ground and burying her head in her hands. Garan squatted next to her and their companions reclined on the ground, looking absurdly as if they were on a picnic.

She noticed Brill looking at her, so she took the opportunity to engage him in conversation. "Who was that man Gercomo?"

Brill sat up straighter, his expression closed. "Only the worst man on Margra. Avoid him at all costs."

"Aye, that's the truth," Danton agreed. "It would have been the death of both of you."

Laidan shuddered once. "But why? What have we done?"

Brill leaned forward. "It's because of your power. He must have heard about it, because he left Vanden in search of you, I think. But actually he's the type of man who doesn't need a reason. You're young and have a rare beauty. You are untouched by the evil world. That alone is enough for him to want to put his dark mark on you."

Laidan's skin broke out in goose flesh as she sensed the truth of his words. Rubbing her upper arms, she realized that Brill sounded like Thurdon, and she recalled how she'd barely paid attention to Thurdon's wise words, so intent had she been on finding love and fawning flattery and a better life than the one she had. What a silly girl she'd been. Yet even as she mulled over what Brill said, she was heartened that he found her beautiful. She'd not been called a rare beauty before and found herself smiling, her eyelashes lowering as she observed Brill surreptitiously.

Suddenly, Garan edged between her and Brill, almost knocking her out of his way. She moved back to give him room, biting back on her resentment. "How do you know so much about him?" Garan asked in a voice layered with suspicion.

Brill and Danton shared a look. "We've been in his power before—" Brill began. He stared at the ground, unable to continue speaking.

Danton sighed heavily and patted his friend on the shoulder. "And we survived—just. We want to stop him, stop him from gaining power and spreading his evil."

"I see," Garan replied before turning to Laidan and giving her hand a quick squeeze.

Danton shifted on the floor, trying to find a more comfortable position. "We can talk more about him later. Now we should rest. We aren't out of this yet."

Laidan found that she couldn't doze but was able to relax. When the others thought it was time to get moving, she was ready to go on. The faint vibration she had detected before was still there, but it was in the opposite direction from where they were headed. Some part of her wanted to follow it, but as she didn't know what it was, she figured that the observatory was the best place to be. It was full of familiar faces and wise men and women. Perhaps the Master Elder could help her with the so-called cadre, or even make it go away. When she thought of that she found herself walking faster, eager to be free of Thurdon's gift.

Garan had to make another choice when they came to a further split in the path. He chose the right-hand fork, arguing that it held true to where the mountains were. It struck her as funny that he could find his way better in the dark and underground than when he was trying to sight Trithorn Peak above.

More stairs loomed ahead, ascending into dark cavities.

"Too bad there aren't any signs," Brill said without any depletion in his good spirits.

Garan sounded severe when he said, "Who said there weren't? Stands to reason that someone made these passages, so they must have had a way of navigating through them."

If Brill took offense at his tone, he didn't show it. "Yes, I'm sure you're right. But could we interpret a sign if we saw it?"

Garan shook his head and smiled sheepishly. "Probably not."

Laidan thought that Garan was easing back on his dislike and distrust of their rescuers. They seemed decent enough to her. But then she'd been out in the world while Garan had spent his life at the observatory, among learned elders and friends he had grown up with. Garan had been very protective of her, too, even though Brill and his friend had been nothing but courteous. Although they were rebels, these two hadn't tried to force-feed them doctrine or tried to enlist them to their cause. Laidan trusted them, and from the way Thurdon had quieted when she was near them, she sensed he did too.

The stairway terminated in another platform. They stood there gaping into the steely haze around them.

Brill said to Danton, "I think we could do with some more light. The glow from Laidan's eyes is too faint now to be of use here."

"I don't have an endless supply of these," Danton said as he lit another fuse. The bright light temporarily blinded her.

"There's a door!" Garan bellowed, making them all start.

Laidan's heart thumped erratically when she caught a glimpse of it herself.

Chapter Eight

TRITHORN PEAK

Brill ran up to the stone archway with Danton close behind, holding the fuse high. Brill slid his hands around the edges. "Yes, he's right. It is another doorway." He turned back to them. "Well, do we risk exiting here?"

Garan responded automatically. "Yes. We should be able to find our way even if it is well short of the observatory."

Brill frowned. "Well, Danton, I trust your judgment. Shall we risk it?"

Danton was rather thoughtful; he rubbed his chin and stared at the door. "If we can open it then I think we should leave. As fascinating as I find it here, I don't want to be lost forever. There's something to be said for sun and air. The real test will be whether we can exit or not."

Brill passed his flask around. "Take a sip of this. It's dragon wine, watered but still good. You'll need your strength." To Danton he said, "We should be ready in case there is trouble on the other side."

Garan nodded even though Brill hadn't included him in the warning. Laidan was shunted to the back of the group. She caught a glimpse of something on the wall. "Wait. What's that? Danton, could you hold your light up so we can see it?"

The others turned to look as Danton moved to where she stood and lifted the sizzling fuse. He stared hard at the wall, a frown etched across his forehead.

"It's a picture, don't you see?" she said, excited by her find.

"Yes, but it makes no sense. There appears to be color—blue sky, though it is a bit flat in this light."

"Never mind the picture," Brill said. "It was probably made before Moonfall. Whatever it shows, the outside won't look anything like that now. It could be covered in lava."

"Or a river," Garan added somberly.

Laidan swallowed spit. "Really, Garan, did you have to say that? You said you thought we were heading in the direction of the mountains. Why would we find a river now? Didn't we just walk under a river?"

Garan shrugged apologetically. "Probably because rivers run under mountains as well as between them."

"He's right," Brill said, positioning himself in front of the portal. "Hold on just in case, because here goes." Brill copied the pattern of depressions in the door Laidan had used to enter the other portal. This one was in much better condition and the notches were easier to see, and the door slid back without effort. There was a wall of black on the other side. A damp, musty smell spilled into the corridor. It was a familiar odor and made Laidan break out in sweat.

Garan peered through the door first. "I am going to see what is in here." He stepped carefully through and stood pressed up against the outer wall adjacent to the door. He was silent for a minute, then he must have picked up and thrown a stone because she heard a dunk-dunk-dunk; the sound of rock bouncing on rock.

"Caves. It leads to some caves, I think." Garan edged out further to allow the rest of them to follow him. "Be careful. The ledge here is narrow."

The one-eyed rebel didn't hesitate. He stepped through and helped Laidan onto the ledge next to him, with Brill at the rear. Danton held up the fuse and asked Garan, "Do you know this place?"

Garan shrugged. "Can't say for sure. The mountains are riddled with cave complexes. I've been through many caves in this area. 'Tis too dark to see if this is one I know."

Brill let the door close behind them. Just then the fuse died and a damp, black wall of nothing hit Laidan in the face. She was reassured by the presence of the three men, but even then she felt the weight of the caves pressing in around her. "How do we know how to get out? We could get lost."

In the darkness, she heard a comforting voice. "Laidan, trust me," Garan said. "If I can't find the way out we'll go back into the corridors. But I have a feeling that this door is here for a reason. You know there was an observatory on Trithorn Peak before Moonfall; perhaps that door led to it."

Garan stayed very still, as if listening. Someone held her elbow while they waited, stroking it with their thumb. Was it Brill's touch that comforted her? Brill didn't speak but waited patiently beside her.

"This way," Garan said. "Walk slowly and put your right hand ahead of you on the wall."

"Can you see?" Danton asked from in front of her.

"Not well. Do you have more light?"

Danton lit another fuse and said, "Another one turns to dust. I don't have an unlimited supply, you know."

In the flare of light, Garan took a slow look around. The rock they were standing on was a large jutting ledge, smoothly carved from the wall. There were other grooved patterns in the rock and the roof dipped to the left of them as if it had collapsed. In the flickering light, she thought she saw engraved columns.

Garan urged them further along the ledge while Danton's light lasted. "Do you see up there in the corner? See that patch of dark?" Garan pointed into the gloom.

"Perhaps," Brill answered uncertainly, his voice echoing in the cave surrounds, overlapping with Garan's. His hand now held hers.

"Well, that could be a way out. And I feel the vaguest of breezes. I'm sure there is an opening not that far away."

"Seems our friend knows a lot about caves," Danton commented. "Just as well; I never found the need to venture into one. I like the sky too much."

Brill laughed lightly, his breath brushing against her neck. "Yes, I know what you mean." He gave Laidan's hand a slight squeeze and asked how she was coping. She smiled, pleased at Brill's attentions.

Garan led the way, taking it very slowly and testing the ledges and footholds as he went. Laidan found herself gripping Brill's hand hard.

She wondered why he didn't complain or make a jest about it.

"I'm right behind you, Laidan," Brill said as he helped her to reach the first foothold.

The climb seemed to take hours. Laidan's knees began to shake and her breath to rasp. "Give me both your hands and I'll pull you up," Danton said. He was lying prone, with his upper body sticking out above her. "It's all right. Garan has my legs. Grab hold of me."

Laidan let go of Brill's hand and let Danton pull her up. She scraped her elbows when he tugged her into the gap in the rock face. Then he assisted her to crawl along it and out onto another ledge.

Garan could barely contain his excitement. "I know where we are! There's light here, but you have to hurry as the sun is going down," Garan said when she and the two men emerged.

"Already? Does that mean we traveled through the night, or many nights?" she asked.

Garan shrugged. "I can't say. It doesn't feel that we were in there that long."

Laidan rubbed her aching back and then massaged her neck. "It seemed like an age to me," she commented with feeling.

Garan leaped a short distance to a round nob of rock and made his way to a bend in the cave. She could make out reddish-hued light that imbued the walls with warmth. The entrance couldn't be too far away. Her spirits lifted as she followed him.

When she caught up, Garan jumped over a crevice in the floor. He leaned toward her, hand outstretched to assist her crossing. Brill came up behind and lifted her round the waist. His touch sent a thrill through her.

"Over you go," he said, making her smile.

On the other side of the crevice Garan guided her round the bend in the cave. He had been correct. The burnished circle of the cave mouth glowed with the sunset; beyond it only the rock of the mountain was visible.

Together they made the last trek over water-eroded stone, dodging holes and fallen boulders to the cave entrance. Garan looked to the sky and smiled.

"We made it," he said with a sigh. Turning his attention to the surrounding landscape and scanning for landmarks, he pointed and said excitedly, "The observatory is not far from here—see, there's Loden Peak. 'Tis a bit of a climb, but when Belle rises there should be sufficient light for us to find our way."

Laidan was ready to sing. As Brill came out of the cave mouth, she turned and hugged him with a squeal of delight. Catching her excitement, Brill let out a cheer and embraced her in return, swinging her in a circle. When he set her down, she clasped his upper arms and realized how strong he was. Their gazes locked momentarily before Brill looked up at the surrounding terrain.

Garan paused, staring at her and Brill standing together. Danton came up behind Garan and slapped him on the back, and said, "Great work, Garan."

"You are welcome."

ᏃᏃᏃᏃᏃ

Garan's heart soared when he saw the familiar pathways. Once free of the caves, they had to climb. It was slow going because even though there was light from Belle moon, the mountains cast long shadows, hiding rock falls and loose stones. He worried for Laidan, as their journey had already taxed her. However, he marveled at how well she had handled the strange roadways beneath the surface and the treacherous path through the cave. The memory of her distress when he had abandoned her in the caves all those months ago, albeit for a short time, still weighed heavily on him.

As he reached out and gripped the ledge above his head, he smiled ruefully. Laidan had matured in many ways during the last year—she was no longer a young girl but a woman. Being beyond the confines of the observatory had shown him how little he knew or understood of the wider world. A groan escaped him as he levered himself upward. Then he quickly slid around on his stomach to offer a hand down to Laidan. She was light, but his tired muscles strained to lift her. Assisted by the tender embrace of Brill, she was soon face to face with him, grasping onto his shoulder so that she could climb onto the ledge behind him. Next came Danton and, lastly, Brill, who leaped up and snagged Garan's forearm with his hand.

As he drew Brill up to the ledge, their eyes met. There was something in Brill's expression, a straight, steadfast gaze that was, to Garan's mind, unashamedly honest. Garan shook himself once when he brought himself to his feet again.

"Tell me," Brill asked softly. "How far is it now?"

Garan pointed along the ledge that they had gained. "Look to that bend and then straight up. You can see the lights of the student wing from here. Above that is the observation gallery, which encircles the uppermost turret; actually, the gallery is part of the summit, crafted from the fabric of the mountain itself. This is the Loden Peak side of the observatory. We'll be safe there."

All of them looked where he pointed. Danton nodded once and Laidan grimaced. It did look like a steep climb. Garan caught Brill looking at him and turned away. Perhaps the young man was worried for Laidan too. But somehow that didn't seem right. What had this young man to do with her? Laidan seemed all too interested in the young rebel.

Beyond the ledge the path was more straightforward, although it was switchback and steep. Garan began to wonder what the Master Elder would say about the strangers. Would he accuse Garan of compromising the observatory's safety? Garan shook his head. If he did, then Garan would have to argue otherwise. He and Laidan would not be here if the two rebels had not come to their aid. And without a doubt, these two had more fighting experience than all the Skywatchers put together. That strange man, Gercomo, worried Garan. What if he and his hardened rebels decided to pursue them all the way to the observatory? What if he joined forces with Lenk and decided to attack? Mentally, Garan did the math and knew they had no chance of withstanding a concerted assault. All the observatory had to aid its defense were its remote position and difficult access route.

They arrived at the Loden Peak side entrance to the observatory and found the gate barred from the inside. Garan thought this strange, because the observatory had many access points leading to different mountain trails and mines. Only one of them led to Klester Valley and Vanden, and that was on the other side of the mountain from where they stood. Garan began to worry that Lenk had already sent men to attack them, and his fellow Skywatchers had secured the building. He doubted that they had been attacked from this side of the Duggan Ranges as there wasn't a settlement nearby.

He stood back from the door and looked up, trying to see if there was movement along the observation gallery formed from Trithorn's mighty summit.

Brill whispered to him, "Are you all right? You're sweating."

He glanced at Brill. Danton edged closer and hissed, "Be ready, Brill."

"No, I'm fine," Garan said hastily. "I thought perhaps because the door is secured that there might be a problem." The sound of the bolt being drawn back cut him off. However, the two rebels tensed. Danton's gaze flicked over their surroundings while he simultaneously pushed back his camouflage coat and placed his hands near his weapons.

Garan saw the pommel of a sword in the folds of the rebel's clothes. "Please, don't do anything hasty. These are my friends." He was going to say that they were peaceful folk and didn't have weapons but then caution wiped the impulse away. No point in laying their weaknesses bare for all to see.

It was Elder Wiley who opened the door a crack, his white whiskered chin visible in the glow of his lantern. He blinked once. "Is that you, young Garan?"

Relief flooded through him. "Yes, 'tis me. I have people with me. Is all well within?"

Elder Wiley sucked in a phlegm-laden breath. "It depends a little on your definition of 'well.' All is well if you can overlook the orders to lock all the doors and for defenses to be built, swift like." Elder Wiley peeped further around the door and caught sight of Laidan and the others. His eyes widened and then he nodded. "I'll take you to the refectory so you can eat and rest." He opened the door and waved them in. "I'll send a message to the Master Elder. I'm sure he'll come to you direct. How do you do, young lady? It is good to see you again."

Laidan smiled weakly and stepped past the old man. Brill and Danton brought up the rear. Garan could hear them whispering to each other. He guessed he had a lot of explaining to do about what went on here.

Elder Wiley led them across the courtyard and in through a narrow arched doorway. From there he took them through a minor vestibule before meeting up with the wide access stairs to the refectory. As Garan strode down the hall and climbed the familiar stairs, he wished that all was as before, that Thurdon was alive, that Laidan had not been infected with power. That there was no Lenk, no rebels. But he knew everything had changed. Life was changing around him, like Shatterwing.

Wiley pushed open the wide, beaten-metal doors and ushered them in. The refectory was fairly quiet and filled with enticing aromas. It was early for evening meal. Soon the place would fill up. Voices in the kitchen, along with the sounds of pots banging and plates clinking, brought Garan an even deeper sense of home. His stomach grumbled loudly. He shrugged and smiled sheepishly at the others as he patted his belly. After all, he hadn't eaten a warm meal in days, and with that thought came the recollection of what had befallen him. Sinking onto a wooden bench he sighed heavily, letting the tension ease out of him. Laidan put her folded arms on the table and rested her head on them. Brill and Danton were wary and stood off to one side, their eyes ranging over the room, the benches, the windows now filled with the soft lilac haze of the rising Belle moon.

Wiley had asked for food and drink to be served up. When the trays appeared, Garan remembered his manners, moving to the servery to bring the food over to the table. It was a warm vegetable stew with mushroom gravy, cacti flat bread and a pitcher of wine. Another loud gurgle from his middle made him blush. "Come and eat it while it is hot. I'm sure we'll have so many questions to answer afterward that we may not see food again for a while."

The two rebels exchanged a glance before sitting down. Danton flashed a smile, his unshuttered eye twinkling with humor. "Yes, must get our priorities right." Then without another word he and Brill got busy eating.

After a few eager mouthfuls of the best-tasting stew he'd ever had, Garan noticed that Laidan wasn't eating. She appeared to be dozing. "Come on, Laidan," he said, nudging her lightly with his elbow. "Just a few spoonfuls and then you can rest. I'll see if I can hold off the Master Elder's questions until you've had a chance to sleep."

A wan face peered at him sideways from the cradle of her elbows. His heart wrenched when he looked at her. If only he could take this burden from her. It made him feel powerless that he couldn't. She mumbled something and he leaned forward to whisper to her, "What is it? How is Thurdon's gift?"

Head still leaning on one folded arm, she grimaced and spooned a small amount of stew into her mouth with the other. Her wrist wobbled and gravy slid down her arm and slopped onto the table top. Apparently oblivious to the mess she was making, she chewed and swallowed. "Quiet for the moment," she said while scooping more stew onto her spoon. "Though I'm so tired that even if Thurdon decided to do a jig inside my head, I'd sleep through it."

Elder Wiley took quiet steps up to their table, his old eyes ranging over them to check on their progress. "How are you all? Do you have enough food?" he asked.

Garan caught his eye and gestured silently toward Laidan. With a nod, Wiley invited her to see her room and assisted her to her feet. She said good night quietly and left the room. Garan watched her leave and then turned his attention once more to the food while they waited for the Master Elder. They didn't have to wait long.

When the Master Elder drew near, Garan stood up to meet him and a knot tightened in his gut. He had achieved his mission by chance more than by design. He felt undeserving of the wide smile and the fierce hug that the older man gave him. Then pleasure was replaced by caution in the old man's expression when he beheld the two rebels.

With one eyebrow raised, the Master Elder said, "Who do we have here? Gentlemen?"

Garan stood to the side, running a hand through his hair. He had been so fixated on eating that he had not given much thought to how he would explain the two strangers he had brought to the observatory. "I...er," he managed to get out.

Brill smiled widely, and Danton laughed once. "Been a long time since someone called me that," the one-eyed rebel said. "Danton's the name, and this is my companion, Brill." Danton spread his arms wide, indicating the observatory. "I'm sure you've got something interesting to tell us about what you do here. I must confess I've never heard of Trithorn Peak or Skywatchers. From the little young Garan has told us, what you do here is truly amazing."

Garan gulped once, his gaze darting between the Master Elder and his friends. Had he said anything he shouldn't? He could not quite recollect. The Master Elder bowed. "I'm glad you see it so, because our role is important and our trust in our visitors is even more so. I take it from your presence among us that you assisted Garan in the rescue of Laidan." Brill nodded. The Master Elder continued, "So far we've had two dubious envoys demanding a ransom for him. I thought them more like bandits, given their dress and manner. But as there was no mention of Laidan we did not bargain with them and sent them on their way. We knew that Garan would have died before letting anything happen to her."

A sudden warmth on his cheeks made Garan look down. He hardly knew what to say to such a compliment. By the fading of Brill's smile, he realized that the young man didn't like the implication of the Elder's words. Garan thought it was time to say something. "When I got to Vanden I found Fillbe dead. Then I was captured by Lenk. We escaped the town only to be caught by bandits, then by another group. In turn, we broke free of them, but wouldn't have succeeded without these two brave men. I tried to rescue Laidan, but things became a little complicated. We owe our safety to these men. I'm not sure why they helped us and whether they realize what kind of trouble may be brewing here."

The Master Elder's eyes widened and narrowed during the course of Garan's speech. He seemed generally surprised when he asked, "And do you know what kind of trouble is brewing, Garan?"

Brill straightened and spoke before Garan could draw breath. "I don't know all the whys and wherefores, but I do know that the Inspector won't give up until he has what he wants. He will suspect you have the lady Laidan here and he knows she has some kind of power."

The Master Elder's face went blank. He neither denied nor confirmed that Laidan might have a power. "I see. The Inspector?"

Brill continued. "Yes, that is the name by which I knew him, but he calls himself Gercomo now. When he finds that we have escaped from him, I don't think it will take him long to work out where we were heading...or at least where Garan was heading. The workings of this place are no secret to the people in Vanden, I suspect, and as the Inspector is holed up there I am sure he knows all that he needs to know by now."

The Master Elder frowned and then responded as if the mountain air had suddenly turned into sewer stench. "So, what you are telling me is that as well as Lenk harassing us and denying us our food and supplies, we now have another party to deal with, one whom I suspect is even more corrupt than Lenk?"

Garan hung his head lower so that his chin brushed against his chest. "This man also has a bigger force than Lenk's. I'm sorry. 'Tis all my fault. If only I hadn't gotten caught. If they attack the observatory, it will be much worse than we can possibly prepare for."

The Master Elder regarded him with his old brown eyes, now surrounded by worry lines. Garan noticed that the old man's skin was flushed from receiving such terrible news. However, his leader smiled and patted him on the shoulder. "Do not blame yourself; others are to blame. How could you know this 'Inspector' was coming? You did your best and that is all that I could ask. You brought Laidan back to us."

Elder Wiley ambled up to the table and stood to the left of Garan. The Master Elder acknowledged him.

"Wiley has prepared some quarters for your friends. After you have cleaned yourself up, Garan, please come to my study." He faced Brill and Danton, opening both his hands in a gesture of greeting. "Please be welcome. I will send for you in the morning, if I may, so that we can talk more. I am sure you have as much to say as you do skill to share. I will leave you now."

Wiley stepped aside as the Master Elder left, then indicated with an extended arm that the two rebels should accompany him. Brill and Danton shared another of their knowing looks and stood up to follow him.

As Danton passed by, he patted Garan companionably on the shoulder. "See you later," Danton said. Garan nodded and then locked gazes with Brill, who nodded once, a smile lurking on his lips.

After they'd departed, Garan headed to his own quarters. He was fatigued, to be sure, but so much had happened that he knew he needed to talk to the Master Elder urgently. Once in his room he shut the door and leaned on it, just taking in his own space again. A familiar scent greeted him and his gaze fell upon the source. Someone had delivered warm, spiced bathing water. That brought a smile to his lips. Such a luxury was a special treat and a wonderful welcome.

Straight away he stripped off his clothes and began the task of washing the dust and grime from his body. He had suspected he might never be clean again. Thoughts of Laidan came to mind. He was glad she was finally safe, though he worried about Thurdon's gift. Surely the Master Elder knew what to do...yet doubt niggled at him. What if the person who knew the most was Brill? He decided he didn't like that idea. Brill and Laidan already liked each other too much. He remembered when he and Laidan had been jammed together in the crevice, how her body had been so close to his and how, when their lips touched, he had burned with deep feeling. She had encouraged him, perhaps influenced by the wine he had tasted on her lips, or perhaps to punish him or to wash away another man's taint from her.

When he thought back to those excruciatingly long moments in which he had struggled to free himself from the cage, he felt overwhelming relief that it was all over. Using sound and a discarded crystal shard, he had worked slowly and quietly to avoid attracting attention. All the time he was working, he'd been imagining Nulf raping her, knowing that every second of delay made the event more likely. On reaching the tent he had expected to find her bloodied and broken. Yet Laidan had said he'd arrived in time.

A chill excited goose flesh across his skin. Coming back to the present, he realized he was standing naked in his room with water dripping to the floor in cold puddles. Even as he dried himself, tension filled every muscle and he knew he needed to let it go. The only problem was that he didn't know if he could let go of her, let go of the hope that she cared for him as much as he did for her. Funny how such a feeling could catch up with one. Now that he had acknowledged it, he suspected it would only hurt him more than it already did.

Chapter Nine

VENTURE

It was with some frustration that Salinda watched Nils's preparation for their journey. To her, he took a great deal of time and was overly fastidious in his attention to detail. He had to find a map. For some reason she thought he would know the Ways by heart, as he appeared to be linked to them in some way. Apparently that was not so, even though he had felt the destruction of a Way Gate from a great distance away.

When she saw his map, she was stunned. She had been thinking it would be a drawn thing of the usual type, only to be surprised by a small hand-held machine that hummed in Nils's palm and projected a maze of lines in the air. Nils explained that it was a two-level map—one level showing the land above and the other the markers of the Way Gates. The Ways were not linear, he explained. In them, time traveled at a slower pace, or the distances were curtailed, he wasn't sure which, only that both explanations satisfactorily explained the result.

"Are the entrances evenly spaced?" she asked him as she walked around the map, tempted to poke at the closely packed glowing dots that she assumed represented the Way Gates. She was thinking that if they were the same distance apart from each other then it would be easy to navigate once one found a familiar landmark. Then abruptly the image sprayed outward and enlarged. With her hands flung up over her head, she jumped back in surprise. Then the image contracted inward again as Nils adjusted it.

"No, not necessarily. They were designed around our work, the places of interest to the Hiem. Large cities could have multiple entrances, smaller towns perhaps only one. Way Gates were also situated in isolated locations where there was some landmark of natural beauty or a useful vantage point." He turned off the mechanism and the map disappeared. "I know how to get there now."

"Let's go then. If we hurry we might catch the intruders," she said, striding to the door.

Before he moved, Nils was seized by a fit of coughing. When he could gain his breath, he stood and continued as if nothing had happened. "Apologies," he added weakly.

Salinda watched in concern as he walked into the Ways and the gloom enveloped them. The gap between them grew as he quickened his pace, so she hastened to keep up with him.

His stiff-backed walk was symbolic of the way he held his feelings in. Even in the act of sexual intercourse, he touched her minimally, seeming neither to want pleasure nor to give it. Did the Hiem not kiss or caress? she wondered as she walked. When she caught up with him, he didn't acknowledge her presence. Salinda walked next to him for hours. Determined to draw him out, she eventually asked, "Was the destroyed Way Gate close to Barrahiem?"

"Any breach of the Ways is too close for the Hiem."

"Oh...that means you don't want to say. You don't trust me."

"Think what you will. For someone who desired great urgency you are remarkably slow." And with that comment he increased his pace.

They climbed several sets of staircases and took two pathways that appeared to be veering left, and then Nils slowed as he came to a junction. His map device sent a warm, yellow glow into the gloom around them, and Salinda could see that the dimness around Nils brightened of its own accord, as if his presence ignited some essential element within the Ways themselves. Pausing, he scanned the area. Salinda stood next to him and did the same. She could see six different Ways heading off into seeming oblivion. All around was a leaden nothingness, a haze...walls? She couldn't tell whether they were made of rock or some other substance.

"There are tracks here." He pointed to one of the Ways. Salinda stared, trying to make out any tell-tale marks. Obviously Nils had better eyesight than she did. He allowed her to move closer. Squatting down she discerned boot-sized smudges in a thin layer of dust illuminated by Nils's map light. She slid her finger along the surface and rubbed the grains against her thumb. If she had been on her own she would have missed it.

Nils faced to the left and sniffed. "There is more dust in that direction. That Way once led to a town called Singala. But I imagine it is gone now." He pointed after the tracks. "Strange, but these seem to be heading toward Trithorn Peak...the observatory I told you about."

Salinda's interest pricked up, like the goose flesh on her skin. She wondered if the people who had used the Way had headed in this direction intentionally. Could they be connected to the observatory? That thought made her think of Shatterwing. Did they study it?

Nils took a few steps in the direction of the ruined Way Gate and sniffed again. "They used chemical explosives to blow up the Way." His voice hitched. "How could they destroy—"

He doubled up and coughed, once, twice. He took a long breath and straightened up. Taking another step he began coughing again. He fought the coughing fit and finally it passed. Salinda noticed a tremble in his hands. She reached out, noting the heat of his skin. Gently, he removed his hand from hers and turned away. "We'd best return now."

"But..." He glided past her and headed back the way they had come. Salinda wanted to follow the path to Trithorn Peak. Before he disappeared from view, she jogged after him, but kept behind him, allowing him his solitude, his exclusion of her. Perhaps he was angry because she was a human and humans had violated the sanctity of the Ways. She could understand that. He valued every artefact of his people and that mysterious race that had preceded them—the Moon Binders.

They reached the bottom of the third staircase. All of a sudden he buckled and fell to his knees. When she reached him, worry dogging her heels, she could see it was bad. He'd slumped forward onto his face. After she turned him over, she touched his face and hands, which were hot and sweaty. His breathing was labored and shallow. His eyes were open, but he didn't respond to her when she called out to him.

"Nils, what am I going to do with you?" She stroked his silver hair out of his face and ran a finger tenderly over his bony brow. A mumbled response was all she got from him. A flash of awareness crossed his face and then he tried to move, to lever himself up, to pull away from her, but he fell back to the ground, slack-faced.

A sliver of fear slid up her spine. How was she supposed to move him? She had to get him back to the city, and then what? Oh, for a flask of dragon wine. Then she remembered the healing tray.

Cradling his head in her lap, she let him rest for a bit, all the while working out the logistics of getting him back to Barrahiem and into the healing tray. After ten minutes or so, he recovered enough to talk. She gave him another five minutes before she attempted to help him to his feet and begin the long, laborious descent to the city. Using her shoulder under his arm to lend him support, they began the lonely trek.

With effort he managed to keep his legs under him as they made slow progress along the Way. Nils's limbs were long and his hand draped down her front and his head sagged. Salinda found his light scent pleasant, but the feel of his bones under thin flesh worried her. How long had he been hiding this illness from her? He'd always been slightly built, but now with this sickness, she recognized the serious nature of his illness. The thought of losing him frightened her, and it wasn't because he was valuable as a keeper of so much knowledge or a possible master of unknown and unfathomable machines. She cared for him.

It seemed to be an interminable time before they reached the outskirts of Barrahiem. The stair was lit by lamps and the lichen dangling from the ceiling. Looking into Nils's face, Salinda could see how ill he was. His eyes lacked luster, his cheeks were sunken and his pale skin had a grayish cast. Nils was wheezing with effort when she assisted him down to the ground to rest. With his eyes closed, he took quick, shallow breaths. Fatigue was evident in every muscle. It must be the air, she thought. Perhaps her lungs were used to it. Nils was from a time when the air had been clean. She remembered the stories he'd read her from the archives...and how so many of them had died from the dust in the air. By the source, don't let him die too.

His silvery-white hair draped across his brow. Brushing it gently off his face she said urgently, "Nils? Nils!"

His eyelids fluttered open again. Stroking his forehead, she said gently, "I want to put you in the healing tray. Are there some instructions somewhere that I need follow?"

He shook his head. Again she knelt next to him, put his arm across her shoulders so that he could use her to lift himself off the ground. "Please, Nils. It's not far now. Help me save you." Gradually, he increased the weight he placed on her. Slowly, she eased him up to a standing position, glad that her dragon wine–induced strength remained. Just the thought of dragon wine made her crave a sip.

With occasional assistance from Nils, she found her way to the room where the healing tray was situated, near the Hall of Elders. Fighting off her attempts to put him on it, Nils staggered to the panel in the center of the wall and made a few adjustments. Sagging to his knees a moan escaped him. Dashing to his aid, Salinda half-dragged him to the tray while he assisted her by crawling. One final heave and Nils slumped his upper body down onto the tray and she helped him lie straight by bringing up his legs and placing his arms by his sides. Immediately lights came into play on the panel in the center of the wall. With a soft sweep of her lips, she kissed his brow and then, feeling a swell of emotion, she kissed his lips too. Would he even remember?

She wondered how long his healing would take. But it was too late to ask Nils. The air under the transparent lid had begun to mist over, obscuring her view of him. She watched until she saw his face relax and the pain slide away. Then she let go of the horrible fear that she had clenched so tight in her gut—the fear that he would die, the fear that all that knowledge he possessed would be out of her people's reach and that the child she carried would be fatherless.

Chapter Ten

A TIME TO STAND

"This isn't getting us any closer to that wine," Danton pointed out as he lay back on the bunk, washed and dressed in a clean robe.

"True," Brill replied, taking a long pull of watered wine as he sat on the bunk next to him. "But this 'observatory' is worth investigating, isn't it? Along with Laidan and that power thing of hers."

Danton huffed. "Are you sure it's the power you're interested in? You've been paying a lot of attention to the vessel itself."

Brill frowned. "I don't know what you mean. Knowledge of such things will be useful for our cause—even if it is only hiding the knowledge of it from others. And now that I know about this place I want to understand what's going on here. These people seem to be good—"

Danton rolled onto his side. "I must confess that I am curious, too. Even if these people are 'good' as you hope, the way they live is unnatural. They keep to themselves, interact little with outsiders. What goes on out there—in the real world—is nothing to them. How can they ignore it?"

"So it was in the Highland Confederacy. This place has a similar feeling, but its isolation sets it apart. Perhaps my father should have hidden his community rather than letting others know of its existence. It was the government of the time that put it down and killed him, you know."

Danton sighed and scratched his elbow before tucking it under the blanket. "I don't think this is the same as your father's set-up. There were other issues involved there, politics and rivalry. This place is almost otherworldly. They aren't here to farm communally or follow a credo. I'd say the mountains are inhospitable at the best of times for agrarian pursuits. There is something else here. Though I agree, they are a cut above the average when it comes to humanity."

Brill peeled of his boots, placed his feet in a bowl of hot water and sighed at the sheer luxury of it. "Maybe they need to remain apart to keep whole and sound. I can't argue with that approach given what I've been through. But it is so exciting to find the kind of people we thought no longer existed, people who are willing to do good for others instead of harm, thinking people rather than creatures of instinct. I say this is the pocket of humankind that is worth saving. Are you afraid that you might lose your skepticism and find some hope?"

Danton had closed his eyes. "No, never afraid of that. In my secret heart I long for it. But I worry about that wine, about what the Inspector is planning, and I think about Salinda. I can't let go of the belief that she is out there, somewhere, alive."

After drying off his feet and putting the bowl outside the door, Brill reclined on his bunk and stared at the ceiling. "I hope she is, Danton. I really do."

೧೦೧೦

If anything, thought Garan, the Master Elder looked more tired than he had previously. As Garan related the events of his journey, he saw the older man's head droop and his face grow more haggard. But when Garan spoke again of Brill and Danton's fighting experience, the Master Elder's head snapped up, his eyes kindling with light. "Do you think they would assist us? Advise us on our defenses?"

Garan shrugged. "We can only ask. I'm sure they could be persuaded to do so. I doubt they would risk the dark paths under the surface again, so to leave they would have to go down through Klester Valley, and I'm sure they don't want to come face to face with an army of rebels."

The Master Elder sighed and then slowly shook his head. "The times we live in. Those dark paths you speak of are called the Ways of the Hiem."

"What—you know about these pathways?" Garan found himself sitting on the edge of his chair.

The Master Elder stood and went to a cabinet behind his desk, unlocked it with a key he kept on a chain around his neck, and drew out an old book. Some of its pages appeared to have separated from the spine and it was held together by a thin strip of leather.

"I know of them from this book." He placed it on the desk and tapped it with his gnarled forefinger. "As far as I knew only the Hiem could traverse them, though you have shown this to be incorrect. The fact that the pathways still exist is quite exceptional. No one has heard from a Hiem since Moonfall. In fact, hardly anyone from our world knew of their existence, either before Moonfall or after. A reclusive people, yet they were known to the observatory."

"The Hiem?" Garan shook his head. "I didn't—I haven't...How did Laidan know how to open the doorway?"

"I cannot confess to know how she opened the Way Gate, Garan. The Hiem were a very old race and according to this book, inhabited cities below the surface of Margra. As to where Laidan got her knowledge, my best guess is that it came from Thurdon. It was he who brought me this book for safekeeping. You must keep what you know to yourself, Garan. Don't speak of these Ways to anyone."

"Of course I will...but the other two ..." Garan grew anxious about the rebels knowing things that should be kept secret. He needed time to reflect so he could work things over in his mind. He noticed how talk of the Hiem seemed to both excite and frighten the Master Elder.

"I will talk to them in the morning. Then we will see."

"But what if they won't help and want to leave?"

The Master Elder shrugged. "We would not prevent them, and can only prevail on their goodwill. They have shown much of this already by bringing you and Laidan here safely. They have asked nothing of us except food and shelter."

Nodding, Garan asked, "Could the fact that they know of these Ways endanger us?"

Their gazes met momentarily. "Not us directly. But the Hiem were keepers of knowledge and who knows what else. In times like these, knowledge can be a powerful weapon. You'd best go to bed now. We will talk further in the morning. Perhaps you will be here when I interview Laidan."

"Of course..." He stood and took two steps toward the door before pausing and looking back. The Master Elder was watching him. "I did have one more question."

The Master Elder's shaggy white eyebrows lowered over a frown. "Our theories are confirmed. 'Tis still on course."

Garan nodded once, his heart lurching. "Oh..." He swallowed around the lump in his throat. "I see." He nodded slowly as he digested that piece of news. "Good night, Master Elder."

As quietly as he could, he drew the door shut behind him and let out a sigh. That was all they needed—an attack to distract them from combating the real threat, a massive lump of rock set to ruin them all.

Garan headed down the corridor, trying to push all his concerns into a corner of his mind. Weariness still hung over him, but he felt too agitated to rest straight away. As a diversion, he decided to check up on Laidan. She was bound to be asleep but he wanted to look in on her just the same.

Laidan's room was on the next level up. He climbed the stairs two at a time and checked the corridor in both directions. It wasn't that he was up to no good, but he didn't want everyone knowing that he was stealing into her quarters. The casual observer would not understand. A grin lingered at the corner of his mouth when he thought that Laidan probably wouldn't understand either.

Stepping quietly down the corridor with exaggerated care he found her door. He knocked gently but there was no answer. Slowly he pushed the door open and poked his head around. Dressed in a cream shift, Laidan lay sprawled on the mattress, her covers twisted around her feet. A lamp still burned by her bedside. Her face looked relaxed, her lips parted slightly—occasionally she murmured and shifted her head from side to side. It was a gentle dream, he thought, not the torment of a nightmare. He swallowed when he thought about how beautiful she looked in the lamplight, with her pale skin marred only by dark shadows around her eyes.

He snicked the door shut behind him and stepped softly up to the bed. Carefully, he moved her feet and disengaged the covers. She groaned slightly and he paused, but she didn't wake. All of a sudden he realized what a fuss it would cause if he was caught here by Laidan herself or someone else. All that time they'd spent together, sleeping so close, he'd become used to seeing to her comfort. He placed the covers over her shoulder, tucked them under her chin and backed away. Then, remembering the lamp, he stepped back to turn it off.

"Is that you, Garan?" a soft, sleep-filled voice said.

"Yes, 'tis me. Sleep well."

Her breathing indicated she had already gone back to sleep. As he pulled the door open to sneak a look down the corridor, he heard the faint swish of someone's robes and froze. All he needed now was for Laidan to wake and scream because he was in her room; all hell would break lose. He shut the door again and stood inside, just behind it. A prickle of fear shot up his spine as the door began to open. Garan held his breath. He saw the outline of someone standing on the threshold, looking in on Laidan.

"Good night, Garan," whispered a voice as the door shut. It was the Master Elder. Garan let out a breath. He waited two minutes, did a quick check of the corridor and bolted down the stairs. He was in his quarters, in his bunk, staring at the ceiling when someone knocked. "Come in," he said, feigning sleepiness.

The door creaked open. "Nice to see that you made it to your bed," the Master Elder said. The light from the corridor kissed the side of his face.

Garan was glad that it was dark in the room because he knew his face was flushed with embarrassment. "Good night, Master Elder."

The door shut softly, and Garan let out a sigh. What was he going to do about Laidan? She would have to decide what she wanted to do with him—if anything. Brill's smiling face came to mind, making him frown. *Go to sleep, you fool*, he said to himself as he turned on his side. There were too many important things going on to worry about a scrawny girl—woman—and her ignorant opinions. Unfortunately his heart didn't agree.

Part 2

A cup of dragon wine fills the heart with vigor; too much destroys the soul

Chapter Eleven

TO BE HOME AGAIN

Pale pink dawn light pierced through the small window in Garan's room. Straight away, he sensed the unease around him. It seemed to permeate the walls of the observatory. He sat up and rubbed sleep out of his eyes. There were different noises and different rhythms in the place. The tenders weren't teaching the young pupils, because he couldn't hear the dull drone of their voices reverberating down the corridors. The normal smells from the refectory were absent. No smell of baking bread to tempt him out of bed. He wondered if they were still making warm porridge and milk. And there was other activity, furniture being moved, people grunting with effort. The Master Elder was right. They were preparing for a siege.

A quick dunk of his head in a bowl of cold water and a dry-off with a clean towel lifted the veil of fatigue. He had a sudden desire to talk to the two rebels. Those two knew fighting ways, and by the Wing, they were going to help.

He went to their room on the next level and, after knocking and pushing the door inward, he found it was empty. Perturbed, he scratched his head until he considered breakfast. His stomach growled at the thought. He jogged down the corridor and slowed at the refectory door. There was no sign of the rebels within; perhaps they were with the Master Elder already. His close friend, Turnet, looked up from his porridge and then leaped to his feet.

"Garan! Come eat with me."

A smile lit Garan's face as he came over and hugged his friend. "Turnet, great to see you."

Turnet shoved Garan down into a seat, then bade him wait while he fetched a serve of porridge for him. "There you go," he said as he slid the bowl in front of Garan. "Now eat up and tell me with your mouth full, as you normally do, what it was like in Vanden. I heard she's here …" His dark gaze flicked sideways. "Do you think you'll study her as intently as you do Shatterwing?"

Garan swallowed a mouthful of hot porridge, and his eyes watered as it singed his throat. "Blast you, Turnet, don't even go there."

"Why not? You get to do the exciting stuff while I stay here. Not a thing to blast in days, and rumors and orders flying about that don't make any sense whatsoever. I was landed with Ruzel to train in your absence—so tedious. How I wish the Master Elder had sent me to Vanden instead. Then I could be the hero and rescuer of the lily-white maiden."

Garan's spoon clinked against the edge of the bowl as he dropped it. "You wanted to go to Vanden?" He closed his mouth, realizing that he was gaping.

"Of course! I could have visited my mother. Seen if my little sister, Eneit, has grown up to be pretty and smart like me. I know my way around." He laughed, but there was concern in his eyes.

"I see." Turnet had been eight years old when he'd been gifted to the observatory. Mutual feelings of loneliness and a sense of abandonment had drawn the two friends together.

"And now she is here without her chaperone…Come on, what happened—did you…?"

Garan put his head down and shoveled a few more spoonfuls of porridge into his mouth, intent on ignoring his friend's impertinent question. He chewed unnecessarily because it gave him an excuse to delay his response. Trust Turnet to find his weak string and pluck it. Wouldn't he be surprised if it snapped?

Turnet, noticing Garan's reluctance, began to tick off his fingers one by one the imaginary milestones that they had invented when they were younger. "Did you…hold her hand?"

Garan kept his gaze steady, trying to bluff his friend.

"Did you cuddle up to her?" Turnet trained his gaze on his friend's face.

Still Garan stared straight ahead.

"Did you kiss her?" Turnet's dark eyes glittered speculatively as they tracked over Garan's face.

Garan blinked.

Turnet clearly took this as an affirmative sign. "You kissed her, didn't you—what was it like? Did she get all soft and pliant? Did you—"

Laidan's laughter trickled into the room from the corridor. Garan and Turnet immediately swung round as she walked in the door, her hand tucked into Brill's elbow. Garan's face grew hot and he saw Turnet pale slightly. His friend had nearly been caught tossing back disrespect along with his warm, watered wine.

Turnet got up and whistled softly. "Now I understand. You brought back competition. No wonder you are keeping quiet. I pity you, my friend. Catch you on shift later." Taking two steps away, he paused and whispered conspiratorially over his shoulder, "Don't let it get to you." He put his bowl on the table next to the servery and headed out the door. A little theatrical wave at Laidan's back and he was gone.

Garan stared at the remains of his porridge while he considered what to do next. Then he stood up, went to fetch another serving of hot porridge, and angled in the direction of Brill and Laidan, who had taken seats not far from the door.

He watched for a few moments as Brill engaged Laidan in low-voiced conversation. Obviously the young rebel didn't have eating on his mind, as neither of them made any move toward the food. The sight of the handsome rebel with Laidan twisted Garan's gut. He studied her face, looking for signs of admiration in her expression. A slight frown marred the smooth line of her brow and her eyes were shrouded with sorrow. Occasionally she would use her hand to rub at her temple, and it was while doing this that her gaze swept the room and she saw him. "Garan!"

Smiling sheepishly, Garan hovered, wondering whether he should join them, just as Danton shoved the refectory doors open and caught sight of him.

"Come on, lad, join us before the real work begins," the one-eyed rebel said.

Brill added similar comments before going to the servery for food. Laden with a large tray full of jostling bowls and mugs sufficient for the three of them, Brill negotiated his way back to the table under the curious gaze of other Skywatchers eating their breakfast.

Garan kept his expression solemn to disguise his concern for Laidan. As he sat down he said softly to the two rebels, "I will, thank you. I need to talk to you both...in private."

Brill gnawed on hard orange bread while Laidan took a few sips of watered wine.

Laidan frowned at him. "In private?" she asked with a slightly wounded edge to her voice. "Do you mean without me listening in?"

Brill lifted an eyebrow, and when he caught Garan's eye, shook his head fractionally—a warning Garan ignored.

Garan faced Laidan square on. If he could spare her more worry then he would.

"Yes, I meant in private. I need to talk about something important and you don't need to hear it."

"Why? Are you being ill-mannered to spite me or don't you trust me?"

Her hurt expression almost shredded his resolve. "'Tis not that ..."

Danton sat down next to Laidan, jug in hand, and poured some more wine into her cup. "What the lad means is that he's worried and he wants reassurance, which is something he's not going to get from us. He doesn't want to expose you to further danger or anxiety. Don't you think that's rather gallant?"

Brill snickered, but when he saw Garan's expression, he stuck his face in his own mug.

Garan fought the urge to bang the two rebels' heads together. How dare Danton tell Laidan what was going on in his own mind and heart? If he wanted her to know what he really thought, he would have said so. He risked a glimpse at her face.

The shock was clear to see. "I don't believe it," she said sharply in reply. "You think I'm a child, Garan. But you're wrong. I'm going to see the Master Elder this morning and then you'll see. I'll be able to use Thurdon's gift and then you'll be sorry you doubted me."

Garan was appalled at her words. If anything he'd ceased thinking of her as a child when he'd tried to kiss her in the cave last year. "I...I don't... I was, er—" He had the choice of apologizing and including her in the discussions with the two rebels or getting up and leaving. He was still weighing up these two choices when he was saved the trouble by the appearance of the Master Elder himself.

"Good morning," he said cheerfully and smiled warmly at them all, as if the observatory wasn't about to be besieged by a hostile force and a celestial body wasn't bearing down on them ready to obliterate what was left of the world. Garan was reassured by the Master Elder's strength and silently wished that one day he could be as wise and as controlled in the face of so much danger. "In the course of the day I wish to speak with you all individually. Laidan, if you have quite finished your breakfast, perhaps you would do me the honor of being my first visitor?"

Garan stared at the table top. He couldn't bear to see her expression or the angry flame that flickered in her gaze. It was enough that he heard her hastily in-drawn breath and the scrape of the chair as she stood up. "I'm no longer hungry, in any case." The men sat quietly until she left the room.

"You sure know how to woo a lady, lad," Danton said with a shake of his head.

"I'm not trying to woo her," Garan replied a little testily. "Sorry, I didn't mean to snap...but she, well...never mind."

Obviously in a good mood, Danton grinned and said, "Don't worry. I know exactly what you mean. So what's troubling you?"

Vastly relieved at this opportunity to change the subject, Garan began, "You've probably already guessed that this place wasn't built for defense. The gate on the Klester Valley side—the access from Vanden—well, 'tis dilapidated and weak. Why, you could probably push it over single-handedly. And the folk here have never fought more than a fist fight over a ration share in their entire lives. No one comes here regularly—no one has ever tried to attack us before. I'm afraid for the people here; they are my friends and I've known them almost my whole life. It would be a tragedy if they were slaughtered, but much more is at stake. If the observatory is destroyed, there will be no way to undertake the vital work we do here, and that could cause the loss of many more innocent lives than those here alone. If this attack is successful, it would destroy not only the observatory but also all the knowledge here." He weighed up telling them about the large asteroid hurtling toward them but hesitated. He'd rather not speak of it because inside he had hope that it would not come to pass. "We stop the meteors and we save lives."

"And?" Brill asked.

Garan turned to the young man and looked into his blue and honest-looking eyes.

"We need your help—to prepare and to fight. If no one has asked you yet, I'm asking you now. We know nothing of tactics or warfare, and you do, plus you know this new threat—this Gercomo—intimately. We need your guidance—no, your leadership—if we are going to make any kind of real defense."

Danton sat still for a while, just staring into space. After a few minutes, he began to stroke his beard. Brill regarded Garan intently.

"Well, are you going to say something?" Garan prompted.

Brill was the one who answered. "We have pressing things to do that would be even further interrupted if we were to stay here and help...but on the other hand this might be an opportunity to get rid of an annoying problem." Garan frowned, shifting his attention between the rebels. Brill's eyes widened, then he added hastily, "I'm not saying we don't appreciate that you work for the greater good, but—"

"I agree," Danton chimed in, his gaze suddenly intense. "The team I have tracking the remainder of the wine will send word to Squab at the rendezvous point if they don't locate us. I guess we can make some time to help out. Do you have any intelligence yet on whether the Inspector is indeed coming here?"

Garan sighed, the tension in his shoulders releasing. "I haven't heard as yet. Though I'm sure we are bound to hear shortly. Our road was rather quicker than the Inspector's, I think. It usually takes at least a day to climb up the Klester Valley from Vanden. We started further away than that and we came up the Loden Peak trail, yet having taken a longer route we arrived in less than a day and night."

"Interesting phenomenon," Danton said. He took a long draft of watered wine and then started on his serve of porridge. "Go on."

"I imagine he would have to determine that we have indeed come here and then round up men and draw up plans of attack. How long would that take?"

"Not nearly long enough," Brill said. "He has his men, and they are ready to mobilize. I'm sure he would have assessed the situation as soon as he heard of the observatory, so we must assume he has already planned the attack. It's reasonable of him to assume that we would head here, given your connection to this place and the absence of other refuges."

Garan's mouth dropped open. "You sound as if you're saying he would attack the observatory whether he thought we were here or not."

Brill nodded. "Trithorn Peak would be a potential threat to him and his plans, an unknown force to be dealt with."

Garan clenched his fist, tapping it on the table. He'd not considered that they would be in danger regardless of their actions. At least now they had the assistance of two knowledgeable rebels and would not be taken by surprise. The guilt he'd been experiencing lessened. It was his fault after all.

"Mmmm," Danton said as if mulling over a set of imaginary plans. Then with a grin he added, "This porridge isn't bad."

"Danton," Brill chided.

"Well, it is good. A man has to enjoy the small things in life now and then. The source knows there is enough going on as it is to gray my hair and make my teeth drop out with fright."

A chuckle burst out of Brill and his smile spread warmth around the table. He was charming and his manner disarming, Garan thought. Even he wasn't immune to it. Garan grinned at them both, toying with the idea of another helping of porridge.

"So how long do you think it will take him to get here if he came straight away?" Brill asked Danton, tapping the table top with a forefinger for emphasis.

"Two days at the earliest, maybe a week if he takes time to prepare," Danton replied with a good deal of foreboding in his voice. "Although sooner is my reckoning."

Brill reached over and clasped Danton's shoulder. "Are we in?"

The one-eyed rebel swallowed another mouthful and smiled. "We are indeed."

Chapter Twelve

LAIDAN'S DILEMNA

Laidan sat on a large, uncomfortable chair in the Master Elder's office and clung to its well-worn arms. On one wall was an old map of the observatory surrounded by mountains. It was from Thurdon's collection. Many a time she'd helped him scrounge among ruins, looking for items of interest, or had been with him while he haggled for some old piece of junk at a market. She gulped back the surge of grief she felt at the thought of him and listened with growing disappointment to the Master Elder as he rambled on to her about what he didn't know.

"So you're saying that you don't know what Thurdon did to me? And that you can't help me?"

The Master Elder frowned at the top of his desk, before looking up and sighing deeply. "I'm sorry, Laidan. I knew Thurdon was special. He hinted at certain things, but he never explained about his power. Not how to use it or how it was passed on...only that someday the world would need it."

"Whore tits!" she blurted before covering her mouth with her hand, appalled. Both of the Master Elder's eyebrows shot up. He lowered one of them, still staring at her. Laidan 's faced heated and said, "I beg your pardon," and coughed into her hand. "Bad company. Thurdon always despaired of me. I picked up any stray expression I heard on the streets, even from a young age."

The Master Elder rubbed the back of his head, making his white hair stand on end. "Do you have any idea how long these glowing eyes..." She tapped her head with both hands, "...and the mental confusion will last?" she asked. "Maybe it will go away on its own." It was wishful thinking.

The Master Elder shook his head. "Forgive me, I feel so inadequate. Perhaps if I study Thurdon's books I could help you, but at present there is much to be done to defend this place, and I have not the time."

Tears stung her eyes. The person she'd looked up to most, after Thurdon, couldn't help her. Her heart lurched in her chest. "Oh, I see." She sniffed and wiped her eyes with the back of her hand. She couldn't live like this, not with Thurdon ranting in her head, with her eyes glowing so that people were afraid of her. She wanted to go back to the way things were.

Although now Thurdon was gone it wouldn't be the same. She thought of the old man, imagined what he'd say in this situation. Then she stopped herself from thinking too deeply lest she incite Thurdon to rise up and overwhelm her mind again. Besides, she knew already what he would suggest. "Maybe I should help myself, research—read books. I don't mean I can do it better than you...I can make a start, though. It is better than sitting around feeling helpless."

The Master Elder lifted the corner of his mouth in an almost smile. "That would be most welcome, and rather wise too. All that reading may teach you something. You were never as keen on books as you should have been."

There was no point in dwelling on that now, she thought to herself, nor was she in the mood to give the Master Elder the satisfaction of being right. "My learning was through doing, Master Elder." She stood up, signaling that she was ready to start, and the Master Elder showed her to a door on the opposite side of the room.

Laidan thought he looked too old for worry. Perhaps the Master Elder was even older than Thurdon had been. She felt a twinge of loss for her master, her father. As she walked behind the Master Elder to a small office off his study, she wondered if her future lay with the observatory. Thoughts of Garan arose and she pushed them away rather easily when Brill's blue-eyed, handsome face came to mind. Could she live a rebel's life? Would Brill give it up for her? Could he take her somewhere safe and care for her and devote himself to her comfort?

Her thoughts dissipated when she entered the office. The air smelled sour and dusty. The room was crammed full of books and scrolls and piles of unbound paper. Shelves rose right to the ceiling and bulged with more papers, maps, heavy leather-bound tomes and thin folded parchments. It was daunting to see all those volumes and realize that she had to go through them, perhaps all of them, before she found something that would help her. And then there was the horrible thought that she might find nothing at all. But a thought like that couldn't be entertained, couldn't be accepted. She was desperate.

When she sat down at the small table, the Master Elder placed a handwritten index in front of her. "This might help you find some reference to Thurdon's gift. I apologize that I can't do more; I can't even stay with you now because I must speak to the others on urgent business. I'll make sure some food is sent to you at lunchtime. And if you find anything, send me a message and I'll come right away. Cedel is in the library and he will alert me if you ask. One of the other elders may drop in on you during the day."

Laidan was instantly overwhelmed and disheartened at the thought of task ahead of her. She was so scared that she could barely think. Yet she didn't want to add to the Master Elder's concerns. With a smile, she lifted her face to his and said in a clear and confident voice, "Thank you, Master Elder. I will be fine here, and I'm sure I'll find something soon."

He smiled slightly before withdrawing back to his study. As soon as the Master Elder shut the door, Laidan put her forehead on the table and groaned. "Oh, Thurdon! Why me? Why did you do this to me?"

After a few minutes of self-pity, she decided the only option available to her was to get started. Looking at the books she let out another groan. She could read but she had never been one to enjoy reading. She found it boring, and hard work. Nor had she, when she'd traveled, had the time. Thurdon was an excellent storyteller and lecturer, and she had never found herself wanting for mental stimulation. He had filled her days and nights with history and had given her a discourse on the natural world around her, a smattering of geography and a few legends from before Ruel moon split.

She thought about what Brill had said about meeting another woman called Salinda whose eyes glowed like hers. He had said that she had the minds—or was it souls?—of the dead within her. Should Laidan herself commence searching for this other woman, Salinda?

The turmoil in her mind didn't lessen, yet she had said she would help research her own problem, so she would. Wearily she stood up and went to a shelf. Perhaps the index would help, but as she didn't know where to begin, picking a volume at random seemed as good an approach as any. The first volume she selected was handwritten in a language she couldn't read. She slipped it back onto the shelf and picked up another called *A Short Discourse on the Fermentation of Wine.*

ᏽᏽᏽᏽ

Garan trailed behind Brill, Danton and the Master Elder as they went over the observatory's defenses. Garan had forgotten about sitting in on Laidan's interview and now that he had missed it, he was relieved. From the few mumbled statements the Master Elder made, it hadn't gone well, and Garan thought it best to leave her alone.

Together they stood in the shade cast by the observation gallery, surveying the wide courtyard, which ranged out to meet the Klester Valley gate.

"Mmm...the fact that the observatory is formed partly from the mountain itself gives you much natural defense, but this is your main weakness," Danton said, pointing at the gate below them. "If you are overrun here, then any other defenses you have will mean nothing. Your only choice then will be to flee into the valleys and caves in the mountain range behind us."

"How will they attack the walls?" Garan asked.

"The Inspector is likely to arm his men with swords, axes, anything he can find. First they'll probably try to climb the walls or break through the lower doors. Then he'll use some kind of heavy weapon, bombs maybe, to blow a hole in the wall. If that succeeds his men will just pour through."

"Bombs?" Garan's heart sank. How could they hold up against that?

"If they have some kind of catapult they could lob boulders instead. The result would be the same: a breach in the walls." Danton looked at them each in turn, his mouth drawn down into a frown.

The Master Elder was nodding. The dilapidated old gate guarding the way to Klester Valley and Vanden stood before them. Piles of rubble were being placed on both sides of it, but those improvements weren't going to be enough, according to the rebel leader. Hope had bloomed in Garan when he'd seen what had been done in his absence, and that hope had suddenly fallen away.

"What do you suggest we do?" the Master Elder asked, looking older now than ever before.

Danton stared at the gate and chewed his bottom lip. "Well...I'd say that they will blow up the gate easily. The rubble reinforcement will slow them, but a few well-made bombs placed strategically will be able to blast a pathway through it. After that there isn't much to stop them, except hand-to-hand combat." The rebel looked up to study the observation gallery. "You have one balcony high up—useful for a lookout, but not for mounting an attack."

Garan couldn't bite back his angry response to Danton's comment. "That's because it is for observing the sky! No one here is trained to fight in hand-to-hand combat. I'm not even sure I know what that is."

Brill was standing further up the incline, staring down into the valley and frowning. "What is it?" Danton asked him.

Their eyes met and Brill nodded once. "I saw something—someone—a scout maybe. Time is running out."

A cold hand of fear wrapped around Garan's heart. "Do you think he saw us? And what about our defenses, will he have seen them too?"

Brill frowned. "I'm sorry, but he probably did. If I were the Inspector I'd want to know what I was heading into so I could prepare the best attack."

The Master Elder's head dropped and he swayed slightly. Garan steadied him with a hand between his shoulder blades. "I was not meant for war or battle. That is not my task," the Master Elder said to no one in particular.

Brill stood up straighter. "We can help with that. I'll not let good people such as you be hurt by men bent on evil. Master Elder, you need to put Danton in charge of the defenses, and we'll do our best to save what we can."

"Kid..." Danton said in a low voice. The older rebel had not been impressed with the observatory's lack of defenses. Garan had watched Danton's frown grow deeper and deeper and hadn't missed the shaking of his head that Brill ignored. Garan surmised that one rebel was a realist and the other an idealist.

Brill turned to his friend. "Don't fret. I have an idea."

Danton stilled. "I'm not fretting," he said, a touch of anger in his tone. "You're talking about a lot of responsibility here. Helping out is one thing, leading is another. And there're no weapons, no means—"

Brill turned his back on his friend and addressed Garan and the Master Elder. "I believe you use explosives occasionally for blasting in your mines, is that so?"

"Well, yes, we do," the Master Elder replied, glancing curiously from one rebel to the other. Garan saw the sparkle kindle in Danton's eye.

༄༄༄༄༄

It was late afternoon by the time Garan went looking for Laidan, leaving the Master Elder with the rebels to make plans and draw supplies from the stores. Brill's idea had sparked a new level of confidence and Garan sensed that morale among the observatory's people had lifted a little. Now he could apply himself to Laidan's welfare. The very thought of battle plans wearied him. Why did this have to happen to them? The observatory worked for the good for all humankind and it wasn't interested in power...unless that power helped their cause.

How had things changed so radically? But he knew the answer. It was the world around them, surging and churning and drawing them along, like the sea during a storm. He frowned at the memory of the ocean. Thurdon had taken him to the coast once, north of Sartell. He'd been so young then, afraid of the waves, but he'd liked the taste of salt. He chewed his bottom lip. He might never see the sea again in this life.

He made his way to the Master Elder's room and quietly opened the door to the little office where Laidan was reading. After poking his head through the door, he stepped into the room with a smile on his face. Laidan was asleep on the desk, her hands hanging limply over the volumes beneath. Garan sighed. Just looking at her was reward enough for his day's work.

Garan stepped quietly up to the desk and brushed a strand of hair away from her face. Her eyelids fluttered and she sat up suddenly, hand over her heart. "Garan! What are you doing here? Is everything all right?"

"I came to see how you were."

Her eyes narrowed, daring him to hide things from her. "And?"

"Everything is all right for the moment. Our two friends are giving advice on the defense of this place. Danton will be in charge of the battle, I believe."

A grin brought dimples to her cheeks. "That's great. I knew they'd help. Brill is so brave and clever."

Garan bit back a nasty comment. He had to work on his jealousy problem. "And how are things with you? Any progress?"

The grin faded into a pout as her lips contracted. She closed the book in front of her with a thud, making no effort to mark her place. A huff of breath blew a stray lock of hair from her face. "I've been trying to find some information about this thing," she slapped the side of her head. "But I'm useless at it—not smart enough. Half these volumes are written in languages I don't understand and the rest are about history or the destruction of the world or the motion of the planets."

"Perhaps you should take a rest. Brill and Danton are coming to watch my shift tonight. Would you like to come too?" Garan's lips lifted in a half-smile. Why did that gaze of hers render him shy and stupid?

With a quick sweep of her straight blonde hair over her left shoulder, she regarded him, expression bland. "Brill and Danton are coming to watch you, are they? Of course I'd like to come. Though I think I'll take your advice and rest beforehand."

After walking past him to the door, she nodded once and was gone. Garan stood there silently, wondering what was going on in her mind. Was she coming because she wanted to see him at work or because Brill was coming too? He growled low in his throat and vowed silently to forget all about her. Of course she was coming because of the young rebel. She'd seen Garan at work before.

Chapter Thirteen

THE POWER WITHIN

The mood was slightly strained on the observation gallery that evening as Brill watched the Skywatchers man their contraptions, their scopes. Two Skywatchers stood on either side of long tubes, each about the thickness of an arm, which were perched on tripods. The preparations for an attack affected everyone. Even the young boys who squatted by baskets of crystals located at the base of the tripods were apprehensive. Garan introduced his co-worker, Turnet, who was a high-spirited young man with eyes that darted everywhere at once. Lithe and with straight dark hair that he frequently brushed from his eyes, Turnet chatted excitedly to them.

"'Tis not often we get visitors. You're in for a treat, I'm sure," Turnet said. "Garan is sure to please." With a bow, he then went to join Garan.

"Garan," Turnet said, leaning close to Garan as he checked the position of the tube and sighted along it. Brill could overhear from where he stood. Turnet was not very quiet. "Did you hear about explosives being placed at the Klester Valley entrance? Or about the old ones being sent to join the children and the tenders, who have been evacuated to the caves?"

Brill didn't hear Garan's mumbled reply.

"Amazing. Who would have thought you coming back from Vanden would cause such a stir." Turnet's grin was wide.

"Concentrate now, Turnet," Garan said as he made adjustments to his scope.

Turnet laughed and bent to his task. Brill couldn't repress a smile. If only he could be that young again himself, he thought. Life had seemed so much simpler then.

The shift had only just begun. He could hear coordinates being shouted by Skywatchers further along the gallery. Garan noticed it too. "Turnet, your head is filled with gossip. Concentrate, will you?" Garan asked a younger lad, Ruzel, to place a basket of crystals beside them. Brill found that he was curious about the preparations going on around him, about the crystals that seemed to be used as tools. He had realized that the Skywatchers' primary concern was to map the sky, and in particular Shatterwing. He found it fascinating.

Elder Newfen, who was in charge of the shift, appeared flustered. One by one the pairs of Skywatchers settled down to work and the gallery became quiet. Brill heard the rustle of clothing, which was Danton's mostly, and the faint whisper of a breeze as it lifted and shook the Skywatchers' cloaks. Dressed in a clean but unflattering robe, Laidan leaned against the wall on the other side of Danton. Her hair hung free, the blonde strands wisping gently around her face.

The line of scopes were trained on the firmament. Four pairs of Skywatchers each patrolled a quadrant of the sky. Brill wandered around the circular gallery, feeling the bustle surrounding him as crystal-filled baskets chinked and crisp maps were unfurled and coordinates called out.

Garan stood before his scope, apparently meditating, separating himself from the noise and activity around him. Brill closed his eyes momentarily and listened. That noise again. Garan hummed briefly then nodded to Turnet.

The Master Elder strode up, acknowledging those around him with a nod of his head. He began to talk quietly to Brill and Danton, explaining in his unobtrusive way what was happening.

"According to the status report," the Master Elder said in a low voice, "nothing unusual was noted on the charts on the previous shift." Brill nodded in understanding. "There has been nothing but the occasional dust flare for the last few days," the Master Elder continued. "Even though the situation appears to be stable, sometimes there are changes during the day so the sky must be checked again at the start of the shift. The Skywatchers cannot be complacent. Only vigilance protects the people of Margra."

A shout down the line quieted the old man. Brill watched and listened as a series of coordinates was called out. Turnet and Garan adjusted their scope to get a fix on the incoming debris. On one side, Elder Newfen muttered calculations under his breath, determining its trajectory. Garan peered into the scope. "Got it."

Brill grew tense as the action unfolded around him. Garan let out an expletive. "Wing dust! This one is huge." After a second look into the scope, Garan said in a tight voice, "Don't worry about the trajectory on that one, Elder. It has to be blown up. 'Tis too big. Luckily not too far out. We can destroy it before it gets too close."

Turnet touched Garan's arm. "Too big for us to destroy?" Brill held his breath as he waited for Garan to consider.

The Master Elder whispered, "A rock that size could well be too big, but the attempt must be made. Splitting it would help."

Garan frowned and checked the scope again. He shouted up the line, "Prepare for a coordinated blast."

Unfortunately there was another call further up and another set of coordinates issued. Brill realized there were two incoming fragments of Ruel and no chance for a coordinated blast.

Danton was restless beside Brill. "How are they going to blast these things?" the older rebel whispered in his ear.

"Don't know. Keep your eyes open, though," Brill whispered back. His gaze was locked keenly on Garan. Something exciting was going on here.

The Master Elder went over to talk to Garan. "There are other ways to deal with this...Can you deflect it?"

"I can try, but I'd rather destroy it. Then there'd be one less rock to fall."

"I know, son, but you can only do what is within your power."

Garan nodded to the Master Elder, his expression solemn.

In Garan's part of the gallery, the pairs of operators dealt with their own meteors. Garan sighted the asteroid again through the scope and confirmed that it was large and at present in a shallow approach.

"It might be a skimmer," Turnet suggested.

"Might and might not." Garan knelt next to the basket of crystals, searching through them. He moved to another basket and savagely thrust his hands in among the stones. Turnet kept calling to him, urging him to hurry. In the third basket, he found what he was looking for. Turnet opened the chute. Garan had chosen a large crystal that appeared to weigh heavily in his hands. Carefully, he eased the crystal into the top of the chute. It wouldn't slide in easily, so he pushed it in with firm pressure. When it was snug, he dropped the chute's cover, which then sat slightly ajar. He nodded to his fellow Skywatcher and took his place on the other side of the scope.

Brill's pulse raced as the tension built. Danton fidgeted beside him. He could no longer share a skeptical look with his rebel friend. He was enthralled by the scene playing out in front of him. Laidan moved closer to him, placing her hand on his forearm. He patted it absently, intent on Garan's work.

Already the Skywatcher hummed. He lowered his tone, reaching bass levels, and put more force into the air passing through his throat. The sound seemed to reach into the structure of the crystal. The other Skywatcher, Turnet, joined in, his hum harmonizing and reinforcing the sound. The glow emanating from the scope brightened. Brill recalled the small explosion in the rebel line when Garan had thrown a handful of burning fragments in the air. Could this be more of the same?

"What's he doing?" he asked Laidan quietly. Then he was drawn by the scent of her and the look of her soft, pale skin and smiled into her face.

With eyes twinkling with excitement and a hint of the glow from her power, she returned his smile. "He reaches into the crystal with sound and that somehow releases the energy within. This meteor's big, though, so even the power from a large crystal may not destroy it."

"Oh?" Brill blinked once. More power? Different from the power Laidan possessed? He looked sideways and saw Danton watching eagerly, speculation glittering in his one dark eye. Who were these people? Before his eyes Brill saw the crystal beginning to react to the vibrations in Garan's and Turnet's voices. It glowed sporadically with a pink and violet warmth.

The Elder took up the tracking with his own scope and began counting them in. Turnet's face was screwed up tight with concentration. The center of the crystal began to glow more intensely and consistently, with darker shades of violet emanating from the center and spreading toward its surface like lightning. Again Garan drew in a deep focusing breath and seemed to force all of his energy into the crystal. Brill could only watch in awe as the thrumming notes from the Skywatchers' throats settled in his bones. The sounds of other scopes discharging around him distracted him from Garan momentarily. He saw thin shafts of intense light bolt up into the heavens. They traveled so quickly he could barely see them once they had left the scopes.

Once again his gaze was drawn to Garan and the crystal visible in the scope's chute. The glow in the crystal was now violet on the exterior and deep red in the center.

"They need more power," Laidan murmured, her eyes now reflecting the glow from the crystal. The chute lid began to jiggle, and a stream of vaporous carmine energy began to ooze from the top of the chute.

With effort, Garan's voice deepened further and he seemed to force even more of himself into the crystal. The air vibrated around them. Brill's hair lifted with static. Laidan's fine hair stuck out from the sides of her head too. The Elder raised his voice, and Brill was dimly aware of him counting four, three, two, one, release. An intense light shot out of the scope, which shuddered once with the force of the explosion of power. Garan was flung back, repulsed by a wave of displaced air caused by the detonation. It swept against Brill too, like a short, sharp wind. Laidan fell against him, her hands clinging to his shoulder. The shot of violet-colored light pierced the sky, aiming for a small glowing meteor just visible to his eye.

When he turned back, he saw that the scope lay shattered into pieces and sprawled among the ruin of it were Garan and Turnet.

Brill raced over to where Garan had crumpled to the ground. As Garan came to, Brill yelled, "That was amazing! I don't believe what I just saw."

He helped Garan to prop himself up on his elbow. The Master Elder nodded and yet there was something sad in his expression. Garan hitched himself higher on his elbow and looked to where the other Skywatcher lay in an unmoving heap. "Turnet?"

The Master Elder was leaning over the other Skywatcher and calling for a physic. Turnet didn't respond to his name or the shaking of his shoulders. Brill could see that his eyes were open and staring. Moving unobtrusively, he blocked Garan's view of his friend. The Master Elder met his gaze and shook his head slightly.

"Turnet!" Garan called weakly, his voice breaking. "What happened? Is he all right?"

Elder Newfen checked his scope hurriedly. "You did it, Garan," the Elder said in revered tones. "'Tis broken up." He pointed to the sky, where shooting stars were diminishing and colored lights marbled the night sky.

Garan was still dazed. Brill thought he registered that the shot had been successful, but understandably he wanted news of his companion. "Turnet?" Garan stared bewilderedly into Brill's face. Brill kept his expression bland. Garan called out then, "Master Elder, tell me of Turnet. Please."

Standing up and letting the physic take over, the Master Elder came to Garan and knelt by his head. He reached out and smoothed Garan's disarrayed curls. "I'm sorry...he could not take the power you released into the crystal."

"The power I released?" Garan asked, the surprise evident in his voice. "But I...we—"

The Master Elder stood after some other men came to carry Turnet away. He looked on sorrowfully as they lifted the dead Skywatcher's body. "Yes, Garan, the power you released," he answered in barely a whisper.

Garan was becoming more aware of the situation, though the full extent of it still escaped him, Brill suspected.

"I don't understand," Garan said with a nervous look at Brill. Danton came over and together they helped Garan to sit up. The young man was unsteady, but unharmed. His curly hair stood at strange angles and his pupils were dilated, his skin white and clammy. Danton supported his back. "Is he..."

"He's in shock," Brill said.

The Master Elder considered them from under his bushy brows. "Apparently. He will be fine after a rest." To Garan, he said, "There is a lot you don't understand. We will talk about this later, when you've recovered. Though I must say you have surprised me. Long have I suspected you had a powerful gift, Garan, one that appeared to elude you. Though, for your sake, I wish you had found it in better circumstances." The Master Elder turned to Brill and Danton again and continued, his voice burdened with troubles, "Please take him to his room so he can sleep. I must see to other things."

Garan tried to fight them off. "No. No. No. Turnet." His voice shook.

Laidan looked on disbelievingly. The Master Elder noticed her standing there, her mouth gaping open, hands worrying her robe. Brill realized he had forgotten about her in the heat of the moment.

"Laidan," the Master Elder said. "Go straight to your room and go to bed. I have enough to worry about at present without concerning myself about you too."

Laidan looked like he had struck her. "But I..." There was a sob readying to burst forth in her voice. To her credit she held on to it, though Brill noted the tears brimming in her eyes.

The Master Elder, seeing that his words had perhaps been too harsh, went over and embraced her across the shoulders. "Come, child, this is a tragic event, and I fear there are more to come. I'll see you to your room and will try to check on you later. There, there, don't cry." And with that the Master Elder escorted Laidan from the gallery.

Without a word, Danton moved to grasp Garan under the arms into a lift, and indicated that Brill should take his feet.

Brill quickly assessed Garan. He was still in shock, but could understand more and more of what had happened. He kept sighing and saying Turnet's name. "Turnet, I didn't mean...I didn't mean...Oh, Turnet, I didn't mean to hurt you..."

"Garan," Brill said sharply. "Help us get you to your room. Can you stand?"

Garan stopped mumbling. "Yes. I can stand." With Danton's and Brill's assistance, Garan sagged between them and took wobbly, misdirected steps. They began the long climb down several flights of stairs. Brill hoped that Garan recovered and that he could come back from the grief he was bound to suffer when the full extent of his loss came crashing down on him. There was simply too much at stake to lose him now. Brill's eyes met Danton's while thoughts of Garan's potential sped across his mind. Danton nodded as if he, too, understood the significance and usefulness of Garan's gift.

♋♋♋♋♋

Sleep eluded Garan. Caught on the cusp of despair and joy, he replayed over and over again the moment when the power had released from the crystal. The afterglow was a potent, burning flame that left his skin and mind tingling. He lay mutely on the bed as time seemed to stagnate around him, feeling every second limp past. The night was reluctantly relinquishing its tenacious grip on the darkness when Garan heard a soft knock at his door. It creaked slowly open like a yawn, and Laidan slipped into his room, a candle in her hand.

Dreamlike, he watched her as she moved toward the bed and placed the candle on the side table. In the buttered candlelight her skin appeared warm and smooth and in his detached state he was mesmerized by her.

"How are you feeling, Garan?" she asked, sitting on the bed and stroking his open palm.

As he stared at her, idle thoughts impacted like darts, punctuating his sense of unreality. Did he have any clothes on? He flinched, glancing down, and saw thankfully that he was wearing his underclothes. His mind was occluded by black spots of amnesia. He recollected Brill and Danton stripping him down; he remembered the smooth taste of dragon wine on his tongue as he collapsed on the bed. After that was the slow turning of time, and of his reveling in a heady mix of enlivened skin and exhilarated mind, wine-induced, he realized.

"Garan?"

"Mmm?" Garan replied vaguely, not quite able to form words. Laidan's radiant face hovered in front on him.

Her soft fingers traced the outline of his bare shoulders and then lingered on his hand again, open and relaxed on top of the blanket. Her index finger touched his open palm. "I asked how you were." She reached out and pushed a curl off his forehead. Her touch was as intoxicating as undiluted dragon wine. His skin burned where her fingers touched him, coaxing him deeper into the moment and the spell of her presence.

"Laidan?" he whispered to her as she flopped against his bare chest and nestled herself there. The warmth of her pressed against him and nearly overwhelmed him. It felt so right for her to be there. Then she gently levered herself up so that she could touch his cheek and run her fingers across his mouth.

"Don't," he heard himself whisper, afraid of the tendrils of desire her touch excited. Another moment and the longing would drive him to the very edge.

"Why?" she said as she ran her forefinger along the contours of his lower lip. With a smile on her face, she watched how he sucked in a breath. Garan couldn't resist the temptation anymore. It was as if he were drunk and a world of storms swirled around in his head. He kissed her fingers the next time she ran them across his lips, then sat forward to kiss her mouth.

With his head swimming, he felt her body against his bare chest, felt her slight resistance as his mouth closed over hers. His hands moved to her head, holding her so he could plunder her soft mouth, revel in her moan. Next his tongue deepened the kiss. His body was alive to the feel of her, the scent of her, and energized by her struggle against him. He broke for breath and dragged her on top of him, caressed her back and waist with eager hands.

"Stop, Garan. Stop!" He heard the panic in her voice over the pounding of blood through his veins. He didn't want to stop. He let her sit up, only to lunge forward and capture her mouth again while his hands found her small tender breasts. The feel of her went to his head. He wanted to pull and rip and tear at the clothes separating skin from skin, wanted her flesh next to his, wanted her to feel the power so alive within him.

Again his tongue ravaged her mouth, eliciting a moan from her.

"Garan!" the Master Elder said peremptorily as he stood by the open door. "Garan, release her now."

As if he'd had cold water thrown over him, Garan's senses came flooding back. Disentangling his fingers from her hair and pushing her gently away, he fell onto the pillows. Laidan sat there with eyes like bruises in her pale face. Her quivering mouth was slightly swollen from his kisses and her gown was askew.

"Forgive me..." he whispered.

Laidan backed away from him. Fear and anger warred on her face. One look at the Master Elder and her face flamed.

"He...he..." She pointed at him, her startled gaze on the Master Elder.

"Go to your room, Laidan. We'll talk about this later."

Choking on a sob she fled the room. Garan met the Master Elder's gaze with the composure of a day-after drunk, and he discerned the accompanying aftertaste of excess.

The old man shook his head. "This isn't good, Garan."

Garan put his hand to his forehead. "I didn't mean it. I feel strange. I—she—"

The Master Elder sat down on the bed. He patted Garan's hand. "You meant it, Garan. You did. You feel desire for her now. It is in the air like the scent of a storm. You hide it from her most of the time. But not from me, and not from Thurdon. Not from any man who has loved and desired."

Garan frowned, knowing the old man spoke true, and flushing with the knowledge that it was obvious to others when he was still coming to turns with it himself. "I can't help it. I hated her for so long it took me by surprise when I found I loved her. Is there no hope for me with her?"

With a sad smile the Master Elder shrugged. "Who can say? Both of you are marked by destiny and power. These can warp a life."

"I could not hurt her. I care for her."

"That may be so when you have your wits about you, which I can see you barely have now. If I hadn't intervened just now what do you think would have happened? Do you even know?"

The blood rushed to his face. Garan knew, even though he had never experienced the act himself. It was as if he'd known instinctively how to touch her, what his reactions would be, what he wanted to do to her. He hadn't wanted to stop, couldn't have stopped if they had continued on alone. All his barriers had been down and his morals in hiding. If she had wanted to she could have had him any way she wanted him, could have drawn from him any vow and he'd have given it to her willingly. He sighed loudly and nodded, letting the old man know he understood.

"Good. And will you promise to leave her be while we work through this situation? Her mind is confused with what has happened to her. She is becoming a woman and being at the hands of Lenk and the bandit, Nulf, has caused some distress and upheaval in her. You know what I mean, Garan? She has experienced things she ought not have and was not prepared for. When this is over you'll have time to work things out between you."

Garan nodded again, feeling as if his heart was bleeding. He knew he was as good as agreeing to let Brill have her if he wanted her, and she him. He clenched his fist. "I will. My work comes first."

The Master Elder sat in silence, regarding him under his bushy white brows. Garan grew more and more aware. The Garan-centric scene that had replayed continuously through the night in his mind expanded. Fractured sounds of exploding equipment, yells filled with emotions: fear, horror and dread. The black spots that blemished his mind contracted, leaving painful holes. "How is Turnet?" His hand trembled but his gaze never wavered from the Master Elder.

The old man's face became haggard and his eyes watered. "You don't remember? Oh, Garan...I'm sorry, but he...he..."

"Dead?"

The Master Elder squeezed Garan's hand, held it in a firm grip, held him anchored to the moment.

"I killed someone," Garan whispered. "I killed Turnet. I killed another human being...my friend."

The Elder sniffed and his lower lip trembled as he nodded.

Garan's body began to jerk. The Master Elder held Garan's hand as a sob burst out of him, as he wailed his despair.

"Oh, Turnet!" he cried, trying to wrench free of the old man's grip, willing himself to sink into oblivion where he could hide from the pain. After a while Garan ceased struggling against the Master Elder as hot tears streaked his cheeks before dampening the pillow.

"Garan," the Master Elder said. "It wasn't your fault. No one could have predicted that surge in your power, no one could have prevented its unleashing. 'Tis right that you should grieve, my boy. But don't stay too long in the shadow. We need you."

As Garan stared at the wall, fighting the impulse to think about his friend yet dwelling nonetheless on all the acute misery of his situation, he didn't hear the old man leave. As the sun rose and sent wan light into the room, Garan was left alone with his despair

Chapter Fourteen

LOVE AND BETRAYAL

The yawing emptiness of the city threatened to overwhelm Salinda as she stepped through the Hall of Elders and continued along the main thoroughfare back to her little house in the Barr family node. The undulating layers of dust parted as she strode along, and the obsidian mouths of the dark windows and doors of the empty houses gaped at her. It was the first time she'd walked alone in the city, and she gained an insight into the horror Nils must have felt upon awakening and how his hope and his capacity for joy had been eroded by what he'd found.

As she entered her abode she remembered that there was no food there. Deciding to turn around and go back to the city, she cast her gaze around the room. On the low table were the cold Pardu pot and two flat drinking bowls with dregs in the bottom of them. Her study notes for the Hiem's coded language sat askew on the floor. Tugging her dark hair over her shoulder, she plaited it idly while she thought of how quiet the place was without Nils.

Once in the gardens, she gathered some of the lairn apples, cut greens and dug up some white tubers, which tasted delicious when slow-baked. She considered entering the food store but didn't feel confident negotiating the contents without Nils's guidance. As she walked back up to the house, she thought of the meal she would prepare and how wonderful a cup of dragon wine would taste with it. She ate slowly with her gaze dancing lazily over her notes on the code. She was in no mood for study, though, and instead turned her thoughts to the people who had invaded the Ways, remembering that tingle of power she had perceived.

When she slept, her dreams were of walking the Ways, puzzling out the maze of pathways so that she could trace the intruders' steps. When she woke she was confident that she could and should pursue them. Cold water from the basin didn't wash away the errant thoughts. She would go—had to go. The cadre was curious. It itched in her mind, and she realized that it was probably the cadre that had put the dreams in her head in the first place.

She began to prepare a note for Nils but then ceased when she failed to find words that would adequately explain her departure or justify breaking her vow. After agonizing over it, she left the house without writing one, shutting the door behind her. She had no idea how long Nils's healing would take. With luck, she would be back before he woke, and if not, her face-to-face explanation would work better than any half-scribbled excuse. Nevertheless, as she left the house she felt as if she was betraying him, her oath and her heart.

As she climbed the stairs to enter the Ways, leaving the confines of the city behind, she found her need for sun and air and breeze growing stronger. And she could not deny that her increasing anticipation included the yearning for a taste of dragon wine.

Traveling alone along the Way made her feel nervous, at first, because she did not have Nils to guide her. It was eerily dark and still. One false choice could see her lost for who knew how long. Yet she found she remembered the paths they had taken previously and the cadre was imbued with confidence. She could see quite well, but even then there were dark places. The strange fabric of the walls glowed a marbly gray. When she reached out to touch it, she found nothing. It was as if the path she stood on was suspended in air, though she knew that to be impossible.

ᏚᏚᏚᏚ

At the Way Gate she found she hovered uncertainly, wondering whether it was the right one. The memory of Nils opening the gate was clear in her mind, but not of how he then had brought her inside to the city. Nils had used gestures and incantations, neither of which she remembered, but where he had pressed along the edge of the door still remained. Cautiously, she slid her hand around the border in the same pattern, triggering the switches. Obviously Nils had used a ritual that was not needed to trigger the lock. She stepped back as the door opened and cold, dank air billowed over her. All seemed quiet and undisturbed so she ventured out, letting the door close behind her. Even in the darkness beyond, she could tell she was in a cave.

With steady breaths she eased along the wall, using her feet to test the ledge beneath her. Ahead and to the right she saw a small patch of dull light, and began edging toward it. The positioning of the Way Gate weighed on her mind. There was probably layer upon layer of rock above it. The upheaval caused by Ruel's fall had been experienced even here.

If there had been an observatory then it might not exist anymore, or not as it had before. Yet the Way Gate had somehow withstood whatever force had been hurled at it at that time. Now with the passing of over a thousand years and the loss of the people who maintained it, the Ways had proved vulnerable to attack. Someone had destroyed a Way Gate. The thought saddened her. Such a great legacy, and it could fall so easily into ruin.

She crawled through the window of ever-brightening light into another cave and continued to follow the curve of the rock wall. There were stalactites and stalagmites in the cave and the faint drip-drip of water on rock. The musty smell eased the closer she came to the entrance and fresh air. When she passed through the cave mouth and saw the open sky above her, joy filled her heart. At first she didn't know whether it was near dawn or dusk. The landscape around her was swathed in orange light.

Waiting a moment to catch her breath, she sat on a rock and rested, unwilling to venture up the mountain if nightfall was imminent. In a few heartbeats the light began to alter its texture, and she saw that what she'd thought was dawn was more like mid-morning as the sunlight slipped above a distant peak and dipped into the tight, narrow cleft she sat in. The faint kiss of moisture was in the breeze. A shiver excited goose flesh on her arms. It was cooler here than at the vineyard and there was no scent of sulphur and no dragon sign. She watched the sun chase the orange light away and deepen the sky to violet. A few red-tinged clouds sped across the sky in small clumps. As the sun warmed the air, Salinda discerned a pathway further up the mountain. There was some climbing to do to reach it, but the cadre pulsed at the sight of it. Smiling to herself, she stood and brushed dirt from her Hiem robes. It was time to seek out those who had traversed the Ways of the Hiem.

⚓⚓⚓⚓

At first Salinda was wary of being seen. In reality she had no idea who had trespassed in the Ways and didn't know who lived on this mountain, only that someone did. There had been signs of habitation around, the sound of distant voices. About halfway up the path she caught a glimpse of a building seemingly carved from the pinnacle of the mountain itself. The cadre's warm reaction to the sight of it confirmed that it must be the observatory.

At a junction of two paths, she heard someone coming and pulled back into the shelter of rocks and a spindly bush whose roots seemed to cling to the air. Two men in plain shirts and trews approached, carrying sacks down the pathway and chatting to each other at the same time. Their voices were a low rumble, unintelligible because the sound was amplified and distorted by the rock. They took the other path, so Salinda edged out and ventured further up the one she was on in order to look back down the other one. The men descended a track that snaked into a valley below.

The path ahead zigzagged steeply. As she climbed further, she found amazement at every turn as more and more of the observatory building was revealed. The land tapered away from the wide base of the structure, narrowing at the peak. It sat like a head on the shoulders of the mountain so that it had a three hundred and sixty degree view of the land. Never had she seen such a sight. The wonder of its construction astounded her. The sun blinded her as she stared into the sky. A sense of awe was growing inside her, one that the cadre clearly shared. Did it know this place? Had one or more of its former carriers seen such a building as this in their lifetimes?

The pathway became more civilized and better constructed—less like a track and more like a pavement cut from stone. Not far along it terminated in an arched doorway. Salinda hitched up her robe in her hand and strode forward. The door was unlocked, perhaps because people such as the men she had seen had been using it to ferry supplies somewhere. Once inside, she negotiated corridors and stairs heading upward. It was eerily quiet. Opening another door, she found herself in a courtyard with walls blocking the view to the mountain range beyond.

Through an archway she found another courtyard that joined others by means of a series of archways. They seemed to ring the building. She paused and listened. Two voices, a girl's and a man's,

132

coming from a courtyard further down, lured her on. Her slippered feet whispered over the paved courtyard as she zeroed in on them.

Through the next archway she came upon them. On a bench sat a pretty girl with white-blonde hair flowing straight down her back. Her sweet face and bright blue eyes were fixed upon the young man who squatted by her knee, holding her hand and staring up at her, obvious admiration in his gaze. Salinda started. "Brill?"

Brill's head jerked around and his mouth dropped open and clicked shut. "Salinda?"

Before she could blink, he was out of the crouch, taking long strides to reach her and surrounding her with his arms. Fiercely, she hugged him, surprised at the joy she experienced on seeing him. Then he pulled back and gazed at her while holding her at arm's length.

"You look different. Better...We thought—" His brow creased. "How? Never mind that—we were so worried about you."

"We?"

"Yes, I'm with Danton—he's around here somewhere laying explosives—but do I have a story to tell you." Brill gave her a recap of their adventures while the girl hovered nearby. Salinda tried to take in what he was saying, but the thought of seeing Danton again left her unexpectedly reeling. What if it had been Danton who had rescued her? How different would her life now be? Then she shook her head, shook away the thought. She would be dead without Nils and she could not regret life, the chance for the cadre to survive.

"What a coincidence that you are here. I've been telling Laidan about you. I thought you could help her."

Salinda shifted her gaze to the young woman. Beneath that frail exterior, Salinda could feel the pull. One glance in Laidan's blue eyes was enough to give her the answers she sought. It was this girl she had detected passing through the Ways.

"Hello, Laidan." Then looking askance at Brill Salinda said, "It was you who traversed the Way?"

"Yes, but it was Laidan here who showed us how to open the portal."

"You carry a cadre," Salinda said simply, turning back to the girl.

The young girl nodded with tears welling up in her eyes.

Instantly, pity welled up within Salinda. She edged closer and soothed Laidan with firm strokes down her back. "What's this? Why do you fret? It is the greatest gift."

Dramatically, the girl threw herself onto the bench and began to cry in earnest, huge sobs racking her body. Raising an eyebrow at Brill, Salinda frowned when he motioned for her to step away. When she neared Brill, he told her what he knew of Laidan's story and how the poor girl was being driven mad and could barely put her own thoughts together let alone tap into the power of the cadre.

Salinda pursed her lips, keeping an eye on the girl as the tale unfolded. Laidan was growing calmer, although her face bore the evidence of her distress. Taking one more look at Brill, Salinda perceived that a few romantic complications were exacerbating the girl's unhappiness. "I will help as best I can, of course."

Salinda edged closer to the girl. Brill stopped her by grasping her hand. "Wait. There's more."

"More?"

"The Inspector's here."

"Here?" It was as if her heart stopped pumping. All of her strength was needed to appear calm—to push away the horror, the memory that was etched like a lacework of scars across her mind. "In the observatory?"

Brill looked at his feet. "Well, not here exactly—yet. He's on his way to attack the place, in pursuit of Laidan. That's the reason Danton is laying explosives. We're preparing the defense of this place."

Salinda's knees weakened and she hastily lowered herself onto the bench beside Laidan, quite aware that a sweat had broken out on her brow and neck. The taste of the tainted dragon essence oozed onto her tongue—a fateful reminder of how low she had sunk.

"Salinda? Are you well?"

Salinda shook her head. "Thank you for your concern, young friend. If you would be so kind as to fetch me some dragon wine, I'm sure I will be restored. This is most heavy news."

"Of course, I'll fetch some right away." His gaze flicked to Laidan.

"I will keep Laidan company while you are gone, Brill. She will be safe with me."

Laidan looked doubtful and confused at first.

Salinda held out her hand to her. "Don't be afraid. I can help you, I'm sure."

Unbidden, Laidan's eyes glowed fractionally, and Salinda's cadre throbbed in sympathy.

"This is a surprise," Salinda said, patting the girl's hand. "You see, I thought I carried the only cadre. When you passed through the Ways I detected you…"

"Yes, I sensed something too. Do you live in the Ways?"

Salinda pushed away thoughts of the Inspector and laughed softly at her words.

"No, not in the Ways, but in a very special place. I hope one day that you will see it."

Just then Brill returned with a tray with two cups on it. One he handed to Salinda and the other he passed to Laidan. Salinda brought the cup to her nose and inhaled the aroma. A tremor of delight ran through her. She let a small amount of wine spill onto her tongue. It was watered, but still potent. Lowering the cup she caught the young couple staring at her and she swallowed then laughed at their expressions.

"It has been a while since I have tasted dragon wine. I wanted to savor the moment, forgive me." And with that she drank the rest of the wine, letting the power of it invigorate her mind and body.

"Brill," Salinda began. "I think you should take me to see the person who is in charge here. I must seek a place of solitude for myself and Laidan if I am to work with her."

The young girl lifted her eyes to Salinda's face. "The Master Elder's room." To Brill, Laidan said, "I'll take her there and you can go and find him. He has already given me the use of his private office to research this—this cadre."

Laidan took the lead and directed them to a hallway and then down one flight of stairs. They continued along the corridor, only to be brought up short by an old man with a shock of white hair. Salinda gasped at first, thinking it was Mez. Same shock of white hair and bushy brows, same hunched shoulders and underlying strength. Laidan introduced him.

"This is the Master Elder."

The old man inclined his head in acknowledgment, and excitement brimmed in his eyes as Laidan introduced Salinda in turn. Salinda found it hard not to smile at such a familiar countenance.

"Brill sent word that you had arrived so I hastened to speak with you," he said. The Master Elder held up his hand as Salinda prepared to interrupt him. "I do not intend to speak at length as there is much to do. I wanted only to extend a welcome to you. We are most honored."

With a slight bow, she said, "Thank you, I am happy to be here."

The old man walked along with them. "Your presence has caused quite a stir. I've been receiving what I thought were idle reports of your arrival since you walked through the gate. I'm afraid I was rather distracted at the time. However, later I would like to spend some time with you. I have it on good authority that you are the only person who can help Laidan."

Salinda nodded, feeling lost for words as they passed people traversing the corridors as they hurried on errands or carried bundles. They walked past doorways where she saw groups of people talking together. She had not expected this awed respect, had not even expected that so many people lived in the observatory. When they reached his study, the Master Elder held the door open for them and invited them to sit down.

"You must forgive me for detaining you, but could you...let me rephrase...are you able to tell me in what way you can help Laidan? Brill was rather vague about the details and mentioned only that you are familiar with this 'cadre'."

Salinda relaxed, feeling nothing but calm respect both for and from the Master Elder. "There is so much to tell and to explain. However, I think a demonstration will be far more effective than lengthy discourse. You have an enemy to fight, and I must help Laidan accept her cadre. I hope there will be time later for a leisurely discussion."

"Of course, if you would be so kind."

Salinda smiled and let herself enter the cadre to draw on some power, enough for it to show in her eyes. It moved within her and the comforting susurration of the cadre's power bathed her mind. She opened her eyes and heard both of them gasp.

The Master Elder sat back in his chair, unable to hide the awe in his expression.

"'Tis true. You have a gift as Thurdon did. I do not understand why all this comes to pass now, as havoc is about to arrive on our doorstep."

Salinda let the power ebb away. "I didn't know Thurdon or even that one such as he existed. However, I was trained to receive my cadre, and I think I can help Laidan adjust to hers, given time. Brill tells me the Inspector is expected to attack. I do not wish to keep you any longer than is necessary."

Laidan, who had been twisting the folds of her robe in her lap, spoke at last. "Yes, please, let's do something other than talk about it. I want my head back the way it was."

Salinda turned and smiled, glad the girl was no longer crying. "Come, Laidan. Show me this place where we can be undisturbed."

A shout in the hallway lifted the Master Elder's eyebrow. He stood. "Time waits for no one. Danton and Brill have been most useful in aiding our defense, but I fear that it will not be enough. And Margra depends on our work. If we fail then this world fails."

He left Salinda agog with curiosity. The essence of truth lingered in the office, leaving her with a desperate urge to consult with Nils, who understood the workings of the heavens better than anyone she knew. Perhaps he could explain what these people did and why the Master Elder seemed concerned not only about an imminent attack but about a greater and more ominous threat.

After Laidan had settled in her seat in the small office off the Master Elder's study, Salinda asked her to talk about her life with Thurdon and the circumstances of the transfer of the cadre. As Laidan went through her life with the old man and revealed her apparent lack of training, Salinda bit her lip in worry. The girl hadn't even known what the old man had given her. Thurdon had hidden the cadre well. When Laidan related the manner of the transfer Salinda sank to the floor in a squat. The pain and the burning light and Thurdon's disturbed consciousness must have been a torment of the acutest kind for both of them. At first she quailed. Could she help after such a disastrous transfer? The cadre and host were both very vulnerable during that procedure. Even after all her training, the cadre had been difficult to mesh in her own mind and even more difficult to access and use. She shuddered as she recalled how her fear had disconnected her from the cadre when she'd been at the Inspector's mercy. Calmly, she quietened her thoughts, realizing that she had to let instinct guide her.

"Bring yourself back to that moment when Thurdon grabbed you and you experienced pain."

Laidan swallowed and paled. "I will try, but it hurts."

"I imagine it does, and will continue to do so. I'll be honest with you. More pain may be involved for you and the cadre before this is done. It was not meant to be thrust into unprepared minds. It can be damaged too. It is as fragile as your own mind and needs to integrate into its new host if it is to survive intact. Even then the cadre can take time to master. I know this from experience. My own self-doubt made me lose my hold on the cadre, so that it fled from me as if I was unworthy."

Laidan nodded her head. "I see. That may be why it is all quiet in there now; it has fled from me. But I still can't think. It is like there is something in the way. I hate it. I wish Thurdon hadn't —"

"Hush, now. All will be well. You will value this gift in time. Now, first we must go back and relive the transfer. I'm sorry, for there will be sorrow and fear and pain in this. But I will talk you through it. It's the best way to tackle it, I think. The cadre helps me. It guides me now with knowledge. It knows best how to care for itself."

"Itself? You sound like you're talking about a single thing, like your cadre is my cadre."

Salinda paused to contemplate the information that the cadre was providing. "Yes. How strange that it thinks of itself as one, when you have one in you and I another. But surely they are different, formed from different experiences." She closed her eyes, trying to glean more information from the cadre. It was the same kind of phenomenon. That was certain. Laidan held a cadre much like her own. It was natural to suppose that her cadre should be able to help in caring for Laidan's. Yet, despite some confirmation of her proposed course of action regarding Laidan's cadre, she could get no more sense of her cadre being part of the other. "I will ponder this further. Now, start by telling me how you came to carry the cadre."

Moment by moment, Laidan described the transfer of the cadre to her, focusing in particular on Thurdon's distress, his worry for her and his hatred of Lenk.

"Can you let Thurdon come to the surface of your mind? Can you call him forward?"

Laidan was frightened and had to be coaxed. After Salinda gripped Laidan's hands, the girl finally marshaled enough courage to cooperate. Thurdon came forward to speak with Salinda, and she was able to assure him that Laidan was well and that she herself was there to help. His essence was very strong and even though he spoke with Laidan's voice, she sensed the wisdom in him and power of his personality. "I searched long for you. My whole life," he said. "I had given up hope and thought it would be the next generation that found the other cadre."

Salinda spoke soothingly, "I'm sorry for your loss and your pain—your tireless and fruitless search. You must cease your struggle. Your time has ended and you must join the cadre so that it can settle into Laidan's mind."

"But I must speak to you to tell you what you need to know. The joining..."

"No, you must listen to me," Salinda said firmly. "When you are fully subsumed into the cadre your knowledge will become Laidan's. You must not fight it anymore—for your struggle harms the cadre as well as Laidan."

"You speak true. I am ashamed for putting this on her without preparation. I thought I had more time...It was cut short by that monster Lenk. I meant to pass it to another." Laidan began to writhe as Thurdon's presence became agitated.

"Another?"

"Yes, my first choice—the Skywatcher, Garan."

Who was this Garan? Time was running short. Thurdon had to agree; he had to dissipate into the cadre. "Forget Lenk now, forget all those deeds you left undone, for we face a greater danger, and Laidan cannot use the cadre to help us. So please repeat this after me."

Salinda said the calming verse of transfer she had learned from Mez while Laidan, slack-faced, let Thurdon speak through her. It was dangerous. She hoped the girl was resilient enough. Thurdon's distinct personality became subdued. Putting her hands on Laidan's head, she could monitor how the cadre was beginning to fray. Abruptly, Thurdon's presence surged toward her, then, as if hooking her, pulled her in before she was thrust violently back as the cadres touched and Thurdon's presence was subsumed.

Salinda picked herself off the floor. "Dragon shit! What was that?"

Thurdon had slipped something into her—a kernel of something. Her brows drew together. She soothed the creases from her forehead with her hand as she paced in the small room. What had that old man done to her?

Laidan's expression began to reform into her own. "Salinda?"

"You're all right now. Thurdon shouldn't trouble you again...I hope."

Salinda's right hand tingled. She held it up. The kernel of knowledge Thurdon had given her began to blossom. A sphere of golden power glowed in her hand, more like a subdued flame. As she gazed at it she saw it had blue lights at its center.

Laidan gasped, her eyes widening with fascination and a touch of horror. "What is that?"

Salinda smiled. "Thurdon, you were a clever man. Let's see what this thing can do." She flicked her hand as if she was flinging off mud and the sphere flew to the wall. It exploded with a loud retort, knocked a picture down and rocked books from the shelves. A blot of soot marred the stone in the wall where the sphere had impacted.

Laidan leaped from her seat with a yell. "Whore tits! Be careful with that. You could blow us up."

Salinda smiled reassuringly. "I apologize. I did not mean to startle you. Thurdon shared a gift with me when he left."

"A gift? He's good at that," Laidan said dryly, though the expression of worry did not leave her face.

Salinda lifted her hand, letting the flame materialize again, turning it as she examined its color and texture. "Now that's useful," Salinda commented to Laidan, who backed away from her, wide-eyed and staring. Taking pity on the girl, Salinda extinguished the flame, then moved to pour some water into a cup. She drank deeply and then offered it to the girl. With shaking hands Laidan drank, but her gaze was wary as she kept Salinda in her line of sight.

"All is well, Laidan. Be calm now."

When Laidan had settled somewhat and taken her seat, Salinda got to work on the next part of the process—settling the cadre within Laidan's mind. The lessons she had taken with Mez had lasted nearly a year. She thought of how to truncate them and use her own experience to teach the girl. Perhaps then Laidan could live normally, but more training would be needed for her to tap into the cadre herself and more still if she was to wield it effectively. As time was of the essence Salinda thought functionality was the first priority. Thurdon had shown her that the cadres could work together, but that could have been because Laidan had no conscious control over it and Thurdon's presence had been so strong and willing. How she would have liked to have known him in life.

Laidan responded well to the series of exercises that Salinda patiently explained to her. She repeated them and after a few hours Salinda detected some improvement in the girl's control. When they stopped to take a short break, there was a soft knock on the door. "Continue with your exercises. I will see who it is."

Salinda opened the door and stepped into the other room. It was Brill, brow creased with worry. "I heard reports of an explosion. I was busy so it took me a while to find out. Is everything all right?"

"Yes...er, a small experiment—" Salinda was glad the damage had been minimal and was still reeling from the sheer possibilities of the uses of such a gift, especially in a fight.

Brill's eyes lit up, and smiling shyly he said, "How is she?"

"Progressing." His hands were clenched so she reached out and patted them. "I will know more in the morning."

Brill's smile disappeared. "The attack may begin tomorrow or the next day."

"The Inspector? So soon. I thought to have more time."

"I'm sorry. He is coming with all his forces from Vanden. If you cannot help her in time, take her into the caves below and keep her safe. Many of the observatory's inhabitants have taken refuge there. You will be well cared for."

"I will, Brill. Now I have to go back—there's no time to waste."

When Brill had gone, a yawn overtook her and she leaned against the door. Despite the dragon wine, she was tired. At least she knew Nils was recovering in the healing tray. She hoped that when he woke and found himself alone he would forgive her, as this visit was going to take longer than she'd originally planned. She'd thought she would merely assuage her curiosity but instead she had become embroiled in the situation.

They worked through the night. Salinda sensed the discharge of some powerful energy close by as they worked, but could spare no time to dwell on it. By the time early morning light filtered through the window, the last hint of glow had faded from Laidan's eyes, and Salinda let her rest. Salinda was confident that together they had put an end to the discomfort the cadre caused the girl. Laidan's hair splayed out on the desk in a fan and her lips mumbled a mangled version of the verse she had learned that night. Worry niggled at Salinda. Laidan hadn't been meant to receive the cadre, and maybe, just maybe, she would never be able to wield it. Only after more training would Salinda be able to tell.

In the next room she heard voices, and leaving Laidan to sleep she quietly opened the door. The Master Elder was at his desk, packing some things away. He looked up when she entered, but did not smile. "Have you made your preparations?" she asked.

Placing a book into a box, he replied, "We will never be ready for an assault like this. I feel as if doom is pressing down on me. Things are happening in Shatterwing. When we can, we strike down meteors that could devastate a city or whose impact would cloud the air with more dust. But the situation will only worsen. I worry how—if—we will cope if we lose this place and must flee. Only here can we do what we need to do."

Salinda sat down, feeling suddenly weak. "You shoot down meteors?" Given events, she'd hardly had time to turn her mind to what went on at the observatory, beyond the vague idea that they studied the heavens.

"Yes, that is our work—to protect Margra and preserve what we can. We do not always win through. Now a worse doom stalks us from the firmament, possibly even Margra's final doom. As yet we do not know how we can tackle it, but if we are forced to leave this place we will have little hope of doing so."

"So the power I sensed discharging around me during the night came from your observatory?"

"Yes, our Skywatchers work during the night hours."

Salinda mulled over all that she had heard. Margra was in danger and these people must be able to continue their work undisturbed. It seemed everything depended on it. "I have made my decision, Master Elder. I had thought that I should leave and take the girl with me out of danger, but now I think we must stay and help in whatever way we can."

At these words from her his brow cleared. "Really? I...We would be most grateful for any assistance. And Laidan, how is she?"

With a glance at the door to the small room where Laidan rested, she answered, "More at peace than she was. She will not be able to wield the power of the cadre immediately, but she may nonetheless be of help." She stood and clasped the Master Elder's shoulder. "I will take her to her room to sleep. Please fetch me when you need me."

A smile lit his face. "I will, and thank you. I'll send breakfast in for you both. And you should try to rest too...we may need your strength. I'll send someone to show you to your room."

At the door to the little office, she turned to him. "We will be ready."

Chapter Fifteen

IN THE SHADOWS BETWEEN THE WALLS

With a satirical eye, Gercomo considered the improvements he had made to the town of Vanden. Now that Lenk was imprisoned inside his own emasculated body, he served as a useful lesson to this household of incompetents. Vanden was his town now, and he strutted down its streets as he had the vine rows of the prison vineyard. He sucked in a lungful of air. There was truly nothing left of Lenk in this town now that he had staffed it with his men and instilled his own brand of obedience. A faint remnant of death taint hung in the air and made him frown—he presumed there was a dead body somewhere that had been overlooked.

One of his men walked past. "You there," he yelled. "Find the source of that stench and get rid of it. I'll not have this place an abode of filth and disease." The guard saluted and ran off at a trot. Gercomo watched him until he turned a corner before swiveling on his heel and returning to his mansion house.

Later, as he sat in the upstairs sitting room watching the sunset, he considered the mountain range which ringed Klester Valley. Outside, he saw the color of the sky shift quickly from pale yellow to blood-orange and then to dark purple across the peaks as the sun's rays died. The countryside around Vanden was not as stark as the vineyard and the plains had been. It was more fertile and the vegetation more varied. The town would be a good base while he put the finishing touches on his next moves. It would be amusing to evict the Skywatchers from their bastion in the mountains. Why should they be untouched by the world around them and hold on to something he wanted?

He sipped his elixir, the pure dragon essence, appreciatively, and it slid like cold liquid fire down his throat. He had drunk an inordinate amount of it lately and it had served him well. Illness didn't touch him, small injuries healed rapidly and he needed little sleep. He wondered if he would have been able to achieve all he had without the support of the essence. It gave him an edge—honed his senses. Vigilance, his watchful eye, put fear into the hearts of those around him. They could not conspire; they could not rebel; they could do nothing but obey.

Once again he glowered when he thought of the power that had escaped him—the puny girl who had tricked them all. The very thought of her both filled him with rage and was tantalizing. Power, any power that was beyond what a mere man could do himself, or through others, was unknown to him. He considered the essence on the table next to him, poured out another dram and gazed at its faint glow. Wasn't this essence a power of sorts? Maybe the power he sought wasn't so alien but had been with him all the time.

Yet the glow that he'd seen in the young girl's eyes was evidence of something else, something unknown and unconquered. For all the advantage the possession of the dragon wine had given him, it was not enough to curb his desire to possess that glowing power, to destroy the innocence of its young possessor, to explore the power measure for measure until he owned it. He would rip it out of her, he would find a way, he would.

Then there was that place, that fortress they called an observatory, perched in the mountains and potentially sheltering a force ready to swoop down at a moment's notice and destroy all he had built. He'd seen their display of power in the night—seen the violet-colored flashes that stained the heavens for almost an hour afterward. They had weapons, pre-Shatterwing technologies, hoarded away. Lenk's assurances that they never shifted from their nest, never so much as squawked, didn't appease his desire to root them out, to pluck from their hands the weapons they could so easily turn against him.

Lenk was a fool. Vanden may have existed in harmony with the observatory for countless years but that was going to change. The occupants, these Skywatchers, may not have had the ability or the will to use their technology for offensive purposes, but he did. Their inertia gave him an edge, their delay an opportunity. They would not, and perhaps could not, fight. That much was obvious, or they would have destroyed Vanden with one of those spears of light before now.

Lenk had been sitting on treasure and a mountain of power. If only he had had the sense to exploit it. Gercomo laughed at the thought. What a mental pipsqueak that man was. Then he thought of what the slaves had done to him, how they had peeled and sliced with their kitchen knives, and he laughed some more.

Already the vanguard of his force, comprised mostly of Lenk's men, had departed for the mountains. Fodder. Delicious fodder, the deployment of which would rid him of the stupidest men in his army as well as those most likely to betray him. To die in battle would be a fitting end for those useless hicks. And with fewer mouths, there would be more wine for his purposes. The remainder of his men would leave in the morning, keeping well behind to guard the siege engine and, incidentally, stay out of harm's way. There was nothing wrong in his strategy—he protected his own. Quiet anticipation filled the air around him and he savored it. Oh, to be moving again after so many years of inaction in that hole of a vineyard, surrounded by society's dregs. Mez had entertained him in the past and Danton had satisfied his more animal lusts. Just thinking about Salinda's recent suffering made him hard, but this was a different kind of satisfaction altogether.

A knock sounded, cutting him off mid-thought. "Come in," he said in a distant way as if he couldn't be bothered. He liked to fain disinterest as it kept those around him on edge. It wasn't hard to fake, either. He was genuinely disengaged most of the time. Something to do with the dragon essence, he expected. It made everything so unimportant and so—miniscule.

"Master Gercomo, sir. The scout has reported back that he was seen. The observatory has been reinforcing its defenses."

Gercomo continued to stare out the window as he watched the brighter jewels of Shatterwing begin to shimmer in the sky. "Of course they have seen us. They are expecting us. Is the access as difficult as the first report indicated?"

He turned to the man standing stiffly by the door. It was Drenker, Fursten's second in command. Fursten was with the vanguard, marshaling them for the trek up the mountain. Drenker jerked his head up and down. "Aye, sir, it is. The main problem is that half the fortress is on the other side of the mountain. It will take a few days to scout around and discover another valley that will allow us to get behind them. If one exists. The people we interrogated said there was no other way from Vanden."

"Yes, yes," Gercomo said in a bored voice, unfeigned. He would not be defeated. He would possess that observatory and discover its secrets at his leisure. "And the deployment of men?"

"It was as you ordered sir. All the former town guards are in the vanguard and will form the front line. My...I mean, your troops are keeping them in order as they drive them forward. There ain't nowhere for them to run."

"Have my team of burden beasts harnessed to my wagon before dawn. I will join you then to oversee the battle. Make sure all is in place or you will find yourself in the very front."

Drenker bobbed his head in deference again. "Yes, sir." If the man showed any surprise that Gercomo was joining the attack, he knew well enough not to show it. Drenker had risen fast through the ranks. Gercomo had had to do a bit of spring cleaning when he had met up with the rebels who had liberated his cache. He smiled thinly, remembering how Salinda had been useful in thwarting the expected double-cross. He could have stayed at the vineyard after the fire and waited for the rebels, but their leader, Waburton, would have killed him as soon as he saw him. The dragon wine was too rich a prize. Waburton neither respected nor was cowed by the Inspector's highly placed friends, or so the last dispatch from them had hinted. The rebel leader had not died well, but then his suffering had inspired loyalty in his men.

After Salinda had saved him and later escaped, the constable in Gunner had served well by assisting in the ambush and execution of Waburton and the others who had threatened to double-cross him. Fursten had been loyal. He was a rebel who knew which was the smarter and stronger side and Gercomo appointed Fursten his number one commander and Drenker his second. Once the remaining rebels understood how it was and who Gercomo was, there had been little trouble. He enjoyed their slavish obedience. The healthy ration of dragon wine he meted out had paved the way, no doubt; that and his ability to act, to root out weak men and opposition and to articulate his vision for the future.

Clenching his hand, a tremor began, a tug in the muscles of his fingers. He shook as he tried to fight the growing cramp. The pain snaked up his arm, up his neck and down into his chest, burning with ferocity. All his fingers curled into claws, seized by a rictus. Pain splayed his legs, sent him tumbling to the floor. Struggling to raise his head, he saw the elixir and reached for it, sucked it hungrily straight from the bottle, and within a minute the pain ebbed and his fingers slowing uncurled. This side effect of the dragon essence had begun in the last few days. Luckily more of the essence put an immediate stop to the cramps.

☙☙☙☙☙

As soon as the lid of the healing tray opened, Nils could tell that Salinda had gone. He had suspected she would go, too, which was why he had set the machine to a short and light heal. One day was sufficient time to assist his breathing, but not to provide a permanent cure. What point was there in health when he was surrounded by death?

Even though he had predicted Salinda would abandon him, it still hurt. Had she not vowed that she was prepared to fulfil her role as his mate? Yet at the first opportunity she had absconded. He raised himself carefully to a sitting position and then lowered his feet to the ground. The shadowed corners of the room seemed so cold now that he was alone. Again. How much harder this loneliness was to bear. He had thought she cared for him and had foolishly let himself believe it. He could not ignore the fact that her absence was like an ache.

Those who had vandalized and then trespassed the Ways had lured Salinda away. Through means unknown, they had exerted some influence over her. At least, these were the excuses he used to balm the pain of her abandonment. Emotion and logic battled it out in his heart and mind. He had to go after her.

Inhaling deeply, he strode out of the Hall of Elders and returned to his home, their home. If he was to seek her in the world of the Sundwellers then he would have to prepare. As his kin had done in times past, he must walk among them unseen, hidden in the shadows and in the spaces between the walls. Once he had manufactured a new shroud, light meter and filter and assembled the other supplies he needed, he set out. In the Ways, he found her tracks easily, as well as the light scent of her and the pull of their bond, the ethereal tie that entwined their lives. Did she feel it too? He thought not, because how could she bear to part from him if she did?

As Nils trod purposefully along the Ways, he thought about how he had pushed her away from his emotional pain. Instead, he had cloaked himself in it, using it to shield himself from further hurt. Yet somehow she had infiltrated his barriers and had crept into his heart.

147

In his younger days, he had been in love's thrall. The image of Luca, in all her beauty, suffused his memory. He had hung on to her every word as if he could not exist without the honeyed sound of her voice. How much longing had there been for her touch, even the tentative brush of fingertips on his hand?

With such recollections as these, he gained a glimmer of understanding into Salinda's behavior. If she cared for him as he had for Luca, then each deflection of her tender affection would have wounded her. Perhaps she had not truly betrayed him after all, but had abandoned him because of his unfeeling ways? He did not know if his thoughts were logical or sound. What logic was there in matters of emotion?

♋♋♋♋♋

Garan had not moved from his bed for a whole night and day. He couldn't face his fellow Skywatchers with what he had done—he couldn't even face himself. A tray of food sat on the side table, cold and untouched, while he lay on his side engrossed in the wall. His appetite had fled along with all happiness and joy, leaving him with only remorse for company.

Without warning, the door swung open and Danton strode in. "Hello, Garan." Garan didn't move. Danton leaned against the back of the door. "Heard you're not wanting to get up. In case you haven't noticed, your help is needed around here."

Garan said nothing and continued to stare at the wall. His eyelids twitched despite his resolve not to react.

Blowing out a breath, Danton hooked the stool with his foot, scraping its legs across the floor, and sat on it. With a big sigh, he said, "I'm tired...so tired."

Garan heard the fatigue in the man's voice, knew for a fact that he'd been working non-stop strengthening the observatory's defenses and laying traps for the siege. Even so, Garan felt disconnected from that. He wouldn't listen to another entreaty for him to get over it or get on with his life. He owed Turnet more than that. Turnet had been his childhood friend.

Danton's breathing eased in and out while he sat there, waiting for a response. When Garan remained quiet and unresponsive, Danton let out an expletive.

"Wing dust! Look here...friend," Danton said, his voice dripping with sarcasm. "You asked for our help—this isn't the time to lie around and think about yourself."

Garan rolled onto his back, a fist clenched at his side and a sob rising in his throat.

"I am not thinking about myself! In case you did not notice, I killed someone—a person—a friend."

Danton didn't even blink at the raw emotion in Garan's voice. "And?"

Garan sat up and pressed his clenched fist to his chest, watching the knuckles whiten. "What do you mean 'and?' Is that not enough? Should I be some kind of hard-nosed killer like you?"

"Ouch!" Danton replied, arrowing his fingers through his dark hair. "Now listen to me, lad."

"Save your breath. Your friend Brill has already been here to talk to me and failed. Leave me alone."

Danton snorted. "I'm not sure Brill has ever killed anyone. But I have." He stood up, moved the stool back to its place by the wall and paced in the narrow space between the bed and the door. Garan couldn't help looking at him. "It marks you, you know, the first time, and you're never the same afterward. And to preserve your soul you should never do it lightly or wantonly. To take another's life is a momentous thing." Danton stopped pacing and faced Garan. "You should feel sorrow as you do. But don't blame yourself, Garan, don't. There was no intent to harm in your actions, you were working for good."

"Danton—"

"No, hear me. Didn't Turnet work for the greater good? Did he not put his mind and soul into protecting Margra?"

Garan ran a hand over his face. "Yes. But he never expected to be wiped out by a fellow Skywatcher."

"Accidents happen. He could have died choking on a crust of bread, but he didn't, he died saving lives."

Garan was drawn to Danton's argument, but it was hard to let go of his anguish. "You put it too simplistically."

Danton shook his head and grinned sheepishly. "No, I don't. Biggest and most complex speech I ever made, so don't you trivialize it."

Garan heard an edge of pain in the rebel's voice. He didn't know much about the two rebels, not the specifics, at least, of their past. Their current deeds had been his guide, the single means by which they had demonstrated that they were good men. Garan suspected that the older man kept his true feelings camouflaged by humor and a smile most of the time. Garan could see that there were shades of light and dark in him, pain mixed in with the joy. At that moment there was honesty in his voice and in his words.

With a sniff and with eyes that burned with unshed tears, he looked the other man in the eye. "It hurts, Danton."

Standing there with hands on hips, Danton replied, "I know...but think on this. Would Turnet want you to abandon your work because he died trying to do his share? Will losing the observatory make your pain less or more?"

"More...but—"

Danton headed for the door and paused with his hand on the latch. "That's all I have time for—I need you, Garan."

Garan swung his legs around and sat on the edge of the bed. It was as if his heart had been chiseled out of his chest like crystal being mined from the caves below. How hard was it to face the truth? How hard was it to keep going when all you wanted to do was crawl into a hole and stay there? Garan locked gazes with Danton.

The older man slid a finger under his eye patch and rubbed gently back and forth along the lower part of the socket. "Let's have breakfast—it's going to be a long day."

⊙⊙⊙⊙

Salinda left Laidan in her room to sleep and went in search of breakfast. Luckily, the aromas of cooking food guided her down the corridors easily enough. After a long, slow drink of dragon wine and a portion of cacti porridge, she ordered some food to be sent to Laidan's room in a couple of hours. May as well let the girl rest, for Salinda knew there was work to be done this day. The refectory was mostly deserted as morning had not yet broken. Out of the window she could see a demi-moon, the sky lightening around it, pale pink and soft mauve—such a gentle dawn for what would be a long and difficult day. How she missed seeing the sky when she was with Nils in Barrahiem. As she looked to the heavens, she was thinking of Nils, could almost feel him near her, could almost detect that light scent of his. She smiled at her own whimsy. *Please be well*, she thought.

The door flapped open behind her, and she half-turned to see two men entering—one in pale blue clothes and a gray cape, and the other...Her heart palpitated painfully.

"Danton?" Salinda suddenly found her knees weak. Her gaze traveled over him as he turned toward her: the beard, the wasted cheeks and the patch over his eye. The remaining one still sparkled and the smile, when she saw it, was just the same, transforming him into a fair representation of the handsome young man she once knew. His face told of much hardship, of battles lost and friends fallen. *Oh Danton!* she thought. Why is there such suffering? How do you bear it?

The rebel leader stood spellbound. He blinked a few times, as if not quite believing what he was seeing. "Sal!" he burst out. "Brill said you were here. But I...well, I was tied up."

The other young man moved away, his shoulders sloping as if weighed down by some great burden.

And next Danton was there, buried in her embrace, his body tense with repressed emotion.

"I thought you were dead," he said with wonder. "I tried not to give up hope."

She ran her hands through his hair and soothed him, felt his tension ease. "Well met, Danton. Well met," she whispered, her voice less than steady.

He loosened his hold on her and took her face into his hands. "Sal...I ..." With his fingertips he caressed her cheek and rubbed his thumb against her chin, urging her lips slowly to his. Gently, he brushed a kiss on her lips and then her brow. His warm lips, so long wanted, eased over hers again and deepened their hold.

Breaking for breath, he whispered in her ear, "I'm so sorry." His voice was hoarse as he held her to him again. "I failed you so many times. But I am better now. I can give myself to you, Sal."

Tears burned in her eyes. How bittersweet this reunion was. She dreaded inflicting more hurt on one who had already suffered enough, but it was inevitable. Tears trickled down her cheeks. She ran her fingertips down his face. "Danton. Your eye."

"It's all right. It doesn't matter, and I can still see you. Sal—we can be together—we can."

"Danton. Danton, I have much to tell you."

His dark eye studied her. "Yes, so much, and so little time just now. But later we will have the rest of our lives."

She shook her head, and watched as pain gradually clenched his brow. "No, Danton. We don't have the rest of our lives."

His expression froze and then he shook his head in denial. "What are you saying? This is nothing. We will live through this..."

She took the opportunity to put some distance between them. "I'm not talking about the attack on the observatory. I'm talking about us. Things have changed."

It was too late for them. Her oath had been given to Nils, and with it her body, and, she acknowledged, even her heart. She found she was unable to look Danton in the face.

Danton's gaze narrowed, his hands dropping to his sides. It was painful to see his emotional withdrawal, the closing away of his heart and the armor of protection with which he surrounded his emotions.

"Danton. Please, I will explain. For now, let us be friends."

His good eye traveled over her as if savoring the memory of her before he would lock it away forever. He swallowed. "Sure." He nodded once, the joy leaving his face. "Friends. Come and meet Garan."

꧅꧅꧅꧅

Nils had entered the observatory in the dead of night, sliding from shadow to shadow, obscured by his shroud. There was much happening within the observatory. He found it hard to fathom how closely this new observatory resembled the old. He stalked Salinda, saw her walking with a weepy girl. Presently, he shadowed an old man, the Master Elder, as he left his office, leaving Salinda behind. What was she doing with the girl?

The old man was hurrying, moving at the best speed his old body could manage. Curiosity drew Nils along behind him. The old man paused and sniffed the air around him, then turned and stared directly at the spot where Nils stood shrouded. The old man shrugged once and walked on, slower this time. Nils crept from shadow to shadow, trailing him, pausing when the old man did.

The Master Elder went into his bedroom and hesitated before

shutting the door. "You are welcome to talk if you will," he said directly to where Nils stood.

In his surprise Nils nearly let himself be seen. Surely this man could not sense him. There was so much power here in the walls; surely it masked something as weak as a Hiem shroud.

Nils held his breath, kept every muscle still. The old man frowned. "Very well then. I hope you will reveal yourself in time. Be not afraid of us." The door shut. Nils was left alone in the corridor, weak with fear. Avoiding the lamps that lit the corridors, Nils swept along as if propelled by the flickering shadows. The old man had unnerved him.

Near dawn he stood in a shadowy corner of the refectory and watched Salinda eat, saw her gaze at the half-mooned sky and heard her sigh. Then her lover came to her. He saw her kiss the man, Danton, saw her enjoy his touch, the caress of his mouth on hers. It transformed her. Her betrayal of him deafened him to their conversation. All he heard was that she wished that they could be friends. Why did that make the man seem so sad, make the energy that had writhed between them a moment before suddenly sour? Then they talked to a tall young man with stunning violet-colored eyes that were framed with grief. Without listening to all that passed between them Nils stayed close, wrapped in his personal pain.

Later, when they climbed to the observation gallery, he followed them, eyes keenly fixed on the rudimentary scopes trained on the sky.

"Will it work at short range?" Danton asked the young man.

"Don't know." He frowned. "I'm sure I can adjust it. But why?"

"Targets—could you hit a target down near the Klester Valley gates?"

Salinda ran her hand along the scope, her brow furrowed in thought. "So this is what you use to focus your power?"

The young man they called Garan looked at her suddenly, a shadow of pain passing across his face. "The power of the crystals."

Salinda sighed and cocked her head to the side. "Hardly. You have much power in you. I can feel it. Not sure what it is, but it is like a beacon."

The man paled. Nils's mind whirled with the revelation that Salinda could sense power. What secrets had she kept from him? He had thought her honest. Now she could add deception along with betrayal to her name. His anger made him quake. Nils's shroud shimmered once, making him momentarily visible.

The man Danton swung around. "What?" his hand went for a weapon.

Salinda yelled and threw herself in front of him. "No. Stop. Don't!" she yelled. "Don't, Danton." Her gaze was fierce.

"Salinda, get out of the way, there is something there."

She faced Danton. "I know who this is. Please be calm. He means no harm." Then, turning her head in Nils's direction she said, "Nils. Please uncloak yourself. There is no need to hide in this place."

Garan was transfixed. "What—who?"

Nils disengaged the shroud and flicked the hood back, his gaze shifting from Salinda to Danton and then to Garan.

Danton tried to edge around Salinda, but she forestalled him. "No, Danton. Leave him. You will only make him afraid. I would not like that, truly."

Danton held still, though his stance was rigid with tension. "Who is it?" He recoiled. "What is it?"

Nils could hear the repugnance in his voice and see the distaste in his expression. Salinda actually cared for this brute of a man?

Salinda came to stand beside Nils. "He's my...husband."

The confession surprised Nils. He allowed himself to admit that the current situation was perhaps not as clear as he had first thought. He stayed by her side, keeping a careful eye on the two men before him. The sense of danger was lessening with Salinda's calm presence.

Danton's eyes widened, then a look of loathing skidded across his face. "But he's not even human..."

Salinda seemed to grow taller in the face of her lover's obvious revulsion. "He is the last of the Hiem—father of my unborn child."

"No!" Danton cried out. "No," he repeated in a whisper. He drove his fingers through his hair and then dropped his arm to his side. His gaze did not stray from Salinda's face.

Nils hardly noticed. A child? His mind struggled to digest what had happened. Salinda had repulsed her lover for him, had defended him. But a child? Emotion rocked him—anger, jealously, fear, horror—and also a strange tenderness. Nils's train of thought was interrupted when he heard Salinda speak.

"I'm sorry, Danton. I need to explain a few things to my husband, and then I will talk to you."

Danton stood transfixed, fists opening and closing. The violet-eyed man strode forward and took Danton by the arm. "We should go now. You need to show me these targets."

With one long look at Salinda, Danton let himself be led away.

Salinda tentatively touched Nils's hand. He withdrew it and stepped back. "You betrayed me."

Her dark gaze never left his face. "No, I didn't," she replied.

"You lied to me."

There was no flicker of her eyelids, just a steady and confident regard. "No, I didn't."

"You embraced him. That brute, Danton, who would kill me in an instant. Kissed him—enjoyed kissing him."

Salinda's cheeks grew pink, and she closed her eyes. "I care for him, Nils—"

Nils turned away.

"Please, Nils. Hear me. Danton and I were once special to each another, a long time ago, before I met you. I care for him, true, but I am bound to you. I was coming back, Nils. I hadn't intended to stay here this long but these people need my help. And they are good people, Nils. Civilized like the Sundwellers of old, like the people you told me about. They aren't cruel or debased but tender and caring and self-sacrificing—all the things you admire so much."

In spite of his roiling emotions, Nils knew from her tone, her steady gaze, that she spoke the truth. Yet there was one thing he found difficult to accept. "You said you carry my child. You know I do not want this...I did not want this ..."

Salinda edged closer, and this time he did not back away. "I know, but I will not change it. We have time to talk about the child later. Right now we have to help these humans."

"I care not for humans. Only dragons interest me."

"You care for Sundwellers, is that not so? You have seen for yourself that I speak the truth. These are the Sundwellers you were seeking when you ventured out into the world. You must help them. Please, Nils."

He was drawn by her gaze and was unable to deny what she said. It was fear, fear of hope that made him deny the possibility. There was more to the observatory than he'd first thought. "I will do what I can to help. But I do not trust these people."

"But you will put that aside for now, yes?"

He was drawn into her spell, his resolve weakening. She had lied to him. But he had never really known how much presence she had, how much assurance. At the same time he knew the end was near and that dragons were the ones who would survive. Why waste the effort in helping these people? "Dragons are the new owners of Margra. There is no point in—"

Her hand reached up to brush his hair from his face, causing him to lose his train of thought. His skin tingled when her finger touched him. He closed his eyes, succumbing to the sensual pleasure of her caress.

"Nils," she whispered, with a new quality in her voice, one that trilled along his nerves. "You can't separate humans from dragons. Their...our destinies are entwined."

With that she took his hand in hers and led him down the stairs. At the sound of other humans, he paused. "Forgive my fear, but I will walk shrouded." Before she could argue with him he slipped away from her. They were her own kind, and she knew how to trust them. Nils did not and could not.

Chapter Sixteen

TESTING THE FOE

In the dark hours of morning, a knock at the door heralded the news that Gercomo's team and wagon were ready. He took a small cask of his elixir under his arm, put a vial of it in his pocket and headed downstairs. It was time to make his mark.

Later, as he considered the valley walls and the road cut into the rock, he brooded on the engineering that had gone into its construction. If the observatory had been built by the same hands, then it was no mean shack simply thrown together. How, then, had it remained secret for so long?

The trek up the valley road was tiresome. In one section the burden beasts had to go two by two and his wagon had to be rigged with rope to haul it around a bend in the road. The siege engine would take longer to bring up, and the road ahead was even worse: precarious and winding.

He did not mind that the engine would be delayed. It was to be the final instrument of despair. With it he would smash the stones around those weak idiots and tear down their edifice, leaving them defenseless. His men would enter, slashing bodies and smashing heads with their swords and axes.

He heard some screams and the sound of light thunder, which he recognized as loose scree tumbling down the side of the mountain. "You there," he indicated a nearby soldier, "find out what's happening."

The corporal nodded and moved ahead. Not long after, Drenker ran up.

"Well, what is it?"

Drenker panted, half bent over. He lifted his head to stare up at Gercomo. "Some idiots from Vanden's guard started to panic, pushing and shoving each other. A bunch of them went over the edge." Drenker spat on the ground. "It's a sheer incline. Not much we could do."

"Hopefully the sound of their screams put the rest of the men in better order."

Drenker's face was held still, hiding whatever emotion he felt, if any. "I believe so."

"Then get on with it."

Drenker turned and jogged away, disappearing among the troops that marched up the steep road. As there were no further mishaps, it appeared the incident had been enough to bring the rest of his men to a proper sense of their peril. In a small part of his mind, he wondered what had started the panic. Had the Vanden men gleaned an inkling of their true fate?

Finally they came in view of the wooden gate that formally marked the boundary of the observatory. Even with the sea of men between him and the building Gercomo saw that the complex was ringed by a wall of bedrock that cradled part of the building's foundations in two arcs. Above it sat the shoulders of the mountain, with the building in between. The observatory had been built like a fortress, part mountain and part construction. He whistled when he thought of how much work must have gone into it and how cleverly the mountain itself was used to effectively divide it into two parts and disguise its true strength. It was an amazing piece of post-Shatterwing architecture.

This part of the Duggan Ranges had been severely convulsed as a result of Moonfall. The upheavals further along were the remains of the collapsed section.

Compared to Sartell and the other towns, whose buildings were utilitarian at best, the construction of the observatory showcased a decadent waste of skill and resources. It was crafted to be beautiful to the eye, which just made Gercomo angry. There was no room for beauty in this world. He clenched his fists as if he wanted to smash it to pieces with his own hands.

He wondered again about the people who inhabited this place. It amazed him afresh that this establishment had escaped the notice of successive governments. Perhaps these so-called Skywatchers had used bribery. No, he realized, it was more likely they used superstition. He'd noticed how people stayed indoors of a night-time in the smaller towns, afraid of what might befall them. He recalled the light display from the other evening and could sympathize with their ignorance. He'd not heard a whisper of Skywatchers in Sartell nor in the vineyard, yet it was now evident that they had been working at this observatory for some time.

"Shall we begin?" he asked Fursten as the man climbed up on the bed of the cart to stand at his elbow. His number one squinted into the sunset and spat onto the ground. The grin on the rebel's scarred face gave the impression of lunacy. *Well, the man had to be dust mad to be a rebel in the first place*, thought Gercomo.

Fursten met his gaze. "Yes, sir." Then he waited patiently for his leader's instructions.

"Give the order."

Drenker yelled. "Send in the troops. Attack!"

Gercomo watched as the order filtered through to the front ranks. He had deployed his men on either side of and behind the Vanden men, forcing the latter forward and into the stony embrace of the observatory's walls. From his position atop his wagon he could see quite well with his viewer. There wasn't a sign of life in the windows that faced in their direction.

He hoped the place had not been abandoned already. That would spoil his fun. The thought of having to pick through the numerous valleys hereabouts, searching mines and caves for the occupants—for the girl with the power—was enough to make him reach for his elixir.

Reducing the building to rubble would be the best way to destroy their power. He could see that clearly. The fortress served as more than shelter. It was a symbol of their supremacy and their separateness. Yet, it was a prize too. Perhaps he would wait and see how the battle progressed before deciding the fate of the building itself. It would make a good hideout, a good place in which to retreat. He scanned the sky and chewed his bottom lip. On second thoughts, maybe it wouldn't be useful with what was coming, so perhaps there was no point in preserving any of it.

As his men began to move it came to him why this building and its occupants offended him so. It was proof that one could exist—thrive, even—without government and vassalage. It had achieved something that he had wanted his whole life.

Gercomo had chosen to work his way through the system, the hierarchy, the art of cheat and lie. He had played the game and not fared as well as he should have—until now, that was. Instinct and intellect had brought him this far, to a point where he now had more potential power than any other. Yet this observatory mocked him, mocked all that he had suffered, all that he had relinquished to get where he was.

The men surged forward, a churning mass of shoulders and heads, of axes and pikes and makeshift weapons brandished aloft, accompanied by shouts and cries. His pulse raced. The wooden fence enclosing the forecourt tumbled with a dull crunch, barely heard above the cries of the men. How easily they rallied to that sound. They would find the building itself rather harder to breach.

Yet he saw how Vanden's men spewed through the opening, forced through by his rebels behind them. They ran forward to avoid being crushed by those following them, only to be pressed against the walls, their access blocked. A wailing cry grew louder from the front lines. Those behind kept pushing forward until a shout cautioned them to slow.

Gercomo looked up to the top of the observatory and to the sky above. Although yesterday's sunset had held no sign of it, clouds were now building slowly among the mountain peaks. A storm would be an infernal nuisance at this point in time, though at present the wind was mild so he shrugged off the thought. The probability was that it would arrive the next day. He'd be long gone by then, the observatory defeated.

Viewer in hand, he scanned the top of the building and made out a balcony circling it. He checked for signs that they were being watched and found none. Had they really escaped and left him to besiege an empty fortress? He shook his head. That was not logical.

With their limited information about his forces and his ability, their first choice should be to fight. In theory, they had a superior position. And they had a girl with power—could she do nothing? Was she worth protecting? Were they getting help from Danton and Brill? This was just the kind of cause that would appeal to the young, royal rebel. He was just like his father, a sucker for assisting the weak.

A series of loud retorts drew his gaze back to his front line. His burden beasts pawed the ground nervously and growled their discontent. Great clouds of dust billowed upward as the air was punctured by screams and shouts. Gercomo smiled. Danton was definitely providing assistance. Explosives: the defense Gercomo himself would have used in the same situation.

Terror reigned among the vanguard until his men restored order to the troops, sometimes savagely if the screams were any indication. Were Vanden's men realizing their predicament now? Did they see that there was no escape for them?

Gercomo scanned the structure, noting that it was undisturbed by the explosions, including the ring walls. More movement from within the observatory brought a thin smile to his face. The men in front surged and more screams issued as stones and other material rained down on them. The Skywatchers were venting debris through chutes and hidden crevices with such force as to waste about half his front line. That they were the useless remnants of Lenk's men made him smile wider. He didn't realize he had laughed out loud until the corporal close to him asked him if he was all right. He ignored him. Just as he had hoped, the Skywatchers had done him a favor, ridding him of these potential malcontents and leaving him with his own highly skilled and very loyal rebel force. Ones with proper rope ladders with which to climb and sharp swords to cut.

The roiling dust cloud obscured the scene for several crucial moments. There was no clear sign that anyone from the observatory had seen the results of their strategically placed explosives. Gercomo leaned out of his wagon and signaled to a courier. "Tell Drenker I want to deploy the siege engine as soon as it arrives and the way is clear. Tell him to leave the dead where they fall and to send in the skirmishers next."

Gercomo steered his cart through the ranks to gain a better vantage point and then aimed his viewer again. He grinned with satisfaction when he saw the dead. They had been useful to spring that trap. His scout had not been able to see much on the first reconnoiter, only the amount of activity in the buildings and that the walls were being reinforced. Enough to know the Skywatchers were preparing for an attack.

Now the little hurdle of the explosives had been jumped he could start his attack in earnest. He noted that no mysterious power had been brought into play as yet, and he wondered at it. Perhaps what they had shown so far was the extent of their defense. If that were true, this battle would be over quite soon.

Ladders were brought up from the rear and carried forward to lean against the walls. As soon as his men were on them, faces appeared in the previously deserted windows and stones were thrown down. Gercomo lifted an eyebrow, impressed by their aim as man after man fell. From the front line, Fursten sent more of Vanden's guard up the ladders and the same thing happened again; all of them were knocked screaming to the ground, only to be crushed by the very men trying to get out of the way of stones and falling bodies. Gercomo smiled at the deadly chaos, almost laughed when he thought about how the observatory was using up all its resources on men he wanted to get rid of.

The last vestiges of the dust cloud dissipated from the blast site and he could make out the remains of the entrance. What he saw made him frown. The explosion had buried the only doorway under rubble. Taking out his riding crop, he allowed it to dance on the end of his knee. If Drenker had come near he would have struck him down. The occupants of the observatory had sealed themselves inside. If he did use the siege engine it could punch a hole in the wall, but he wasn't sure that would give him access to the inhabitants. It would take time, precious time in which they could flee into the valleys and caves behind.

Once again Gercomo looked at the men dropping to their deaths as they were pelted by rocks. He had patience and intelligence and knew his tactics would win through. Drenker came forward with a status report. Gercomo resisted the urge to smite him and relaxed his grip on the riding crop. The siege engine was still a few hours away on the mountain road.

"Excavate the doorway to gain entry," Gercomo said. "Use explosives. That should unnerve them."

His second in command Drenker nodded. "We will need to destroy the resistance before we can lay explosives. They seem to be quite firmly embedded where they are now. Archers may do the trick—make them think twice about staying put."

Gercomo listened to his second in command and decided this was a reasonable tactic. "Fursten will provide some archers. Coordinate with his attack."

Drenker disappeared into the throng of men, dispatching messages to the front line. A few attendants stood idly by so Gercomo issued some instructions to them. He took a sip of his elixir and then another, savoring it as he swallowed.

The third attempt to gain entry via the ladders failed, and Vanden's dross was nearly spent. *Time to turn the tables*, thought Gercomo. After ordering his men to disassemble the sides of his wagon, converting it into a flat-topped cart, he strutted along it, hurling orders.

Gercomo was not going to be thwarted. He would show the Skywatchers that escaping from him was not permissible. If the observatory could not be his, then he would destroy it and rejoice in doing so. That fortress harbored the vessel of power he desired, his property, his prisoner.

He had not forgotten Fursten's tale of the collapsed cave with no trace of exit. Power. She had wielded it somehow to escape as if by magic. The very thought of something so intangible tantalized him. He wanted it, whatever it was, because it was rare, it was unknown and it was forbidden. And it was a tool. He had the dragon wine and soon he would have that girl's power and that was more than he had ever dreamed possible.

The passive resistance from the observatory continued as the afternoon wore on. They only fought back when attacked. There were no offensive maneuvers from those gutless, peace-loving hermits. No one had even offered parley. After an hour or two Drenker strode toward Gercomo, his face streaked with brown dust and his clothes besmirched with blood. Not that Gercomo cared, but the man seemed whole so the blood must not have been his own.

"Sir, this is serving no purpose. Should we not wait until the siege engine arrives?"

"Confound it. It serves my purpose." Gercomo glanced over his shoulder. "The siege engine is nearly here in any case. We can breach the walls then. Keep going. I see you have some of Vanden's resources remaining."

Drenker's gaze turned to the road behind them, where a line of men and burden beasts were pulling and heaving on the ropes that had dragged the engine up from Klester Valley.

He nodded. "Yes, sir. Then we will breach the walls. Do you prefer that we attack with boulders or the bombs?"

Gercomo clenched a fist. "Start with boulders. We have plenty of those at hand. We will see what their response is. Hopefully they are chicken-hearted enough to surrender when the walls begin to shake and crumble. If they do not, watch for my signal, and hurl a bomb into the breach."

Drenker ducked his head. "Understood, sir. When we've prepared the engine we will start the bombardment. I'll have raiding parties standing by to penetrate the building."

Chapter Seventeen

THE BRAVEST HEART

"Things are looking serious," Danton said to Brill in hushed tones as they stood on the gallery watching the battle. Unattended scopes stood along the rail, still aimed at the sky. Brill was becoming increasingly worried. Though he knew he should probably not have been surprised, the blatant disregard the Inspector had showed for the lives of his own men was unnerving, and his persistence in pressing his attack when there had been no aggressive move from the observatory even more so.

The Master Elder had suggested parleying, but both Brill and Danton agreed it was unwise to cast any potential captives the Inspector's way. The two rebels were sure they could stand firm if such hostages were taken and used, but they doubted any of the observatory's inhabitants could bear to see another suffer, even if giving in to the Inspector's demands meant their own deaths. The two men understood the type of tactics the Inspector and his Infra-pact rebels would employ.

The siege engine's apparatus groaned and whined as it was heaved into position. Brill couldn't suppress a shudder as he watched the rebels crawl over it like flies on rotting meat. He also found that the knot of dread in his gut was getting tighter. Fear—he was afraid of what could happen, for the people who might die, who had already died or been seriously injured. It had become horribly clear that this battle was for survival—it was not a minor skirmish to rattle the cage of some tyrant or a foray to attack a supply line. This was real, this was life or death, good against evil, and if Garan and the Master Elder were to be believed, the beginning of the end if they failed.

Danton had not taken his eye off the invaders. "If they hit the right spot the wall will come down, and they'll have free access to the place. Damn, I wish we had more weapons, more time." He shook his head. "I need to mobilize more men to throw rocks onto the invaders once they breach the wall. But more importantly, we have to put that siege engine out of action." Danton called for Elder Wylie, who hurried over to them.

"Elder, use the remainder of the tenders to gather rocks and get ready to attack." The older man nodded, but his skin was pale and his hands shaky.

"Yes. I will go right now."

"Where is the Master Elder?" Danton asked before Elder Wylie reached the door.

"Overseeing the evacuation. Elder Titina is being difficult. She does not wish to go with the evacuees. She says her place is here." He shrugged. "She can be very forceful and a little too brave."

Brill got the impression the old Elder would rather be looking after the evacuees than staying here to face a battle. All around, he could see the wide eyes and stunned expressions of the runners, who brought food and water, news from the battle front and carried messages within the complex.

Brill commented quietly, "What do we do if he decides to level the place with bombs?"

"We can save the people, but I'm not sure about the building, unless..." Danton's eyes glowed with enthusiasm. "We use Garan."

"Yes, but it's risky. We need to talk to Garan and the Master Elder and we need to do that now."

"I've already spoken to Garan. He agrees it is possible to hit a closer target."

Brill's spirts lifted slightly. "That's good to know. I didn't think he was ready to kill."

Danton frowned and rubbed at his bearded chin. "He's not, but he will have to be. Let's get on with it. The Master Elder will have to convince him." Danton slapped the younger man on the shoulder and then moved down the gallery to find a runner to relay his messages

It wouldn't do for them to take their eyes off the Inspector, so Brill stayed where he was and fretted, his eyes surveying the terrible scene below. Such waste. Such wanton destruction. He looked at the roof overhead and the structure displayed below. He believed in this place. It had to be protected.

His friend returned shortly afterward and stood behind him, taking in the scene below. Brill said, "Won't be long, but we'll need to take precautions in case your plan doesn't work. I can see that the siege engine is nearly ready. It won't take them long to deploy it. If they get through—when they get through, we'll need to slow them down or, better yet, eliminate any pursuit. We can't afford to have the observatory's people harried from one cave to the next. They'll die from exposure and exhaustion within a month, maybe less."

"I know. We will have to be prepared to make a last stand. You, me, a few others to help."

"That sounds very final." Brill stilled. This was it. The final battle, the chance to die for the greater good. He exhaled, readying himself.

"It is."

Brill took another look at the men milling below, some at the rear parting to let the siege engine through, others dragging a sizable boulder for hitching to its lever arm, then turned away. Instead he took in the Skywatchers and tenders throwing debris from the windows onto the skirmishers. Their aim was deadly accurate.

Danton sighed as he stood next to him. "It can't happen, Brill." He turned to face him. "We can't let it happen. The Master Elder told us about that asteroid thing coming into the Wing, ready to rain down destruction on us, and if what he says is true then nothing except maybe the dragons will survive it. If we don't win here, Brill, then there's no point to anything. We may as well throw ourselves into the path of that boulder and die right here, right now."

Brill nodded and his brow creased with a frown. "I haven't quite accepted that our fate is out of humankind's hands. I always thought there was hope for redemption, and now it all hinges on the Inspector and his pursuit of power."

"So, there are some more explosives in the stores. I hate to think it will come to that, but once they fire the siege engine, we prepare our retreat ..."

"And blow up the place around them, with us still in it…"

Danton nodded. "It's not a nice thought, but there's no other way."

"I agree."

A door opened, heralding the entrance of Garan and the Master Elder, both of whom wore drawn expressions and had dark circles around their eyes. They too had done their share of rock gathering and stone hurling. Brill nodded once and went to watch the attack's progress, keeping one ear on the conversation. He shook himself slightly, throwing off his dire thoughts and omens. Danton hadn't revealed much about his discussion with Salinda. Garan had been more forthcoming, and what the Skywatcher had related had been bad. Brill felt for his friend. He suspected how deep Danton's feelings went and was proud of the way his friend had put the task ahead of his own personal feelings.

The scopes were being packed up and transported to a cave for storage and possible evacuation, but a few items of furniture remained in the gallery. Danton dragged two short wooden benches to face each other and sat down. Inviting the two Skywatchers to sit, he relayed his concerns about the potential outcomes of the deployment of the siege engine. "If their aim is good, they could breach the lower wall with their first shot. If we are lucky it could be the second or third." Brill glanced over as dismay and fear exchanged places on the other men's expressions.

"Where did they get a siege engine?" the Master Elder asked. "To my knowledge, Vanden didn't possess one."

"Not sure. Could be a cannibalized dragon harpoon," Danton explained. "They had those on the town walls."

Garan nodded then shook his head disbelievingly.

Brill thought about the spring action of a harpoon and what alterations might be made to convert it into a siege engine. He added his views to the discussion. "Yes, has to be. If we are lucky it won't work—"

"Don't get your hopes up, Brill," Danton responded. "We have to be ready in case their first shot is right on target and punches a hole right through that wall. We have to plan for that contingency."

The Master Elder and Garan sucked in audible breaths. The older man reached over and squeezed Garan's hand as it clenched and unclenched the material of his trousers.

"I know," Brill agreed. "I doubt we can put a plan into place before they make the first shot."

Danton leaned forward, engaging directly with the Master Elder. "This is where we need your help, Master Elder. You remember your suggestion about a parley?"

Snowy eyebrows lowered over the old man's red eyes, his complexion paling. "Yes," he said in a voice tinged with exhaustion. "I think I know what you want. After they have broken through the wall you want me to step into the breach, attract the attention of the...er... and—" He swallowed once and dragged a shaking hand through his shock of white hair. "Delay."

"Yes, call out that you seek a parley with Gercomo. It will take time for the message to filter through to him and some little more time for him to respond to you. We also need to draw their attention away from the observation gallery, so we'll need extra help."

"Such as?"

Brill called to them. "Hurry, I think they are nearly ready."

Danton leaned forward. "Get Elder Wylie to commandeer more tenders to create a diversion—something dramatic, like wailing, screams—out there on the walkways rimming the courtyard. Also, station some people at the windows waving hands, acting panicked and overplaying their fear."

"I do not think they will need to act a part. Most are terrified, but at least they will still respond to direction. I will direct Elder Wylie accordingly," the Master Elder replied.

Danton nodded. "Good. It will be worth it. It will distract the enemy, make them think they have caused a lot of damage and add weight to your seemingly desperate attempt at parley. Do you think you can manage it?"

The old man smiled, as if he was finally relieved of a burden. "Yes, I will do it gladly. 'Tis time for me to be useful."

"Brill and I need time to prepare if they breach the wall—about ten minutes. It will take that long for any rock fall to stabilize and dust to settle. Then when it is safe, we need you to step out. We need to draw Gercomo into the open."

"Wait a minute. I thought you wanted me to target the engine, but now it sounds like you want me to aim for Gercomo," Garan said, gaping with growing horror at Brill and Danton.

"Well," Danton said. "If we take him out, then the rest of them will go. Disabling the siege engine will only remove the weapon, not the rebel force—and not the instigator. We may only have one chance at this, Garan. If you miss, he may well stay out of range."

"Not if he senses our defeat," Brill added. "You may get another shot if you miss the first time."

Garan stood up suddenly. Danton tried to pull him back down to his seat but gave up when Garan shook his hand off. "I won't kill. You can't ask me to do that. We are meant to save lives, not take them. Master Elder?"

The Master Elder frowned into his lap, his eyebrows lifting and dropping as he grappled with his thoughts. Danton and Brill waited, bridling their impatience.

"Garan," the Master Elder finally said, his voice gravelly from fatigue and deep sadness. "You are right when you say we use our skills to save lives. But in this case, killing this man will save lives: our lives, these men's lives, and the countless lives of others if we can defeat him and continue our work."

With one last look at the scene below, Brill came to stand opposite Garan.

"Taking him out will mean this place will remain whole and functioning; there will be no delays in your work and minimal casualties. Please, you have to see that it is the best course. I wouldn't ask it of you if it weren't necessary. You know I understand—"

Garan was nodding to himself while he sniffed and wiped a tear from his cheek with his forefinger. "I will do as you ask, though the source will reject my soul for the deeds I have done."

Nobody had anything to say in reply to this. With a heavy heart Garan went away to prepare himself and to set up his scope. When the Master Elder shuffled out the door, Garan watched him leave, his expression solemn.

Danton lifted an eyebrow in query and Brill nodded. It was time to ready things for their final retreat. Brill and Danton started setting the explosives and marking their positions so that they could be progressively blown as they retreated through the building and out to the Loden Peak side. Strategically set against support pillars and doorways, the blast should severely hinder pursuit. Hopefully they wouldn't have to use them, but if they did, they would take out as many of their pursuers as they could and block those who remained.

Not that the Master Elder had agreed to that course of action, but it would increase their chances of survival later. What the Master Elder didn't know couldn't hurt at this point, thought Brill ruefully. Brill hoped that they wouldn't have to destroy the observatory and cast its reclusive inhabitants out into the wider world.

As he worked, Brill remembered the look Garan had given him. The Skywatcher knew that they had probably sent the old man to his death. If their ploy didn't work, Brill and Danton would have a lot to answer for. It didn't take them long to finish up and then they headed back to take up their positions.

Several men reported to them at various points as they were heading back to the observation gallery with news that Elder Wylie had the tenders he needed. Danton instructed each one to be ready to gather rocks if and when the wall was breached, and how they were to pelt any invaders after the signal was given. Then he told them to pull back out of harm's way if the rebels stormed through into the observatory. The runners headed back to Elder Wylie to pass on the instructions.

"Do you think the balcony will hold up if the lower wall comes down?" Brill asked as they viewed the observation gallery from below on their way back.

"I hope so. Let's pray the first shot misses. That would give us breathing space," Danton replied, but without a hint of his usual smile.

☙☙☙☙☙

The tension in the air was palpable to Salinda. The noise of the battle reached them but it was muted through the stone of the walls. She wished they had more time to prepare, to explore what they were capable of, what the cadre could do. Laidan was at peace now, but there was no time left to teach her how to use the cadre, let alone to practice. Salinda had not used her gift for attack before either, only for knowledge. The ball of flame that Thurdon had transferred to her could be useful, but as yet it was untried. The only thing the poor girl, Laidan, could master was putting her mind into contact with the cadre in a passive way. That was going to have to be enough.

Garan popped his head round the door. "Sorry to disturb you, but

171

I had to see you. Orders are for non-essential people to evacuate. I am to try to kill this Gercomo fellow with my scope."

In spite of his casual tone, Salinda could feel Garan's distress. Laidan gave him a weak smile.

"Are you better now, Laidan?" Garan asked with a soft timbre to his voice which he reserved for Laidan, Salinda noticed.

"I am, thanks to Salinda."

Garan came in and closed the door behind him, then he blushed to the roots of his hair, clearly uncomfortable. "Laidan, may I ask you to forgive me. I acted wrongly toward you and I—"

Laidan pursed her lips together and frowned. "Garan, I'm not sure..." Laidan's gaze flicked to Salinda and her pale skin flushed scarlet. "It would be better to talk about this later."

Salinda regarded her charge with a calculating eye and gathered that something was going on between the two young people. She frowned when she recollected that she had interrupted a somewhat romantic interlude between Laidan and Brill. A love triangle would make their relationships complicated, to say the least.

Laidan glanced at her and shrugged. With a flick of her blonde hair, she stood and walked over to Garan with a confidence that made his eyes grow wide. She embraced him in a sisterly way. "It's all right," she said, patting him on the back. "Be well, Garan."

Salinda turned her gaze on Garan. He had something about him, something that Salinda hadn't come across before. The number of extraordinary things she had encountered mounted up. Along with her meeting with Nils, there was too much coincidence for these to be random events. The feeling that the cadre was manipulating her was strong. Yet how could it? She ached to discuss it with Nils, to explore the idea of predestination, but her husband was elsewhere in the observatory recording events, hiding in the spaces between the walls and hopefully staying out of harm's way.

The young man had opened the door to depart but paused when she began to speak. "Garan, we will come to watch you and assist you if we can," Salinda said.

Garan surged forward to grasp Salinda's hand and squeezed lightly. "Your offer is most welcome, though I do not know how you can help. Have you used a scope before, or a crystal?"

Salinda shook her head. "No, but through Laidan, Thurdon gave me this." She held out a sphere of power in her hand, faint and fading as they watched. She let the power leak harmlessly away.

Garan's eyes widened and he swallowed. "Come then—the observation gallery, as quickly as you can." Then he left, breaking into a trot and disappearing from view.

Salinda added Garan to her list of people she would take into the Ways with her regardless of the battle's outcome. All she needed now was for Nils to make an appearance, for he could escort them while she stayed behind and helped with the defense.

Then she paused in her thinking. Garan was needed for the battle for the observatory. He could not leave just yet. And Nils would almost certainly oppose visitors to Barrahiem so she'd have to manage his objections.

How she wished Nils would unshroud again. She couldn't feel him nearby. Surely there was more Nils could do to help them than record what was going on while remaining shrouded? Yet there was no time to be cross with him, or wish he had some magical device that would obliterate their attackers, so she put those thoughts from her mind.

Before they left the room, Salinda made sure Laidan took a nice long draft of watered dragon wine to bolster her strength, while she downed her own portion of wine and then sighed. How she had missed the taste and effect of the dragon wine.

"Now, are you ready to join Garan and the fight? I will do what I can to protect you."

Laidan nodded, but said, "What can I do? Being burdened with the cadre has left me feeling weak. And I can't throw balls of fire like you."

"I know how you feel...but I think you'll find just one full night of sleep will be enough to restore you. As for helping, I'm not entirely sure. But you have a cadre and I have mine and together I think we will be able to help. We can but try."

Laidan chewed her lips and wrung her hands. "I don't want to be captured again. Or die."

"I understand, but..."

The girl stood up straighter as if gathering her strength. "All right then. I'll help. Let's go."

They made their way along the corridor and took the flight of stairs to the next level and the next. Salinda hitched up the hem of her tunic in her hand so she could climb faster. They loped along past three doors until they came to an archway that led to the observation gallery.

When they entered the gallery, Garan was making adjustments to a short scope, sighting along it over the balcony. Beside its tripod legs was a basket of crystals, placed by two assistants. To her eyes they glowed faintly mauve in the afternoon sun. Interesting.

"Where are Brill and Danton?" she asked Garan.

Without looking up from his preparations, he said, "They have given me my instructions and have gone to check whether the rest of their preparations are in place. Danton said he'd be back shortly."

With a shiver of trepidation, she looked over the edge of the railing and saw the milling men below, bellowing and waving weapons, the dull glint of metal catching the sunlight. Smoke wafted in the air like thin clouds and she could taste a pungent smell in the back of her mouth. Explosive residue, she assumed. She ducked instinctively, realizing that she could be seen.

Laidan hovered by the door, her mouth ajar as she took in the chaos. The noise was overwhelming. There were so many men there, and they were like a heaving mass. Risking another peak, Salinda rose. Bodies littered the ground, being trod into the earth. Her stomach churned. So much death. Would it ever end?

Laidan groped along the wall and slid down to sit on the ground, her head resting on her folded arms which lay across her knees. Salinda went to sit down next to her. She needed the time to think and consult with the cadre. She had little idea how to help Garan if his assassination attempt failed. Could she use that ball of power Thurdon had showed her? Could she thread the two cadres together and fuse their strength to Garan's? That had been her plan, to access Laidan's cadre where Laidan could not. The girl could connect with it, and as Salinda could sense that when she was assisting Laidan, then in theory it should allow her access to both entities.

The sound of a winch being agonizingly turned echoed below. Curious shouts and orders flew about and the tension around her seemed to grow taut as a string ready to snap. A great boom sounded and the building shuddered and rocked. Laidan screamed once, grabbing hold of Salinda, her eyes wide with fear. Salinda soothed her hands and brushed her hair off her forehead. "It's all right. They have hit the wall, I expect."

She turned her head to see Garan climbing to his feet after being knocked down by the tremor. He shook his head a couple of times, grabbing the balustrade to steady himself. His assistants fled when he waved them away. Brown dust billowed up past the railing, roiling and roiling. Laidan coughed and Salinda tried to breathe shallowly.

The dust coated Garan's dark curls but he seemed to ignore it, occasionally wiping his nose on his sleeve. He sighted along the scope. There was so much dust it was difficult to see. When he shook his head decisively, Salinda realized his target hadn't come into range.

The rebel attackers below were hushed. They hadn't yet stormed the walls, as if they were waiting for something, perhaps the dust to clear. And then it began. Moans and wails were interrupted by the occasional scream. It was close by and the terrible sound chilled her heart. It was the tenders and the elders who were caught in the attack on the wall, she realized. They made so much noise, tears trickled down her cheeks. She squinted over the railing. The rebels were poised and ready, but held their ground, waiting for the stone from the breach in the wall to settle, she suspected. The air was clearing. Occasionally, she heard a cough as those near the front hacked up dust from their throats.

There was a ripple of murmuring among the attackers. Salinda listened hard. There were breaks in the moans. "I am the Master Elder," yelled a voice below her. "I wish to parley."

Salinda nearly choked on her fear for the old man. Surely they hadn't sent him out, the fools. By the Wing, Danton! What have you done?

"I wish to speak to...to Gercomo!" He repeated the call, louder this time, and it carried. Then the caterwauling erupted again. All the attention was being drawn below. Salinda saw that she could help Garan by pointing out the Inspector. She pushed her face close to the railing and searched for him. He'd be at the rear, she thought.

Again and again her vision ranged over the men clustered at the rear of the attack force. She watched one push his way back through the ranks and kept her gaze on him, occasionally jumping ahead to see if she could spot the Inspector in his path. Around a bend in the road a flat-topped wagon was inching forward and the men surged in front of it like a slow wave. That was him. Even from this distance she was sure. A chill rippled up Salinda's spine at the sight of him and her skin prickled with sweat. She did her best to quell her reaction and was able to draw upon the cadre for assistance. To see him there, alive, unharmed, wreaking harm and oozing evil, made her bury her fingernails into the palms of her hands.

"Garan!" she called, pointing at their target. "There he is, just coming around the bend on top of that cart. Can you see him? He's the one gesturing and issuing orders."

The young Skywatcher knelt beside her and followed her directions. "The one who is strutting on top of the cart?"

"Yes." Her heart rate kicked up a beat.

With a nod, he stood and went to his scope, adjusting and sighting along it. She could hear him begin to hum, and, detecting a tingle of power on the edge of her tongue, she stared at him in wonder.

The young man worked alone. Salinda turned her gaze from Garan to the increasingly glowing crystal that sat in a square chamber in the scope. She could feel the power now in her teeth, like an ache, and her eyes began to water. It was so different from her cadre, whose power was like a soft perfume, gentle to the touch. The power Garan wielded was sharp and clean.

Salinda's eyes stung, and her sinuses ached as the volume and intensity of Garan's hum increased. Over the noise she could hear the Master Elder. His voice sounded feeble and full of fear as he repeated his request to parley. Salinda's heart filled with anguish when she thought of his probable fate.

Gercomo's soldiers had begun to chant menacingly, and their voices grew inexorably louder and fiercer. The clink of their weapons as they banged them together added to the threat. A quick glance at Laidan confirmed its effect on her. The girl's eyes were wild and her chest heaved as if she was struggling to breathe. Salinda understood her fear. The sound made her heart palpitate too. Just then Danton appeared in the doorway. Salinda surged to her feet and went to him.

"Garan, if he's in range, do it now," Danton hissed, getting ready to turn away.

She grasped Danton's hand and tugged. He swung toward her, his face creased with worry. "Danton?"

"There's no time, Salinda. This place needs my help if it is to survive—"

"You have to save the Master Elder."

Danton's gaze narrowed. "I said I don't have time for this, Salinda." He tugged his hand free from hers.

"The Master Elder?" she asked.

"It was his choice." He shook his head and walked off. She knew then that he would die. The Master Elder had put his life on the line for them all. Let it be worth it, she prayed. By the Wing, let this place live.

♋♋♋♋♋

Nils had been near the wall when the boulder hit. His skill in navigating narrow cavities saved him from being crushed and his shroud let him breathe through the dust and debris that showered down on him. He followed the Master Elder, wondering at his quiet air of determination, his calm composure. The old man fascinated him because he was able to sense Nils's presence, and he seemed to know what Nils was without being afraid of him.

Nils had watched while the Master Elder worked tirelessly in the defense of the observatory. Shadowing him, Nils was there when he gave orders, hurled rocks at the attackers and as he struggled to make difficult decisions. Nils found that he admired the Master Elder, and he had begun to write down the old man's actions and deeds, noting them in his pocket book. Here was a Sundweller worthy of inclusion in the Barr family's archive.

The Master Elder was nearby. He'd been knocked down by the impact. Nils crept over to him and saw that his leg was pinned by a piece of wall. With a hesitant look around him, Nils tried to help. The sound of the troops outside was unnerving. Nils would have to be quick.

"I knew you were near," the old man said when he felt the rubble lifting off his leg. "Thank you—I wish we could have met in better circumstances."

The dull thud of rocks tumbling and bouncing echoed around them. The tenders began to move, some seeking shelter by climbing up the staircase, others approaching the gaping hole in the wall itself, screaming and shouting and making so much noise that Nils's skin

177

prickled. Through the breach, Nils could see the others, the rebels, who were bent on destruction and death.

The old man tried to climb to his feet but his leg was badly injured and he fell back down. Nils admired his bravery. How did he do it, how did he go on in the face of death? "Please help me."

Nils shuddered. He was so exposed with all these humans around him. Yet how could he refuse the old man's plea, this man who seemed to fear nothing? With a shaking hand, he disengaged his shroud. Wonder filled the old man's eyes and tears leaked unashamedly down his wrinkled cheeks. "Praise the source!"

With Nils's assistance the old man got to his feet. "I must walk forward. I must muster my strength. You have filled my heart with hope. I know now that I can face this, knowing that your kind still exist." The old man let go of Nils's steadying hand and limped carefully over the uneven ground.

"I am the last of my kind," Nils replied.

The Master Elder looked back and swayed. "I am sorry for it, but that makes this moment even more special." Turning his back on Nils, he stepped into the breach as the last of the dust cleared. "I am the Master Elder of this observatory. I wish to parley," he boomed out, his voice unexpectedly loud and strong.

Nils drew back and reengaged his shroud. Noise filled the cavity, noise from those wailing and screaming within and noise from the men gathered outside. The rebel men's chant fell away and they began jeering the Master Elder, flinging insults and graphic descriptions of what they would do with his entrails.

Faces marred by anger. Arms thrusting spears and axes into the air. Nils recorded the events, detailing them in his mind for later preservation in the archive. Too much was going on to jot them down. He used a chant to note key points so that he could be as accurate as possible. If he had had the forethought he could have brought a recorder to dictate the event blow by blow. Time limped by as he watched with growing horror at the scene before him.

The Master Elder stood proud and unafraid as he waited for his request to be acknowledged. Some of the rebels in the front lines, who were standing on the remains of their fellows, took offense at that. Leaning down, they picked up fist-sized rocks. One struck the Master Elder in the hip, making him stagger. He stood taller, a hand held over the injury, and then another stone struck. And another. Nils watched each one, helpless despair seeping through his being as he bore witness from the shadows. Finally a stone landed square in the old man's chest and he was flung backward, arms outstretched. Nils saw him fall and wept.

The men were shoving against each other, shouting, and behind them orders came to move forward. Nils saw the Master Elder's hand twitch and realized that he lived still. But the rebels were now leaking in through the breach. They would chop him, cut him, cudgel him until nothing remained but a bloody mass of tissue. Nils could not stand by and let that happen. Still enshrouded, he crept forward.

The rebel men were closing in, shuffling and sliding over broken stone, their clothes bloodied and torn. "There he is!" cried one gruff voice. Tenders crept back from the stairwells where they had sought refuge and hurled rocks in retaliation, halting the rebels' advance. They succeeded long enough for Nils to reach the injured man.

Nils shuddered as he bent down and lifted the Master Elder. All his instincts were to hide, to flee, but he couldn't let them dishonor the Master Elder. The rebels saw the Master Elder rise into the air. Nils caught a glimpse of wide staring eyes and heard with pleasure the strange, strangled gurgling that emerged from their throats. "Ware!" one screamed, but was pushed to the ground from behind. Another rebel took his place, but stood there too stupefied to attack. He was mercilessly shoved to the ground by the men behind him. Nils retreated back into the shadows, further and further back until he found a protected place to lay the old man down.

The Master Elder revived slightly when he realized Nils was there, but it was clear he was dying. As a courtesy to the man, Nils removed the hood of his shroud. The old man smiled despite his suffering. "Thank you," he whispered.

Dark red blood tricked down the elder's neck. "How do you know me?" Nils asked as he tried to stop the blood flow.

"A book. Your kind was known here once...What is your name?"

"Nils of Barr. And yours?"

The man's eyes were losing focus. "Jalen...my name is Jalen. Barr...I know that name. There was a Hiem who went by that name here before the moon split ..."

Nils leaned forward as the man's voice grew fainter. "Barr?"

"Trell of Barr...tried ..." The old man struggled to speak. "He had a plan...wouldn't listen."

"My grandsire—"

But the man was gone. The Master Elder had died. Nils wept as he recorded the last moments of his life, taking note of the details that would make the documentation of this moment vivid and true.

Chapter Eighteen

IN DEFENSE OF HOME

The sound of Garan's hum brought Salinda back to the present scene and away from Danton's departure. Soon her hair began to lift with the charge building in the air. She held her breath as Garan released the crystal's power. A blast of air sizzled as the crystal discharged, spitting light out of the end of the scope with a blinding flash. So much was happening. Garan immediately began to reload his weapon, dropping the spent crystal from the base of the scope before reloading it with a fresh one from the basket at his feet. Salinda peered over the railing, searching for the Inspector, hoping beyond hope that he was dead. Through the cloud of billowing smoke surrounding the wagon she saw first a leg and then an arm appear. The Inspector stepped forward, his clothes reduced to burning tatters but his skin gleaming white underneath, miraculously unharmed. She heard Garan's incredulous intake of breath. "But I hit him."

"He's impervious to the blow—how can that be possible? Are you sure you hit him square on?"

"Yes." Garan's voice was almost a sob. "I aimed to kill."

The observatory was crumbling around her. The screaming beneath them was more than staged now. She could hear the cut of swords and the dull thumps as people were bludgeoned. She became aware that she hadn't heard the Master Elder's voice for a while.

"Is that thing loaded again?" she shot at Garan.

"Yes, but he...withstood—"

"Laidan, get up. We must do something, we must destroy him or this observatory will fall."

"But how? What can I do?" She pulled her arm out of Salinda's hold, her eyes widening when she got to her feet and saw the churning mass of rebels below.

"Come on, Laidan, just focus on me, listen to me. We can do this. I know it."

Garan stood staring at her, his violet eyes brilliant. Reassuringly, she smiled back at him. "Young man, I will use the cadre's power to assist you. I think we can add a little something to your blast."

He looked doubtfully at Laidan. "We?"

"Yes, we. She knows enough to be of help to me. Go ahead, begin your humming."

Salinda didn't know what the combination of power would do, yet it wasn't logical that the Inspector had withstood Garan's blast. She began to worry about the reasons for such a phenomenon as well as the consequences for them all of this new experiment. Laidan commenced the chant she had been taught to assist her to tap into the cadre. Already Salinda was in contact with hers; she only had to reach out to Laidan and draw hers forth. She began to weave them together, feeling the sweet warmth of her cadre's power mingle and thread with the spicy tang of the one Laidan carried. It was a pity she didn't have time to savor it, to examine it. She let the power flow over her so that she could shape it.

Keeping in sync with the Skywatcher, Salinda gritted her teeth through Garan's build-up of power. The sound of the arm of the siege engine winding back meant that they were out of time. Garan re-sighted his scope on the Inspector who, somewhat to Salinda's surprise, was still standing on the cart giving orders. He had not withdrawn from range as any sane man would. Was it because they had failed to harm him with that blast? Was that enough to give him such confidence?

Astonishingly, the Inspector appeared equal to their attack. Did he think himself invincible? Salinda wondered. As he strutted without fear, she saw him drink from a small flask. It reminded her of when he had imbibed the concentrated dragon wine elixir—his pure dragon essence—and something fell into place in her mind. Just then she noted Garan's power nearing its peak, detected him near the release point. Putting her thoughts aside, she fed the cadre's power into the crystal and into the discharge of energy that emanated from it, lengthening the spear of light, prolonging the bolt of power that hit the Inspector.

The power coming from Laidan's cadre rocked Salinda back on her heels. Laidan was rigid, her eyes rolling back and the long strands of her hair haloed around her head. Salinda hadn't been prepared for the strength of it, the sudden flood of it through her mind. Laidan could not control hers, only tap into it to allow Salinda to channel it. Salinda had not attempted such a feat before and for a fleeting moment she hoped it would not harm the girl. The power release threatened to escape her control, to erupt around them. She struggled and reasserted herself, riding it as she would a bucking burden beast.

The stream of power expired explosively. Salinda was thrown flat on her back and struggled to breathe. She blinked a few times, heard a change in the sounds coming from the scene below and rolled onto her side. Then she lifted herself to peer over the railing. The power had hit the Inspector full on, yet he still lived. Fascinated and horrified in equal measure, she watched as he writhed. A purple glow erupted on the outside of his skin, as if the beam of light from the crystal had ignited something within him. In the bright glare of the light she noticed that there was a small barrel on the cart behind him. Could that be the dragon essence he kept so near? It too caught alight, feeding the violet and red flame that engulfed the Inspector.

Laidan sobbed, sucking in lungfuls of air on the ground behind Garan. She'd been winded and her clothes were singed, but otherwise she looked hale. Garan crawled over to the girl and cradled her head in his lap, all the while speaking to her and soothing her with his quiet words.

Salinda gaped at the Inspector. The sense of power building—a new, strange sort of power—drew her groggily to her feet. He seemed to be growing in size, contorting. The air filled with his screech. Then the timbre of it changed, deepened and became familiar. Her heart thumped hard in her chest, lurching as the scene below her unfolded.

Something emerged out of the Inspector's back. He hunched over, screaming hoarsely, and then she saw them—wings. They sprouted and grew, fragile membranes unfolding, flapping over the heads of the men surrounding the wagon. Those looking on began to shriek in fear. Others, sensing panic, began to push and shove in an effort to flee. The men trying to climb through the breach in the wall began to slow, then stopped and turned and quailed at the sight that met their eyes.

The Inspector's altered form contorted again, bulging outward as he spasmed in apparent pain. His feet curled and clawed, his head lengthened into a snout.

Clasping the rail, Salinda cried, "By the Wing! What have we done?"

The phenomenon had a life of its own. A spiral of color bathed the Inspector, mauve and green, colors she knew well, and then began to settle in a well-known pattern of scales.

Salinda was biting down on her fist. She could see more and more of Gercomo's men turning toward the cart, pausing in their charge as they watched, dumbfounded.

The Inspector heaved, sloughing off the remainder of his skin as if he were shedding his human flesh, revealing a small dragon form. The wings beat. Salinda sensed the creature's mind, like the dragon minds she had touched in desperation. He clutched at her, recognized her. His mind was confused, humbled, angry and powerful. With great beats of its wings, the newly formed beast leaped from the cart and came directly for her.

"Your globes of power—use them!" Now on his feet, Garan screamed at her, clutching Laidan to his chest.

The creature was moving closer, screeching. The sphere of power appeared in her hand. She poured strength into it and hurled. It exploded against the dragon's snout. He faltered, wings flapping urgently as he strove to maintain height, and then he veered away. The sound of his wing beats receded.

He was gone.

Garan collapsed to the floor, dumbstruck, but still nursing a frightened Laidan. The young girl's body shook, her clawed hands embedded in Garan's vest. "What happened?" she screamed.

He shook his head. "I don't understand what happened." His confused gaze sought Salinda. "Was that a dragon? Where did Gercomo go?"

Salinda crawled into a squat and breathed deeply a few times before dragging herself to stand. "Garan..." The implications were beyond explaining, beyond comprehending. "He didn't go anywhere... he transformed into the dragon you saw."

"Transformed? But...but how? Why?" He stroked Laidan's hair from her face. "Crystals do not transform; they destroy or repel."

His raised his eyes, seeking hers again. "It must have been you. You transformed him into a dragon—"

"No, it's not as simple as that." She frowned. The dragon essence ignited. He'd been imbibing it for months, maybe longer. It was too potent for human consumption. Had she really transformed him, or merely hastened a transition already in progress? Whatever the cause, the outcome was terrible.

"You have lied to me," said a familiar voice.

Salinda stared into the shadows and took a step forward. Close to sobbing, she didn't know whether to rejoice at their salvation or despair at what had happened. They had lost so much. "Nils? Oh, Nils!"

The shroud shimmered into view and then disengaged. Nils stood there staring at her, his expression a curious mixture of loathing and fascination. His robes floated around his feet in the gentle breeze and there was blood splattered on his shoulder. His eyes glowed silver in the setting sun, and he looked even more otherworldly than usual with his white hair strewn about his shoulders. She rushed forward. He opened his arms to her, and she fell into his embrace as a sob burst out of her. It was relief—pure relief that they had survived, and relief that he had finally let her in.

He lifted the hood of the shroud over his head, hiding his alien features from the aghast gazes of Garan and Laidan. "You have much to tell me, Salinda. But there is too much light here. May we go inside?"

Salinda hesitated. She wondered about the battle. Catching her look, Garan got up to peer over the railing. "They are pulling back. If you could manage a few more of those blasts, they would probably scurry faster."

With a quick nod to Garan, Salinda wiped her tears and stepped to the railing, feeling Nils behind her. She aimed the balls of power slightly short of the wall of retreating backs. And for good measure, she flung one at the siege engine. It exploded into flame with a satisfying pop.

Danton came in at a run. "You did it!" His euphoric gaze swept them all, pausing when he noticed Nils. "They are retreating." He noticed Salinda at the rail and Garan holding Laidan. "That was you just now?" he asked Salinda.

"Yes. How are things below? Is ..."

Danton lowered his gaze. "Brill is managing the situation below, but I'm sorry to say the Master Elder is dead." He looked directly at Garan. "I'm sorry." Garan's shoulders drooped at the news. Laidan put her arm around him, supported him.

"He was a good Master Elder—a brave man. Braver than I could have been," Garan said, burying his face into Laidan's pale hair.

"His name was Jalen," Nils said to no one in particular.

Salinda gazed at Nils, saw again the blood on his shoulder, and realized that he hadn't been hiding away keeping himself safe but had been there in the thick of it, learning the Master Elder's name.

A surge of emotion was ready to burst out of her—relief and joy and pride. In the future, when Nils recounted the tale of the last moments of the Master Elder's life, she would weep. She was glad he had found something worthy to record in the archives.

His bravery made her realize, too, that the barriers Nils had hidden behind were starting to crumble, and the more they fell away the more she could love and respect him.

Danton looked out over the railing then turned back. He couldn't suppress a grin. The Inspector was gone. She wasn't sure he'd seen the transformation, but knew it wouldn't be long before he heard, before he demanded an explanation. Danton's remaining eye glittered with the light of victory. "I can't believe we've done it," he breathed in amazement. "Though if one of you could tell me what just happened out there I'd be grateful."

Seeing that Laidan was near to collapse, Salinda said, "Garan, please take Laidan to her room to rest. Stay with her, if you will, in case she needs anything. I'll be along soon."

Garan nodded solemnly, put his arm around Laidan's waist and supported her from the room. Before he passed through the doorway, he said, "But you will explain it all to me later? I saw but I still don't understand it."

"Later, in the refectory. We'll meet there," Danton suggested. "I wonder how long it will take the staff there to prepare a meal? There will be many hungry people to feed."

Brill came in at a run, making way for Laidan and Garan. He embraced Danton briefly, slapping him soundly on the back. "Did you mention food?"

Danton laughed. "No food for you. You need to make sure those

Infra-pact rebels make a full retreat." They all turned to the scene below. Rebels were fleeing, scrambling over rocks and bodies in their haste. Salinda couldn't quite believe that the worst was over. Burden beasts, some still wearing their traces, balked and lunged in among the mass of people trying to flee down the road. No one was seeking to enter the observatory. What appalled her most, though, was the number of dead and dying they were leaving behind. As more and more of them retreated, the number of corpses was revealed.

Brill backed away from the railing. "I'll do that now then."

"Good," Danton said, grinning with almost savage delight now and rubbing his hands together. "I had better disarm those explosives we laid for our retreat before someone accidentally sets them off. Excuse us for now, Salinda, but I expect an interesting explanation later."

"Yes, of course," Salinda replied, trying to compose herself as she wiped at the tears that still leaked down to her chin.

Danton nodded but before he could leave, Elder Wylie wandered onto the gallery, looking dazed. "Is it over?"

"We think so, Elder Wylie," Danton said quietly. "Give us a few hours to confirm that the rebels are gone and then you can bring people back. Could you also see that we have some food ready? We will hold a meeting in the refectory in two hours."

"Of course, Danton." Elder Wylie turned to Salinda. "If you will excuse me, my lady." Danton glanced fleetingly at Nils before exiting, ushering Brill and Elder Wylie ahead of him.

And then they were gone, leaving Salinda standing with Nils, the last rays of the setting sun turning his white hair mauve.

"I didn't lie to you, Nils. I just didn't tell you everything. I've kept the power within me a secret for so long. It's a hard habit to break."

Nils touched her hair, trailing his fingers through the strands and shaking dust free. "You are an intriguing woman...Salinda."

👁👁👁👁👁

Later, in Laidan's bedchamber, Salinda found both Garan and Brill tending the girl. Garan assured Salinda that Laidan had rested before Brill had entered. Earlier, Brill had confirmed that the retreat was in full swing. He'd set a couple of tenders to keep watch on the road, in case they doubled back, but with the Inspector gone, they had no reason to attack again. They were free to leave, to take the wine, to do whatever they wished.

On entering, Salinda noted the tension in the air and watched as the girl responded to her two admirers' attention. Laidan was beginning to understand her sexual nature and the power she had over those who were attracted to her. It was clear Garan was smitten by her. Salinda's gaze flicked to Brill, and she wondered about him. Perhaps he hadn't had time for love before. How could he? He was barely older than Laidan.

All Salinda could see for these three was heartbreak. Salinda had to teach this girl that there was more to self-esteem than being admired, than letting men use her for short-term gain. But would the girl even listen?

Chapter Nineteen

A RECKONING

It was close to midnight by the time Salinda joined the others gathered in the refectory. The smell of stew and fresh-baked bread caught her attention and banished unpleasant thoughts.

When the all clear was given some of the inhabitants had returned to the observatory right away, with the remainder due back over the next few days. Immediately they set to work returning the observatory to its usual order. The Master Elder's body had mysteriously appeared in his room, reverently laid out on his bed so that those who had loved him could pay their respects before the funeral service and ritual burning.

She suspected it had been Nils who had paid the Master Elder, Jalen, such an honor. Citing his fear of humans he continued to shroud himself, but had agreed to meet Salinda later in the refectory.

After tending Laidan, Salinda had found her way back to her room where she could sleep for a few hours. She needed to think a few things over, too—such as what she was going to tell Nils and the others about the cadre and what she thought had happened to the Inspector.

Nils joined her before long. As he held her in his arms, she reveled in his closeness. It was as if he had let all his barriers down and she could open to him.

"Nils. I want to ask you something."

"What do you wish to ask me?"

"Could I bring Laidan and Garan to Barrahiem?"

He grew still. "You wish to bring humans to my city. For what purpose?"

"Laidan has a cadre, like mine. But she needs help. She's had no training. And Garan, well, he has a power I do not understand and I really need to do so. They are good people, Nils. Please say yes."

"You ask a lot of me. I will think on it, but even if I agree, it is possible they will refuse. Both of them have a life here on the surface."

Salinda sensed that he would agree, for his response was nowhere near as negative as she had expected. He really had softened in the last day or so. "Yes, you are right. They will not be easily persuaded."

ᏬᏬᏬᏬᏬ

Salinda took a seat near Danton, who was brooding over a cup of dragon wine. Like her, Danton had been appalled at the number of casualties on the rebels' side and despite the euphoria of winning and still being alive, the loss of life had hit him hard.

Surprisingly, they had sustained only a small number of dead and wounded, although the loss of the Master Elder was a huge blow. Brill and Garan entered with Laidan in tow. And then Nils disengaged his shroud beside her, causing the others to gasp at his unexpected appearance.

Elder Wylie sat at the table behind them with a number of Skywatchers and tenders who had either assisted in the battle or were newly returned from their refuge. Salinda was rather daunted by the larger audience, but she accepted that all would want to know about the events that had unfolded and as the Master Elder was dead, she was unsure who would lead the observatory in future.

Salinda noted that Laidan made no move to get food for herself. "You should eat, Laidan. You will need your strength."

"Strength for what?" the girl replied a tad saucily before taking the seat next to her. Salinda continued to watch her. Laidan flicked up her eyelids from staring at the table top and saw Salinda's expression. With a slight acknowledging nod, the girl got up to obtain her own portion of food and sat down again. The looks she cast the two young men were in stark contrast to the little scene that had been playing out in her room previously. Salinda knew she would have to tread carefully with this girl. She turned her attention to Danton.

"Danton, I don't think I was able to introduce you properly to Nils before. Nils saved me from the witch's pyre at Gunner. I was near death, and he was able to take me to a place of safety and cure me." Nils opened his mouth as if to correct her, but she shook her head slightly, hoping he understood the need to keep his legacy a secret for now. "He is the last of a very old race that existed before Ruel split."

Danton had trimmed his beard and washed the dust from himself and his clothes. He turned to Nils. "You saved her? I thank you—"

"Danton, please listen to what I have to say. We need each other in this time of growing peril. We have beaten this attack, but I fear there is worse to come in the future. I ask you as my friend to listen and choose your course wisely."

Danton watched her face and nodded. If he was angry still, he hid it well. As she stood and faced them, her gaze took in the gathered crowd, and her friends directly in front of her. "Some of you have heard part of this already. Laidan and I each carry an entity called a cadre. The cadre was created more than a thousand years ago by a group of people who somehow formed their minds into a single cohesive force that could be carried within a living being.

"As each carrier passed it on to the next on their death, their essence joined with the cadre, bringing their knowledge and experience to it. At each exchange of carrier the 'cadre' grew in knowledge and accrued power over time. I'm not certain of its origins as it is so old it is hard to tell. But some of the things it reveals indicate that it existed, or the minds that form part of it were alive, when Ruel split and the world was all but destroyed."

"So you have access to the minds, knowledge and power of those who have held it previously," Garan asked, and his look included Laidan.

"Yes," Salinda answered. "Though the expression of power I wielded today was shown to me by Laidan's cadre, by Thurdon in particular. I have not had cause to use such a force before. My cadre contains mostly knowledge, and as I am still new to it I have not fully explored the depths of it. However, I can tell that I will have to tackle that next if we are to prepare for what is to come."

"You hid this power from me? This treasure trove of knowledge?" Nils said grimly.

"Yes. I'm sorry, Nils. The cadre has always wanted and needed to be kept a secret. I have no doubt I would have been killed, and the cadre destroyed, if I had revealed it to anyone at the vineyard.

"When the Inspector kidnapped me, I endured much to keep from dying. Letting the Inspector know of the cadre or obtain it was the worst possible thing I could imagine.

"So great was my fear that I naturally hid its existence from everyone else, too. If I hadn't detected Laidan passing through the Ways, I would have stayed quiet about it. And praise the Wing that I did detect it, and was forced to speak of it, for what would have happened here if I had stayed with you? If I hadn't acted the way I did?"

There was silence while Nils digested this information. Salinda's attention shifted to the others.

"So," Danton said, catching her eye with a wave of his hand. "What happened to the Inspector? Did he really transform into a dragon?"

Brill's eyes brightened. "Do explain it if you can."

Salinda steepled her fingers. "I am not fully convinced I know exactly what happened, not precisely. I can only deduce from what I know. When the Inspector caught me at the vineyard—" She paused, swallowed once. "Forgive me—it is difficult to speak about that time." She paced in front of them slowly, letting the memories flow. "As we fled the prison vineyard, he revealed to me that he had distilled a pure essence from dragon wine." She skipped over the part in the story where she had been addicted to a tainted blend. "He drank this often, and I observed that it affected him. His skin was cold, he didn't eat or sleep, he didn't behave normally—"

Brill scoffed. "There's nothing normal about him. He's drunk on power."

"That may be. But I think what happened was an extraordinary confluence of elements: he had imbibed so much dragon essence that when hit with our combined power, a transformation was triggered."

Danton was shaking his head. "I don't know. But he did change, and your explanation is as good as any. The main thing is that he's gone now and can't harm us anymore."

"I wish that was so, Danton. But I fear our danger has only increased."

Danton leaned forward, his fingers turning his cup of dragon wine. "How?"

Salinda gazed at each of them in turn, seeing the concern, the hope, the joy mixed in their faces. "I cannot say for certain what the outcome will be. I fear we have put an evil mind inside a dragon's body. That must impact on other dragons."

"Don't care. We'll just hunt him down," Brill quipped.

"After we retrieve that wine and get it to the people who need it," Danton said. Brill acknowledged the point with a nod.

Salinda closed her eyes, felt the glow of the cadre as she consulted with it. "Yes, you must follow the wine." She looked quickly at Nils. "And Garan and Laidan must come with me."

Garan and Laidan gasped. Garan said, "What?"

"You will come with Nils and me to a very special place. There we can help you study your power, Laidan, and see if we can learn more about what happened to the Inspector. We will return to the observatory often as there are other threats yet to be conquered."

"But what if I don't want to go?" Laidan said, sniffing back tears.

Salinda patted her arm and whispered, "We'll discuss this later until you are comfortable with the idea."

Laidan's eyes widened and she sought Brill's. Salinda didn't miss the forlorn and beseeching nature of the look. Garan said nothing, but he nodded once and spooned stew into his mouth.

"Salinda—may I talk with you?" Nils said, stepping away from the table. Salinda met Danton's eye, and he winked at her.

She and Nils went to the window. Outside, clouds obscured the sky and the occasional flash of lightning lit the distant mountain peaks.

"You have deceived me in so many ways," Nils began.

Salinda took his hands in hers. He didn't pull away, so she edged slightly closer, pressing her body to his. "I have explained myself to you," she said softly. "I have omitted details, I admit, but I have never lied to you."

"I never realized how clever you are until I saw you at work today. You have them bending to your will, even Danton, who seems so full of fire and spark. Yet you have subdued him without offering anything in return. I confess I do not understand this breed of Sundwellers you have discovered."

"I like them, too, Nils." She smiled at him.

Nils frowned at her. "You ask much of me if you wish me to allow other humans into Barrahiem."

"I know. It can't be helped."

Nils tool a deep breath. "I consent for the reasons you outlined earlier. There will be strict conditions, though."

"I understand and I'm sure Garan and Laidan will agree to them... in the end."

He inclined his head.

"But I tell you this. I will honor my vow to you, Nils of Barr, because I want to—strange fickle creature that you are."

His eyes widened, enhancing the silver in his irises. "I am glad to hear it." He lifted his hand and stroked her cheek.

The End

The story continues in Deathwings, Dragon Wine Part Three

Preview of Dragon Wine Part 3 Deathwings

Chapter One

Wings

He was falling.

Air rushed past. Breath stolen. Sharp rocks below. Fear spearing into his lungs, his heart.

A blur of the world around him.

Gercomo opened his mouth to scream. No air. No sound, his mind white with panic.

His arms and legs flailed. He tried to fly.

It was like swimming against the tide, limbs useless, clumsy. A great, burning surge of blood trammeled every muscle, undoing his human-ness, remaking him, remaking his mind. Dulling it, smashing it, obliterating it. He sucked in a lungful of air snatched from the wind rushing past.

A guttural cry vibrated against his hardened skin. His own fear haloed him. He struggled to maintain height, wrenching his shoulders, clenching his jaws in the effort to crawl through the air, yet he continued to drop.

Throwing his senses out, the world around him spun and slowed and came into conical focus. Valleys and rifts and eroded peaks loomed large beneath him, all jagged, with the capacity to rend flesh.

He flapped. Wings moved, halting his plummet.

With a desperate heave, he threw more of his strength into his wings until his muscles burned, the sensation as if the flesh was being ripped from his bones. It wasn't working. He was falling, still. But slower, now.

With a last ditch effort, he fought to recall the dance of dragons, remembering how they skimmed thermals and glided above the prison vineyard. Effortlessly they used the membranes on their wings to trap the air and slide. That was what Gercomo was doing wrong. He was fighting against the air instead of working with it. He ceased his struggling and stretched out his arms, no, his wings, and air billowed underneath them. The headlong rush to the ground slowed as the wind caught and gently lifted him. A relieved laugh turned to a screech that was alien in his mouth as he soared higher.

He was no longer falling, but he was too tired to stay aloft for long. Already the muscles between his shoulder blades ached.

Beyond the treacherous foothills of the Duggan Ranges, the desert plain stretched out in a muted pink, mauve and brown. He tilted his body in that direction, the hues of the landscape strange and his vision distorted while he tried to process a greater range of colors and a spectrum of light he'd not experienced before, a fierce violet glow and other alien ripples of energy that radiated and bent as he turned his head from side to side. He wasn't seeing with his own eyes. It wasn't the same. These were his eyes now. He had to adapt.

The flat stretches of wasteland gave him an uninterrupted view of his surroundings. Yet he could not tell if objects were near or far. At times he thought he could, but his brain was having trouble interpreting the new information.

Drifting lower, the wind grew precarious and, like a cough, the air pushed out from under his wings. In a panic, he tried to maintain his height, to stop himself from falling, and failed. Instead, the clawed foot he extended to the earth clasped emptiness and he rolled and tumbled. Over and over he went, his bones bending and his tendons twisting. Fear and agony intermingled and robbed him of even a scream. When he finally came to a halt, he lay there stunned, pain shafting through every part of him, while he waited to breathe again.

Gercomo uncurled his claw and then dragged a torn wing from underneath his ungainly, scaled body. Every movement radiated hurt and increased his confusion. He no longer had hands that could touch. All he could do was lick his skin. It was then he noticed his size.

He was puny. Even he could tell that he was small compared to the immense dragons. He was hardly larger than a man. What horrible twist of fate was this? To be cursed to exist as a beast, but not a real one, just a semblance of one.

Looking down at his body, he knew it was terribly wrong. He was nothing like the huge winged beasts that overflew the vineyard. He was pitiful. What if another dragon found him? They would know he was different, alien. Instinctively he understood the danger. With one wing dragging in the dirt, he scrabbled across the stony ground, scooping loose earth with his claws as he waddled, driven by the need to hide before Margra's sun set, bleeding the sky of light.

The desert was barren and there was no sign of human habitation. Turning to glance behind, he saw that nothing followed on land or sky. The changes in his body had slowed. He found his sense of smell enhanced. As the light faded, the tortuous jigsaw of his vision settled and honed to a rare acuteness. He could see the warmth of the day's sun radiating off the sand. Above, the dark purple of the sky was marred only by Shatterwing blinking pinkly above the horizon. Ripples of red and violet caressed the sky far into the distance. The colors confused him. *Why do I see in this strange spectrum?*

During the night, Gercomo found a patch of ground, layered with rough, loose sand. A nudge of his snout revealed it was littered with large, round stones, as though a river had once flowed along the plain. Within the soft folds of earth, he found he could wriggle down and cover himself with the sand. Delving deep enough to keep safe, he finally allowed himself to rest. After a few hours, pale pink sunlight swept over the horizon. Then as the sun climbed higher, the sand began to warm his skin. The pain eased as if the dirt provided healing. And as he lay there his mind began to relax and to warp.

The human concerns began to wane, but a few knots of anger did not disappear entirely. He held on to the important things and would not let them fade—anger, envy and lust. They were what defined him, and they melded well with the animal desires surfacing within him. He was hungry, and he was lonely. He had never needed another person before, but now there was something burning in his blood, something driving like stakes through his brain. He needed kin.

In the late afternoon, Gercomo was rested, but a cavernous hunger had grown inside him. He needed to eat. Needed to move. Simple as that.

Thoughts of food, of starvation, began to dominate his mind. What did dragons eat? Was he a dragon or dragon enough to eat raw burden beast? He lifted his head and sniffed. There wasn't much of anything except dust on the breeze. He would need to search out prey.

The sand dropped silkily from his scaled hide as he clawed his way out of his resting place. Tentatively, he stretched a wing and tested it. It no longer sang with pain yet it was still tender in places, particularly the elbow joint. Fortunately it functioned. In the growing shadows, he stepped confidently, his strange vision still pink and mauve with flashes of vermilion. He remembered there were other colors in the spectrum of light and that the world wasn't nearly as contoured as it seemed now. The small stones around him were so clear and precise, and the distant peaks loomed so large and felt so near he imagined he could breathe onto their slopes. Even these human thoughts of what he'd lost slid to the back of his mind as the need for food took over.

The sun's rays began to cool as night shrouded him. A scent drifted on the light breeze. He turned his head and concentrated. In the distance, he heard something, a *clink, clink*, as if someone was throwing stones against a rock. Perhaps it was an animal, something he could eat. He inhaled, hoping what he smelled was food.

While the aroma called to his olfactory senses, Gercomo zeroed in on the sound, learning with each step how to control his various body parts. The more he walked the more natural his gait became. He was almost elegant as he slowly stepped toward his prey.

Ahead he saw that there was a tumble of boulders, spread in a circle like thrown dice. Further on he could see the mark of flame burning across his vision. Beyond that was a settlement or a dwelling of some kind. But there amid the standing boulders was a boy, tossing stone after stone. Stealthily, Gercomo angled around to get a better view and to see if any adults were about, to see if there were any dragon lances or harpoons. The boy was aiming for a target, a crudely drawn circle on one of the boulders, the outline faint in the dim light emanating from the small fire. *Tick, tick.*

Gercomo sniffed and realized the boy was the food he'd smelt. His stomach churned and saliva filled his mouth, dripped off his tongue. He wanted to surge forward and swallow the boy whole. But he held that impulse in check when he detected a new scent and then heard the sound of a woman's voice.

The urgent call was distant but growing closer. The boy paused as if hearing the voice but then shrugged once and kept aiming at the target. So far he had not noticed Gercomo standing behind the surrounding boulders, not twenty paces away. The boy looked about ten years old, maybe younger. Gercomo blinked and saw that the child had a faint violet glow about him as well as the tantalizing scent of food. Another cry from the woman and the boy laughed and scooped in the dirt at his feet to pick up more stones.

As Gercomo crept forward to within striking distance, the boy stiffened and turned around. With a faint squeak of surprise, the open-mouthed boy stood stock-still.

Hot piss wet his bare feet and stained the ground. Gercomo snatched at the boy, grabbing him around his small waist and clasping him tight in his grip.

Looking down at the scaly appendage that held him, the child screamed and struggled. Gercomo liked the sound; it made him drool.

The woman's voice was suddenly closer—after a pause, there was a sharp intake of breath from just outside the ring of boulders. A frantic wail cleaved the night.

Swinging his head round, Gercomo saw her jerk as she entered the circle of stones, saw her recoil at what he was holding in his claws and stop dead, her eyes like large dark holes. When he had her full attention, he bit off the boy's head and upper torso and swallowed. Next he ate the remainder, enjoying the crunch of bones in his snout, the sharp gnash of his fangs and serrated back teeth as he chomped and chomped and then swallowed. His laugh echoed around him, sounding like a roar.

With a guttural scream, the woman pulled her hair and fell to her knees, lost in a moment of grief. She should have run. It would have made better sport.

Gercomo threw his gaze toward the settlement, but no one stirred. She was alone and unprotected. The boy's life blood filled his stomach with warmth, spreading out and reaching his extremities with a tingling sensation that enlivened him. Eating humans was good.

Like a dart he lunged at the woman and pinioned her against the target her son had painted. She fainted so he let her go. After falling to the ground, she came to, shook her head and began to crawl away. He let her go at first, seeing that she found hope in that pointless exercise.

Then, reaching out, he pierced her dress with his index claw and drew her slowly toward him as the cloth fell from her shoulders. With the other claw, he flipped her over and drew a line down her front. The sharp tip cut the skin. A fine red gash opened up. The scent of blood teased his hunger and made his pulse throb.

A howl like the lonely wind tearing across the plains rose from her mouth. How he wanted to taste her and yet play with her and draw the moment out. This hesitation was both invigorating and excruciating, priming his taste buds until he drooled hot saliva across her face and shoulders.

The woman struggled and tried to break free. She turned on her stomach and scrabbled in the dirt on all fours. At his screech, his victim shivered and shrieked. He liked her fear, reveled in it. He flipped her over and her screams became music and then she stopped, her eyes wide and staring, though the life had not quite left her body.

When she quieted, he played with her some more, exciting that melody once again from her throat. A bite of her arm was a tasty morsel, raising the tune to a new pitch. As he lapped the blood from her wounds with care, savoring each drop, her voice became low and husky. He began again, this time at the legs. Her scream flowed over him, filling him with joy as he licked at the arterial blood gushing into his mouth. As he gulped down a thigh, her voice grew whisper-thin. Another bite and there was a visceral grunt and then a low moan as her last breath eased out of her throat.

Gercomo didn't know if she could see his grin, see how happy she had made him. He had found a new source of power—human flesh.

Acknowledgements

Skywatcher is part two of the Dragon wine series. I hope you find it a satisfying read and love it as much as I do.

Many thanks to the great team at Momentum who have been very professional and supportive in getting *Skywatcher* out quick so quickly after *Shatterwing*. You guys are a dream team.

A special thank you to my editors Brianne Collins and Tara Goedjen who did a great job and made me sweat a bit and made the book better for it.

Thank you to my supportive friends and fellow writers Nicole Murphy, Kylie Seluka, Kaaron Warren, Trudi Canavan, Glenda Larke, Karen Miller, Cat Sparks and Amanda Bridgeman and the mob at the Canberra Speculative Fiction Guild.

I'm also grateful for the support of my partner, Matthew Farrer, who is also a writer and gets the whole "I must do this now" deal.

To my children, Taamati, Shireen, Erana and James, I believe you can read this book.

Thank you, Russell Kirkpatrick, for the maps.

Donna Maree Hanson

September 2014.

Addendum

It is now April 2017 and *Skywatcher* is being published by me as I managed to get my rights back after Momentum Books closed. Now the whole story of Dragon Wine will be told.